MATING SEASON

BEN

YAEL MAREE

Mating Season - Ben

Editing by: Shay Laurent

Cover design: Jennifer Demeter

Interior Formatting: Dawn Lucous, Yours Truly Book Services

For Megan

Ben pushed a lock of fuzzy hair away from his forehead and studied his best friend as she fingered the pages of the book. Her young face glowed with excitement when she told him how she had discovered this hidden treasure, breaking into a smile as the words gushed from her mouth. It made him laugh, his friend loving a book so much, but seeing her happy made him feel warm and content. He lay down and watched Ariel's eyes grow wide, expanding with wonder, mumbling to herself as she read.

"Ben? Ben!"

His head jerked towards her and he focused on the sound. His name became sharper and the words clearer as her mouth moved.

"What?"

"Have you been listening to anything I've said?"

"Not really." He jumped to his feet, and idly kicked his ball about, then balanced it on his knee.

"I'm done," she said as the falling darkness swallowed her face.

"Was it good?"

"I think so."

"You're not sure?" His face wrinkled like old parchment.

She traced her fingers along the book's leather cover, trailing both letters and emblems. "There are some words I don't understand. I need to ask Mama Beth what they mean."

"Are you sure you want to do that?"

"Why wouldn't I?" She grabbed the book and clutched it between her hands and chest. Cradling her newly found treasure.

"Because it's Mama Beth. You know how she gets."

"This is different. It's a book."

"Okay, if you say so." Ben shrugged and continued to kick the ball.

Ariel nodded, scanning the dark horizon. "Will you come with me?"

"Of course." Without hesitation he tucked the worn ball under his arm and rested it on his hip. Ariel stood and stretched her gangly limbs and brushed the sand from her lithe frame.

Ben fell into step next to her and they meandered in easy silence down the path. They spotted the orange glow rising above the thick shrubbery from the beach below.

When they neared the beach, Ariel stopped and turned to Ben. "Maybe you should wait for me here."

"But I thought you wanted me to come with you?"

"I do, it's just that…." Ariel shuffled from one foot to the other, "After what happened last week Mama Beth won't be too happy to see you."

He covered his mouth, stifling the giggle that escaped him. "Yeah, you're probably right." He put the ball down and sat on it, a smirk set on his face. "I'll wait right here."

Ariel nodded and turned toward the beach, disappearing behind the long shrubbery.

A cackle of laughter drifted by him, carried by the wind, then died away in the sudden hush that followed.

The distinct voice of Mama Beth sounded harsh and

muffled, followed by Ariel's. Ben balanced on the ball, his hips rolled as he shifted his weight against its movements. He huffed, looked up at the dark night and studied the specked blanket of the sky. Ben sighed and drummed his restless fingers on his knee. He spotted a lone, reedy twig, a singular leaf, clung to it. He reached over and yanked it. The twig bent with force and broke off with a crisp snap.

He gripped the long leaf and stripped it idly as he strained to hear the distant conversation. He pulled apart the veins one at a time following the precise construct from stem to tip. He waited, entirely absorbed in stripping and deconstructing the leaf layer by perfect layer.

Another heavy silence fell before the muffled conversation of old women rose once more.

When Ariel returned, she no longer had the book and her smile had been wiped away. She clenched her jaw, her arms folded across her chest. Ben leapt up and raced to his friend, wanting to ease her pain.

"What did she say?" he blurted.

"She burnt it."

"It'll be okay, Ariel." He slung his arms around her, stretching his lanky eight-year-old frame so that he could blanket her with comfort.

"I'm fine, I'm fine." She wiped the welling tears. "It's just smoke in my eyes."

Silence accompanied them as they walked to Ariel's house. When they climbed the porch stairs, she whispered a good night. He waited until the red door closed behind her, then sat on the porch wondering if he could ever help mend her broken heart.

Sweat poured down Ben's forehead as he weaved and sidestepped. His feet kicked up sand as the ball glided between them, as if it was the most natural place for it to be.

He noticed Ariel the minute she arrived. She sat and stretched her long body on the golden beach, her hands raked and pulled through the sand, letting it sift through her fingers. He knew she would come. He counted on it. He knew her like he knew the tides. Seeing them both every day of his thirteen years. His core coiled with the sight of her, stealing glances up at the shape of her face and down along the curves of her body.

Ariel's presence melted away his intense concentration. Consumed by thoughts of her, he found himself yearning for her attention. Wanting her to admire his skills, his speed and accuracy. But each time he looked up, her face remained buried in thought, her eyes glazed, sand shifting between her fingers.

He wiped sweat from his brow and was caught off guard when Jacob advanced and in a swift move stole the ball away. Ben gritted his teeth and scowled. He was too distracted. He needed to remain in control. He couldn't let her see him rattled, flustered, lost. Ben re-joined the game, when a wayward kick sailed through the air. His gaze followed the trajectory, the guys already shouting their warnings, but she was so lost.

His entire body shivered and pivoted. He bolted towards Ariel.

He wasn't going to make it.

He didn't.

He cringed when he heard the thud. The impact area turned bright red as the rest of her face turned crimson. He reached her a few seconds too late. Ben dived and threw a hand across her back.

His heart slammed in his chest and he winced at the red welt that had formed on her cheek. "I'm so sorry, Ariel. Are you okay?"

She swatted his hand away and sat up. "I'm fine, didn't even hurt."

He heard the quiver in her voice. His veins flooded with anger. He should have protected her. Her face grew scarlet and swollen.

"That was George. I'm going to kill him." Ben's body shook as he turned to face the group of boys who had resumed their game.

"Just leave it alone Ben." Ariel stood up, pushed away from him and turned to walk towards the village.

He let it go, swallowed down his frustration and ran after her.

"Ariel, wait!" He caught up to her easily.

Ariel swivelled to face him. "I'm fine, just leave me alone. I have to go home anyway, Rosalie needs help preparing for tonight."

He realised he'd forgotten all about Rosalie's ceremony. No wonder Ariel was so tense.

"Your face looks really red…" He wanted to reach over and soothe the pain.

Her nostrils flared and her lips clenched. "Luckily, it's not my ceremony night then, isn't it?" she hissed, then turned away, and marched up the path.

He stood motionless as he watched her disappear down the path. Heat crept across his cheeks, his fists clenched.

Ariel told him to leave it alone, but he couldn't. Anger flared in his veins, until he no longer had control. Ben wasn't certain whether it was because she'd rejected him again, or because he'd failed to protect her and was made to look like a fool. Either way, George was going to pay for what he'd done.

Ben raced back to the beach, his strides long and powerful. When he burst onto the foreshore, he saw the group of boys still playing. He spotted George easily. He was a year younger than Ben, but stood a half a head taller. His black long hair billowed over his shoulders as he tackled the ball away from Jacob.

Fury roared through his mind, quietening reason. A fresh swell of rage rose in him as he recalled the red welt on Ariel's face. He bared his teeth and broke into a sprint then launched himself onto George. He tackled the bigger boy into the sand. Fine white granules showered both boys, coating them in a fine white powder.

"What the hell?" George gasped for air as he fought Ben off. "Wait," a smirk spread across his face. "Is this because I hit your girlfriend with the ball?'

"She's not my girlfriend." Irritation pricked at Ben.

"Sure she's not."

Ben rushed at George once more and hurled a fist which connected with the boy's jaw. Ben winced at the pain that shot through his knuckles but continued to punch, penetrating his opponents' defenses.

"Get off me! Get off me!" George screamed.

The rest of the group surrounded the fighters as they wrestled. The two boys rolled in the sand until Ben managed to regain control and straddle George.

Blinded by rage, his fists pounded against George's face. He heard the dim noise of screaming, then the chanting of his name, the call to war. His blood ran cold with the thought. His hand froze mid-air as he saw the blood leak from George's mouth. The red stain across his own hand, splatters of crimson seeping into the golden sand.

Ben climbed off the younger boy whose body curled on the sand. The beach fell silent as Ben's gaze sliced through the group of boys, fear and confusion flashing in his eyes. He shouldered past them.

Then he ran.

Ben sprinted along the beach until the group was out of sight. He ran to the water and collapsed in the shallow wake, the waves breaking against his sandy knees, his breath ragged.

He studied his torn knuckles, then dipped them in the sea. The salt stung the broken skin. He clenched and unclenched his aching fists, steadying the quiver.

He looked across the tranquil ocean and calmed his breathing. He had never done that before. Had never had the desire to do that. He didn't know what overtook him. He questioned where the need to hurt George had come from and why was his need to protect Ariel so strong?

Ben knew he would have to find George later and apologise, and he would, but first he needed to talk to Mama Cath about what had happened. He knew it wasn't right, yet protecting Ariel had felt like the most natural thing to do, the right thing to do.

He was sullen when he reached home. He burst through the door and walked until he found Mama Cath in the lounge. She was sewing the pants he'd torn the previous week. She looked up at her son and set the sewing aside.

They stared at one another in silence. When her eyes flickered to his inflamed hands, he shoved them behind his back and held her gaze. He clenched his jaw, locking all his emotion in place. But her eyes full of questions penetrated his defenses and the tears he held back flooded out.

Mama Cath shot up and winged her arms around him, she navigated him to the couch where she sat and allowed his body to fall against hers. His body shook and quivered while he sobbed into her chest.

"Shush, shush" She rocked him gently until he settled. "What's wrong Ben? What's happened"

He looked up at her. His young face marred by tears and angst.

"I did something."

Mama Cath pushed away from him the lines around her eyes tightening. "What did you do?"

"I hurt someone."

"Benjen?"

"I punched George. He kicked a ball into Ariel's face and she got hurt. And then they all started laughing like it was nothing at all..." His voice rose as he spoke, echoes of his anger coursed through him once more.

"Ben," her harsh voice cut through his anger. "Calm down."

He took a long steading breath and looked at his mother.

"I didn't mean to, it just sort of happened. One minute I was looking at him, the next..." he looked at his hand and clenched it. "The next I was on top of him, there was blood everywhere... I got scared. I came home..." he looked to his mother who took his hand in hers, her soft skin an instant balm for the turmoil of his mind. "I didn't mean it..."

"I know."

"But I did, I had no control."

She nodded.

"But why?"

"It's in your nature."

His young face twisted with confusion, "but you've taught me better than that."

"I tried, but you can't fight nature, you can't fight thousands of years of evolution."

"What are you talking about?"

"Mankind."

"Humankind?" he brushed a hand over his face trying to comprehend his mother's words.

"No just men."

"What are you—"

She raised hand and sighed deeply as she let his hand drop. "Why do you think men and women live on separate islands?"

He spotted Ariel leaving her sister's ceremony. Though boys were not allowed to join in, he would often hide inside a shrubbery cove he had created, so he could recite the words of parting along with the women. From his vantage point, he could spy almost the entire beach, but he most liked to see the new vessels dressed in white, their bodies exposed through the light material. His body reacted in a way that excited and scared him. His heart pumped blood through his veins, flooding him with a craving, a need to be touched. Perspiration prickled his skin when the wind blew against the white dresses and pinned them to the sweet, tender flesh beneath. He swallowed hard, his eyes feasting on the bodies of the vessels. He felt his body tighten at the thought of Ariel becoming one of them. He bit his lip fighting the ache in his groin.

He watched as the farewell ceremony ended and the

group separated. Some of the women sat around fires and drank, while others walked back to the village. He pulled his legs closer to his abdomen to make himself smaller as they walked by, unaware of his presence.

He spotted Ariel walking along the shore. He needed to see her. He always needed to see her.

He allowed a few more minutes for the crowd to thin then climbed from his hiding spot and ran to the beach. He watched her sunken shoulders and slow walk for a moment before speaking.

"So, Rosalie left?"

Ariel swivelled on her heels, her eyes wide. "Shit, Ben, you scared me!"

"Sorry, Ariel."

She left him behind and continued walking. Ben took a long breath and started after her again.

"So, Rosalie?" Ben tried again, speaking softly.

"Yes, she's gone." Ariel bit her lip, her eyes swelled with unshed tears.

"Are you okay?" His fingers prickled with the urge to comfort her.

"I think so, I just hope she'll be okay."

"Of course she will."

Ariel fell to her knees, releasing a resigned huff. Ben shuffled next to her and banded an arm across her shoulders.

"Of course she will," he repeated and squeezed her shoulder gently. "How's your face?"

"Still looks better than yours, that's for sure."

She nudged him softly, her elbow connecting with his ribs. Seizing the opportunity to gain her attention, Ben winced and fell backwards into the sand in mock agony. He waited for her to turn to him, realising he wanted her to feel for him, in the same agonising way that he felt for her. When she continued to stare at the waves, sunken in her thought, he gave up competing for her attention.

"Do you want to go hiking tomorrow? It might take your mind off things."

"Sure, I'll be done with chores by mid-morning."

"Great, me too. I'll come and get you from your house." Ben rose to his feet.

"Sure."

He gave her a wide grin which she missed entirely, her gaze fixed on the dark ocean.

"See you tomorrow." He called over his shoulder as he ran off towards the village.

3

"**K**eep up slowpoke," Ben teased from the peak. He offered Ariel his hand, which she took, and with a powerful yank he pulled her to the top of the rock. He wiped his sweaty hand on his shorts then lay down on the hot rock panting. He threw an arm across his eyes, shielding them from the sun.

Ariel perched herself on the edge of the cliff, catching her breath. "Rosalie is out there somewhere."

"She is. She'll be back next week."

"Do you think…"

"What?"

"Never mind." Her cheeks flushed red.

"What is it?" He prodded, his curiosity peeked.

"Do you think it hurts?"

"What?"

"You know… it?"

Ben sat up and scrunched his face, his mouth suddenly dry. "I don't really know. But I don't think humans would have to do it if it did." He jumped up, trying to hide the bulge that was beginning to grow in his pants, and extended his hand. "Come on, let's keep going."

He kept a gruelling pace. Not because he wanted to tire Ariel out, but because he needed his mind to focus elsewhere. It was getting harder and harder to control the tight discomfort in his shorts. His constant obsession with Ariel and the other women on this island was starting to become a problem he wouldn't be able to continue to hide for much longer.

When they reached the turquoise pool in the clearing, he bit his lower lip for fear of breaking into wild laughter. He had scared Ariel that first day they discovered the pool, and he knew she still harboured some ill feelings towards him. He ran a hand over his face trying to settle his features. He needed to get away from her before she caught him laughing.

"Race you." He didn't wait for an answer. He took off, leaving her behind, his face exploding into a childish grin he could no longer contain. When he reached the water's edge, he looked behind him. Ariel wasn't running. Hot in all the wrong places, he threw himself into the pool and let his body sink into the cool water.

By the time she arrived, he was floating on the surface. He watched as she peeled off her dress. Her slight bikini clung to her body and instantly his mind was flooded with thoughts he knew he shouldn't be having. She padded into the water and stopped at hip height.

The clear, cool water did nothing to sate his desire, he wanted to be close to her. Closer. He sucked in a deep breath and sunk under the water once more then came up for air right by her and splashing her, knowing what her reaction would be.

"Ben!" She stood frozen for a moment then leapt at him pushing his head under water. He grinned, reached for her hands then pulled her down with him. Their eyes locked momentarily as they floated, suspended. The sun speckled surface above them pierced the water with shards of brilliant light. Frozen in time, they sank, anchored together. When their feet touched the muddy bottom, Ariel wrung her hands free and swam away. He chased her, diving and reaching, wanting more, but she evaded him easily. She swam back to the shore leaving him with his thoughts.

Beads of water sparkled along Ariel's tanned skin and her tangled, wet hair fell behind her in a frenzy. Ben lay next to her swallowing hard. His heart thumping in his chest. He had to tell her.

He broke the sleepy silence. "Are you going to miss me when I leave?"

"You're not leaving yet."

"No, but I will, one day soon." His insides constricted with the thought.

"Of course I'll miss you, you're my best friend."

"What if one day I could be more than that?" His eyes focused on her face.

"What are you talking about?"

"Well you know, one day I'll go to Dagon, and you'll stay here, but you will be summoned for the ceremony and maybe we... you know..." His pulse hammered as he said the words. Almost telling. Almost confessing.

"Oh gross, don't even think about that."

He winced but his gaze remained rooted on her face. "Why not?"

"It's just gross. Anyway, I wouldn't want you touching me with your thing." He watched her turn a shade of red.

"How do you know? Have you even seen one?" His mouth felt dry, adrenalin rushing through his veins.

"Yeah." She gave him a sardonic look. "I work in the nursery you know. All the boy babies have them. Anyway, you used to pee in front of me all the time when we were little."

"Well I'm not a baby anymore, am I?" His chest expanded as he pushed it out hoping his thirteen years of growth would make him look like more of a man than the boy he was.

"You sure do act like one half the time." She giggled as he scowled at her.

"Well do you want to see it or not? I'll show you mine if you show me yours." His skin flushed and he held his breath. Ariel's face squinted as she considered his words. He swallowed hard trying to find moisture in his mouth.

Ariel stood on shaky legs and cocked her head at him, daring him to change his mind.

He stood up, awed at her bravery. He knew he should tell he that she didn't have to do it. But he felt selfish, and needy. He wanted this.

"Well, are we doing this or what?" Her voice quivered.

Ariel reached behind her back, released the slim strap of her bikini top and slid her free hand under the loose fabric, covering up her chest. His eyes followed her every move as his throat threatened to close, his breathing becoming harsher.

Ariel allowed her hand to fall away, exposing her perky nipples on small swollen mounds that were no more than budding breasts. Ben held his breath mesmerised by their simple beauty.

Ariel slipped two thumbs into the elastic of her bikini bottoms, Ben followed her lead and mirrored her actions. Every muscle tight and rigid, stretched to its limits like an elastic band.

"On three," she mumbled breaking his trance.

"One..." He didn't really hear the word so much as noted her lips move, quiver.

"Two..." The tremor in her voice matched the one of his heart

"Three." His breath stalled.

Ben pulled down his pants and shot up to watch Ariel slip out of her bikini bottoms. His world stopped moving.

He feasted on her body with wild, uncertain eyes, his chest tightened as if he had forgotten how to breathe. His eyes traced each curve and dip of her long body. Aware of the shapely apex of her legs, the rosy colour of her cheeks. The sudden movement of Ariel's hand weaving through her hair, drew his attention, unnerved him. His stomach clenched and his body simmered with desire. He sucked in a long breath ignoring the swelling between his legs.

"I told you I wasn't so small anymore." His chest puffed out rising and falling in erratic breaths as he caught her looking.

"You call that thin worm big?"

Ben's ears flooded with heat.

"Bigger than that flat chest of yours." He covered his mouth as soon as he'd said it, but Ariel was already gathering her bikini, slamming her legs through the bottoms. "No wait, I was only joking."

"Yeah well, it wasn't funny."

"Ariel, wait." He stepped closer wanting to take away the words, the pain on her face. "I didn't mean anything by it. You are beautiful."

"Well I did! I don't care what you think! You have a piddly little worm, and I never want that thing near me again."

She ran off before he had a chance to dress. In his haste to get his pants back on, he tumbled.

"Stupid, stupid, stupid!" Ben cursed himself as he managed to dress, then chased Ariel. She had gotten a head start but he could catch her. He had to catch her.

He searched for an hour, but he found no trace of her. He reached her home and saw the light from her bedroom, his heart twisted and sunk with regret. Ben sucked in a deep breath, his slender fingers dug into the skin of his forearms as he stared at the light. Like a beacon, but not of hope. He could have called to her or climbed up to her window but the possibility of running into Mama Beth was a deterrent.

Especially if she saw Ariel cry. Despite what Ariel thought, her mother was fierce when it came to her. Ben stood beneath her window until the light went out. He stood in the dark a few minutes longer admonishing himself.

He kicked red sand as he walked home. "Stupid, stupid, stupid," he whispered to himself as he scrubbed a hand over his face. Jaw clenched, he shook his head.

He snuck into his house where he heard his mother's calm, shallow breathing from the next room. He made his way to his bedroom and closed the door behind him. Ben fell back onto his bed and stared at the black ceiling above.

He replayed the afternoon in his head cringing as he heard himself belittle her. He wanted to punish himself but instead he found his mind drawing Ariel, then moulding her as if out of sand or soft clay. Each of her flawless features formed and smoothed out to perfection. He licked his lips as he etched the memory deep inside his mind.

The sensation between his legs tugged at him. Lately, when he was alone in the darkness with his thoughts, he found himself thinking of the bodies of the vessels he spied on the beach.

Today he could think only of Ariel. Bewitched, possessed by her naked form. The small buds of her breasts dotted by delicate pink nipples. The thin white scar across her abdomen, the one he'd given her when they'd tumbled on the rocks at the age of ten. The clean delicate skin at the apex of her legs, the round curve of her hips and buttocks.

He groaned as he thought of her, his breathing accelerated, desperate to release the need that had hijacked the body he once knew. Ben spilled himself across his belly, the hot liquid matching the heat of his desire.

4

A week had passed, and Ariel maintained her distance. He had seen her leave her home and head to the nursery and from there straight to the hospital where no doubt Mama Beth kept her busy.

His regret visited him throughout his day, it sat with him in the foreground of his mind, reminding him of his words, of her wounded look, of the aching pang he felt as he tried to defend his actions. Ben grew tired of re-examining it, he knew he couldn't take the words back. He needed a chance to apologise, to make things right, to make everything like it was before.

He needed to fix it.

"Ben?"

He looked up to see his mother studying him.

"Are you okay?"

"Sure. Why wouldn't I be?" He grinned at her hoping it would mask his torment.

"You just seem to be on another island somewhere."

"No, no, all here, everything's great."

Mama Cath sat on the couch forcing her son to make

room for her. She placed her hand on his leg and squeezed. Ben looked to his mother's face, for the first time seeing a hint of concern.

"Mama Beth is on her way to see you." Her voice was steady but he sensed the undercurrent of something else.

"Why?" His heart pounded in his chest while his mind reeled with questions, landing on Ariel's naked form. He squirmed on the sofa clenching his jaw.

"She says she brings news."

"What news?"

"We will soon find out." She squeezed his thigh softly and got up. "Go wash. She will be here soon."

"Why do I need to wash for her?"

"Darling, the wash is for me."

"What do you mean?"

"I mean you stink and I am the one that has to live with you." She winked and gave him a slight shove toward the shower room.

When he emerged, he heard the women in the living area. He recognised his mother's soft voice against Mama Beth's harsh one. He steeled himself, drawing in a long calming breath. He would face whatever punishment came his way.

He stepped into the room and gave the newcomer his most charming grin. "Good evening Mama Beth."

She looked him up and down and nodded. "Ben."

His smiled wavered. Mama Beth had pulled him into this life form his mother's womb. She'd watched him grow, as had the other women on Inan. But she was, more than most, a mentor, a mother. She'd comforted him in his times of need and often admonished him when he'd deserved it, and despite her harsh demeanour, she had always held a soft spot for the boy. Yet the tone and curt manner she used now were new. A stake of fear buried itself in his chest as he inhaled.

"Sit. Join us." Mama Beth gestured for him to come further into the room. She removed her tin of tobacco and expertly rolled out a thin cigarette. Mama Cath and Ben sat in silence watching as she licked the sticky paper sealing it and tucking the roll up between her lips. She struck a match, the flame flickered and grew until it glowed yellow. Mama Beth took a long drag, the tip of her cigarette burning bright orange. She extinguished the match with a smoky blow, the twirling smoke hanging in the air like a light veil.

"I have news." She looked at Ben as she spoke, sucking at the cigarette once more. "Benjen, son of Catherine, your name has been Called."

Ben drew a frayed breath choking on the smoke.

Mama Cath gasped. "That is not possible, he is only thirteen, that can't be..."

Mama Beth held out her hand silencing Mama Cath's protest.

Ben sat silent. His heart hammered in his chest like a mallet, threatening to bludgeon his insides.

"Ben, as The Called I need you to acknowledge that you have heard what I have said."

He nodded. His head felt heavy, as if it might fall off his neck.

"Good." Her eyes didn't leave his face. "Catherine, I think the boy could use a drink."

Mama Cath dipped her chin, stood and walked to the kitchen. She returned with a glass, golden liquid swished within as she handed it to her son. Ben took a small sip. His eyes glazed and his brow furrowed in deep creases.

Mama Beth waited, inhaling another lungful of smoke. "On the next full moon, you and your fellow men will be transported to Dagon where you belong. Take this time to sever your last bonds to this place, say your goodbyes and prepare yourself as best you can for your new life."

"The next full moon is in four days." Mama Cath covered her mouth, tears welling in her eyes.

"Indeed." Mama Beth nodded lightly. Her eyes fixed on Ben who sat motionless. "Catherine, I'd like a minute alone with the boy."

Mama Cath looked at Mama Beth then turned to Ben. "I'll be right outside." Her voice quivered as she spoke. Ben didn't seem to hear her as she stepped out of the room.

"Look at me boy."

Ben shot up at Mama Beth's sharp tone, focusing on the woman sitting before him.

"You have always meant a great deal to me, and I would like to think that I have meant something to you, which is why you will take this advice. Take these last days to heal open wounds and sever ties. Do not allow feelings to linger, do not make empty promises. Do you understand what I am saying to you Ben?"

Ben swallowed, his mouth dry, "Yes, Mama Beth."

"Are you sure?"

"Yes, Mama Beth."

"Good." She rose to leave, "And Ben?"

The boy looked up at her, "When you do these things, best to do them with your clothes on."

His mouth fell open and his eyes grew wide, his gaze followed Mama Beth's advance towards the door. He heard her exchange a few words with his mother before Mama Cath stepped back inside.

He was shivering by the time she reached him. "Oh Ben," she wailed and wrapped her arms around his smaller body. He clenched his jaw to stop his tears from falling, wanting to seem strong enough, old enough. But as his mother's arms tightened around him, he let go, fear engulfing him where bravery should have been. An emptiness creeping all around him.

5

Ben woke earlier than usual that morning. Maybe it was the stillness of the wind or the emptiness that gnawed at him that lulled him out of sleep. His body coiled with tension, as he climbed from his bed and got ready, the unknown closing in on him. Life as he knew it was soon to end. He needed comfort, to sever ties, to heal open wounds. To find Ariel and talk to her even if it killed him.

He headed to the farm. The crops had come early that year and picking season had arrived in earnest. He spent the early morning harvesting bananas from trees. The sticky sap flowing along his back and onto his shoulders. He carried the heavy bunches to the waiting baskets, his muscles aching with the effort.

He heaved in a long breath as the women who worked with him, hauled the heavy bunch off his shoulder, and placed it gently into a basket. He wiped sweat from his forehead, straightened and savoured a drink. He froze when he spotted Ariel leave the nursery. His stomach knotted and churned. His eyes followed her as she weaved her way through the village and towards the beach. She disappeared behind buildings and shrubbery. He knew where she was going.

This was his chance.

Heal open wounds. Sever old ties.

He threw down his gloves and found Mama Cass among the trees.

"Mama Cass," he called.

She glared down at him from her ladder, a saw in her muscular hands, brown sap staining her arm.

"I'm busy Ben." She turned back to the tree and continued sawing the branch, heavy with bananas. "It's coming down." She called to the women who stood beneath the tree prepared to catch the weight of the hefty batch. With a snap and a shaking of leaves it severed from the tree and fell into their waiting hands. They shouldered the bough and carried it swiftly away.

"Mama Cass, I need a quick break." He charmed her with a desperate smile.

"Not break time yet," she said, descending the ladder.

"I know, but I need to go." The young woman reached the ground and studied his face. "Please." He tried smiling again.

"Ten minutes boy and you better be back and catch up on your load."

"Thank you." He jumped up and gave her a quick hug taking her by surprise, her hard features softening into a smile.

"Just go already before I change my mind."

Without further discussion he ran, shedding his stained, long-sleeved shirt. Ben careened his way through the village following Ariel. He kicked up dust and sand as he ran, his heart throbbing in his chest, Mama Beth's words echoing in his ears.

He climbed the rock face, his sore muscles protesting the exertion, sweat leaked down his back. His head peeked above the rim and he saw her as he knew he would. Sucking in breath, he pulled himself up and watched.

Ariel lay on the rock like a lizard leeching heat from the sun. Her white singlet clung to her soft bronzed, features, an arm shielded her face and covered her eyes.

She was yet to notice him, and he relished in seeing her there, natural, wild, real, no boundaries or fears. He trailed the movement of her hand with his eyes swallowing hard as it plunged into her pants. He licked his lips, eyes glued to her every move. Within seconds she yanked it out with an angry moan.

He took a steadying breath. "Not happy to see me then?"

Ariel's eyes flew open and she scrambled to sit up. "How long have you been standing there?"

"Just got here." He smiled at her, hoping the beating of his heart and the bulge in his pants wouldn't give him away.

He waited for her to speak, but she turned her gaze towards the ocean avoiding his eyes.

Ben cleared his throat. "I'm sorry."

"You've already said that." Her voice clipped, the hurt still dangling on her words.

"I mean it." He tried again, taking a small step towards her.

"I know."

"So why have you been avoiding me?" He squatted, picked up a discarded twig and drew lines into the sand.

"I haven't, my mum has had more for me to do with Rosalie away…."

He looked up at her. "Don't lie to me."

Ariel didn't respond.

Ben walked over and sat beside her, shuffling over until their legs touched. His skin prickled with the sensation. He had to tell her. He wanted to reach for her, take her hand, instead he wrung his hands and begun.

"So… I've been called."

Ariel's body whipped around to meet his face. "What? Already? But you should have at least another year—"

"I know."

"So why have they called you now?"

"Because I look too much like a man..." his expression was torn between pride and annoyance.

"Well, I beg to differ." Ariel jabbed him in the ribs, yet neither laughed. "You can't go..." she whispered.

"I don't want to go..." He wrapped a hand around her shoulder, the sensation sending his body reeling.

"It's going to be so boring without you. What am I going to do when you're gone?" She pulled her knees to her chest and leaned her forehead into them.

"I don't know, chores? Anyway, you'll probably be an aunt soon and you'll have to help Rosalie with her baby."

She nodded as silence descended upon them once more.

"I'm going to miss you Ben."

Her words stabbed his aching heart. "Not nearly as much as I'm going to miss you." He raked a hand through his hair.

Heal old wounds. Sever ties.

"How can you possibly say that?"

He swallowed hard. *Sever ties*. His pulse hammered in his veins.

"Because it's true. I..." he cleared his throat feeling heat rise to his face. "I love you Ariel." His voice quivered his eyes locked on hers.

Ariel gasped. Crimson coloured her face, but she didn't back away. Encouraged, Ben drew her closer, then leaned in, his entire body tingling. His gaze shifted, transfixed on her lips before closing the distance, no longer able to fight against the tidal wave of emotions washing over him. His mouth grazed hers, stealing a short, soft peck from her warm lips.

His heart smashed against his chest as he released her.

Warmth flooded his senses and a drunken smile spreading across his lips.

He jumped to his feet. "I have to go."

"Right now?"

"My ten-minute break has already been an hour too long, and Mama Cass is going to kill me."

"She will," Ariel scoffed. "When do you leave?"

"The day after tomorrow."

Ariel nodded as if in a daze.

"Can I see you tomorrow? Can you meet me by the pool?" He needed her to say yes, there were so many more words to say.

"I'll try," she mumbled.

"I'll wait." Ben grinned at her, his insides in turmoil.

He descended the rock face, his heart threatening to give way then ran back to the farm knowing Mama Cass would unleash all sorts of hell on him. He didn't care. He felt like fireworks were going off inside him, his entire body alight in a way he had never felt before.

Ben found his shirt on the path and shucked it on as he continued to run. He entered the small banana plantation, hoping to avoid Mama Cass. He ran to the equipment basket and searched for his gloves. They were gone.

Running through the rows of naked trees he searched.

"Looking for something?" He froze. Mama Cass leaned against a tree, his gloves tucked into her belt.

They stood in silence and eyed one another. Her glare pierced his sheepish look.

"That was a long ten minutes."

He stood and brought his hands to his mouth, trying to cover the smile that crept up uninvited.

"Do you have anything to say for yourself Benjen, son of Catherine?"

He shook his head, afraid to speak. Afraid that he might spill out the happiness that bubbled inside him and that the feeling of joy would subside. He didn't want to share it, but to hold on to it for as long as he could.

"You are to finish your row and then you will go to Mama Ed, she has some chores for you up at the animal farm."

He nodded.

Mama Cass scowled. If she was expecting a protest, she wasn't going to get one.

He held his hand out for his gloves, the smile on his face spreading like wildfire.

"Don't worry boy, by the end of the day we will wipe that smile from your face." Mama Cass studied him for a moment longer, her stern expression cracking a fraction before she placed the gloves in his hands and walked away.

B en stank of manure and sweat, his muscles ached in a way he hadn't dreamed possible. After he had helped shove manure at the pig farm with Mama Ed, he'd helped Mama Layla with the fish, gutting and cleaning scales from the slippery animals. His hair and body shimmered with flakes that embedded themselves all over him. He pushed the door open and walked to the couch where he collapsed in a reeking heap.

"What do you think you're doing?" Mama Cath shrieked. He looked up at her with heavy eyes. "Get the hell off the couch and go shower."

He hauled himself up and cocked his chin at his mother, too tired to speak.

Ben stood under the scalding deluge, staring at the pebbled floor at his feet. He massaged burning muscles and tired limbs, fish scales fell from his body like stars from the sky.

When the heat lifted the heavy fog from his mind he was back on the rock with Ariel. His tired body suddenly set alight. He bit his lips trying to remember the feel of hers, the softness and warmth of the moment, the soaring of his heart and the sealing of his fate. He would be forever hers and she forever his. Even if forever meant two more days.

He let the water run over him as he let Mama Beth's words wash from him.

Sever old ties.

How could he sever their bond? It was as deep and endless as the ocean itself.

6

Ben studied the red door of the house he had come to know almost as his own. He knew how the hinges creaked and how each floorboard sat just slightly outside its comfort zone. He knew that if he was to swing the door open, he would find the tattered blue couch that sat along the living room wall, and that to the left would be the small kitchen and round table with four wooden chairs. He knew where Mama Beth kept the pots and pans and where she hid her gummy drops and whisky.

He knew which bedroom belonged to Ariel and how it smelt faintly musty with her sweat in the mornings. By late afternoon it was airy and fresh and the sunlight that poured in through the window coloured the room white and yellow. In the evening it would smell fruity, like her wet hair, but the air would be sweltering in the tiny space.

He knew the house as well as he knew himself and he knew its occupants as if they were his own family.

He watched the door knowing that when it opened Mama Beth would step out first shouting profanities and swearing at the gods as she urged her daughters to hurry their sorry assess up.

On his last day on Inan, he didn't want to watch Ariel peel potatoes from afar or cut meat or prepare fruit for his final meal. The thought tightened the rock in his stomach, worsening his already sour mood.

"Sever old ties," he recited to himself staring at the door.

It flew open, and Mama Beth sprawled out, "Come on you two, we have a lot to do today."

Rosalie and Ariel stepped out behind her, giggling to themselves. His body stiffened as he caught a glimpse of Ariel.

Ben ran up to Ariel and grabbed her by the hand.

"And what do you think you're doing?" Mama Beth's sharp tongue lashed out at the boy.

"Morning, Mama Beth." Ben gave her a weak grin. "I just wanted to speak to Ariel for a minute."

Mama Beth raised an eyebrow and nodded slightly. "Don't take all day about it." Her lip rose slightly at the corner in a sneer, and she walked off waving for Rosalie to follow.

Ben pulled Ariel by the hand. "Let's go."

Ariel held her ground, causing her hand to drop out of his. "What are you doing?"

"Come on."

"Come where?"

"Does it matter? We only have one day left."

"For what?"

Ben shrugged and looked at her blankly. "Just come on, will you? Or do you want to spend our last day together by the door to your house?"

The pool was their place, therefore inevitable that they would end up there. They sat with their feet dangling in the cold water as the hot sun shimmered across its turquoise surface.

Ariel sucked in a breath through gritted teeth. "Mama is going to kill me."

"Probably." Ben smirked. "Lucky for me I'll be gone, so I'm kind of leaving you high and dry."

"So what else is new?" She gulped down her giggle. "You're always gone when Mama comes to find us." Her lips downturned at the thought. This time was different.

Ben cleared his throat and changed the subject. "So, have you found my replacement yet?"

"I'm working on it, there are some sweet eleven-year-olds that seem up to the task. Maybe, Jacob. He might do," she jibbed.

"He'll never be able to keep up with you." He knew she was joking but his heart raced as she named Jacob as his replacement.

"Maybe not, but he may have to do."

"My replacement doesn't have to be a boy, you know."

"Why? Are you going to be jealous?"

"Like you won't believe." His voice suddenly raspy, his face rigid.

Ariel giggled. Ben's hard eyes snapped to her face and silenced her.

"Oh Ben, just stop." She balled her fists. "I can't spend this whole day with you walking on eggshells. We both know what happens tomorrow. We can't pretend that every single thing we say isn't goodbye."

Ben nodded. His eyes flickered from the water to Ariel. He leaned back resting his body on his elbows and turned towards her.

"I wasn't joking just now."

"When you said Jacob won't be able to keep up?"

He fought the urge to touch her as he spoke. "When I said I'll be jealous."

"Of what?"

"Of every other person that gets to spend a minute with you that I don't." His chest rose and fell in rapid breaths.

"Ben." It was barely a whisper.

"I meant what I said the other day Ariel. I love you." He drew in a long breath, his fingers itching to reach for her.

"What could you possibly love about this?" She gestured at her body, her lips pursed.

He frowned, gathering his eyebrows over thoughtful eyes. "You are the smartest, most fun person I know. You never back down from a challenge. Fierce like Mama Beth taught you to be. You are kind and compassionate, and you are so beautiful." He felt the heat rise to his face as he said the last.

He met Ariel's eyes and his insides coiled with desire. With a fierce unyielding need.

With one swift move, he snatched her arm out from behind her and caught her head as she fell onto her back, her legs still dangling in the water. He rolled himself above her, their faces inches from one another. His heart thrashed in his chest as he swept an errant hair from her cheek.

He leaned his face into hers, their foreheads touched, mingling sweat and skin. He closed his eyes and all he could feel was her. The heat her body radiated, carried a secret he wanted to uncover. He swallowed hard, feeling himself swell, filling with forbidden temptation.

Sever. All. Ties.

Her chest rose and fell in unison with his own, her warm breath skated over his skin as he leaned in closer. He opened his eyes to see her mouth part ever so slowly, her tongue darting out to lick her top lip, an invitation. A summoning he could not deny. He leaned in, her breath hitched.

And then the world shattered.

"Ariel, daughter of Elizabeth, Mama Beth is going to kill you!" Rosalie's irate voice sliced their silence as she burst through the shrubbery, her red face swollen with effort, her hair wild and sticky, her shirt clinging to her like a second skin.

"Oh, sorry." Rosalie's sudden interruption turned apologetic as scanned the scene she had stumbled upon. She cleared her throat, then looked at her younger sister whose eyes pooled with angry tears.

"Hi Ben," Rosalie greeted him.

He rolled away from Ariel and waved in reply, heat burning his face.

"Come on Ariel we better go, I think you took it too far today. I have rarely seen Mama so upset."

Ariel frowned, biting her bottom lip. She plucked her feet from the water and stood up.

Ben clung to her arm as she looked at him apologetically.

"No," he mouthed to her.

She jerked her hand away and followed Rosalie out of the clearing.

He wanted to call after her, run after her, but he knew that her fear of Mama Beth was stronger than any summons he might make.

He fell onto the grass, his heart unsettled, unsure of how to return to normal. If there would ever be such a thing now that he had felt Ariel beneath him.

He sucked in air and felt the regret seep under his skin. All the things he could have done and said, all the wasted time playing games, skirting around the truth. He could have kissed her a hundred times over. He could have tasted her skin and run his hands through her hair, he could have felt her touch on his body. Instead the only thing left was an empty promise of all he would never know.

He grabbed a fist full of grass, his despair turned to anger, the anger to anguish. He wiped the tears that welled in his eyes and swore to leave the heart break and desire here. He would drown them in this pool of cool turquoise water where they would be held frozen for all of time. They would remain on Inan, not haunt him across the ocean. The idea of Ariel and these feelings would be just a dream, a childhood crush he must shake.

Sever all ties.

He jumped into the lake and sank to the muddy bottom where he cried out, a muffled, aching scream. In his despair, bubbles burst from his mouth like a pent-up flood. He breached the surface, his lungs empty and his heart like lead, held in a dark void of hopelessness.

He strode away from the hidden pool, knowing he would never see it again. Without a backwards glance he promised himself that he was done.

"Where have you been?" Mama Cath froze mid-step as Ben entered the house.

"Out." He didn't look up.

"Are you okay?" She stepped toward her son and cupped his chin in her hand, lifting his face to hers.

He snatched it away, "I'm fine." He strode toward the back rooms.

"Where are you going?"

He turned to his mother, his face flushed, his fists clenched. "What's with all the questions? I'm just going to my room. What do you want from me?"

"I just thought you might want to spend some time with me before you go." Her voice was soft as she looked into his swollen eyes.

He took a half a step forward then stilled. Torn between heart ache and misery. "Of course, I do, I just…"

"I know." Her soft features were tender, her voice calm. "I'll be here when you're ready." Not allowing him a rebuke, she stepped outside and left him with his guilt and grief.

He washed his face then searched for his mom. Her found her on the porch admiring the ocean as it curled and fell endlessly on the sand bar bellow.

"I'm sorry about before."

"I know."

"It's just—"

"I know."

"Since Liam and Mason left, it's been only you and me, and now I'll have to go too, and you'll be all alone."

"I'll be fine my sweet boy."

"Will you?" Concern marred his boyish features.

She nodded slightly and laced her hand through his, squeezing softly.

"Do you think they could be there? On Dagon?"

"I hope so, but I don't know darling. There have been two Shuffelings since they left..." She sighed and looked at the ocean as if her sons' faces were drawn in the blue waves.

"I don't want to leave you. I want to stay and look after you."

"You are a beautiful boy, but there is nothing for you to protect me from. I am safe here and I have everything I need."

"But not your kids."

"No." Tears pooled in her eyes as she kept her gaze on the undulating ocean.

They sat in silence for a short while, a light breeze carrying with it the smell of spiced meat and brewed ale. Preparations for the night's feast would be near done.

Ben broke their silence. "What will it be like? Over there?"

"I don't know my darling, I suspect it would be similar."

"But I will be all alone."

"Yes. But you must not be afraid."

"But what if I am?"

She winged an arm around his small body and pulled him close to her. "Then you must find courage in yourself."

"What does that mean?"

Mama Cath sucked in a long breath, pushed away from her son and looked into his eyes. "It means do your best to be true to yourself. Don't be a fool. Listen, learn, observe every-one. Know your place and protect yourself and what is yours. Don't pick fights but stand up for yourself. Fail. Fail and try again. Don't give up." She gave him a faint smile. "You are a clever and loyal boy, compassionate and sweet. Don't lose those traits as you grow into a man."

"A man?"

"Yes."

"You mean when I am eighteen?"

"Yes."

"So that I can—"

"Do the right thing."

"How?"

"Be kind, be gentle, and don't ever take something away from someone that wasn't yours to take."

"What does that mean?"

"You will know."

"How?"

"You just will." She stood up stretching her hand out to him. He took it and she pulled him into an embrace.

His head was full of questions, his heart thumped in his chest as it chipped away, pieces falling to the wayside as his mother's grip loosened around him.

The darkening sky signalled the drift of music on the wind and the villagers began to assemble on the beach. One last party. One final goodbye.

He grabbed his worn soccer ball and tucked it under his arm, then laced the other into his mother's as they made their way down to the beach.

The party was like so many others before it, excessive and unnecessary, and yet it seemed there were always reasons to feast and celebrate, to say goodbye.

A group of young boys were standing around in a circle talking and laughing. Their faces lifted as they saw Ben and they ran towards him eyeing the ball. Ben lobbed the ball to his friends then looked to his mother in a silent question. Mama Cath squeezed then released his arm as the boys scattered in an organised mess and kicked the ball around, trading shouts and curses.

Ben looked about the darkening beach, searching for Ariel's familiar face. In his distraction he missed a kick and cost his team a goal. He tried to force himself back into the game, but couldn't help scanning, searching for her. An overwhelming pit of disappointment gripped his insides, growing and gnawing at him.

A slow, gradual horn blew, calling the assembled to gather in a semi-circle around the feast table. Ben and two others were called out then stood facing the crowd. Ben's heart thumped in his ears, as he waited for familiar words. Words he had said to his brothers and countless others, words which made you disappear. Words that meant that the end was here and there was no coming back. He licked the sweat from his upper lip as he let the words wash over him.

> *May the sun shine always upon you.*
> *May love and serenity always surround you.*
> *May righteousness always guide you.*
> *Though we say farewell,*
> *you, our sons, are always with us.*
> *You are in the stars, and sun and moon,*
> *you are the seeds sent into the world.*
> *Go sew new roots and prosper,*
> *For soon it is your time for harvest.*

He found himself scouring the faces in the crowd aching to see Ariel, the comfort her smile could bring. He swept a hand through his hair and ground his teeth. He couldn't see her.

Why wasn't she there?

The crowd grew silent. Just a murmuring as they helped themselves to food and drink now that the words had been said. Their shallow goodbye as dry as the cold meat and bitter brew.

They sat in smaller groups eating and laughing. Most would go on with their lives. Tomorrow and the next day would look much the same as any other. He hated them. How his departure didn't fracture anything in their existence and yet shattered his and his mother's completely. And Ariel. Where was she?

He flung his full plate on a table and marched up the path. On this, of all days he couldn't bare not to be with her. Not finish what was started that morning. He knew she felt it too, how the earth moved ever so slightly, how the world hummed a quiet melody, how the air stood still and held its breath.

Ben smelt the smoke even before he rounded the corner. He stepped into view and saw Mama Beth. She was sitting on the porch, her long body leaning against a post, her legs stretched before her resting on the first step. A book in one hand a smoke rolled up in the other, hiding her face behind a bluish mist.

She looked up at him, her face expressionless. Mama Beth brought the cigarette to her mouth and inhaled deeply, the hot ember burning orange as it singed the paper.

"Mama Beth," Ben took a tentative step forward and straightened his spine, "where's Ariel?"

"She's doing her chores. Chores she would have finished this morning if you hadn't run off with her." She sucked the cigarette again, her face scrutinising the boy.

"When will she be done?"

"Not today." Her voice held a frosty edge.

"I want to see her."

Mama Beth put her book down and rose to her full height

letting the roll up drop from her fingers. She tramped the smoking tip, mashed it into the ground then stepped off the porch and stood over Ben, who at thirteen, almost matched her height.

"I told you to sever all ties."

"I tried."

"Not hard enough."

"I love her."

"I forbid it." Her eyes blazed like lightning.

"But you can't. I love her." His nose flared and he stood taller folding his arms across his chest.

"You must stop."

He held Mama Beth's gaze. She studied him, her face stern, showing a hint of amusement.

She sighed and took a step back running a hand across her eyes. "Please, let her go."

"I can't, I don't want to."

"Your love is a selfish thing, it can never be reciprocated or enjoyed or explored. You will both end up hurting." She turned her back to him and climbed back onto her porch.

"I'll never hurt her."

"You already have, more than you know."

"But—"

"Benjen!"

He stopped talking and looked to her face as she shook her head.

"Tomorrow you will go to Dagon, and in a few weeks or months your memory will fade, your life will move on and you will forget what you had here. Ariel must live here her whole life. Everything that you have touched holds you in it. If you make her any promises, she will hold on to them dearly, even when she goes to Ishmin, in her eyes you would always be her first. You have tainted her youth and her innocence, do not rob her of happiness. Do not say words you can never show, do not make promises you can never keep, for she would live in pain and anguish each day, until her last day."

Ben looked at Mama Beth, her hard exterior melted away. For the first time in his thirteen years he saw a glimpse of Elizabeth, daughter of Irma. She seemed smaller, fragile, vulnerable, as if the words spoken were not for her daughter at all.

He climbed the steps of the porch and sat gingerly next to the older woman whose eyes were swollen with tears.

He swung his arm around her. He felt her body stiffen for a second before allowing him to comfort her.

"You must go now Ben, go say your goodbyes."

"I'm not leaving till I see Ariel."

"Then you will spend your last night on this porch with me." The cold edge returned. Mama Beth straightened, letting his arm fall from her back, and rubbed the tears from her eyes.

His gaze flickered from her to the door.

"Don't try it boy." Her tone was arctic. "And don't bother with the back either. Mama Ronda is a very good watch dog. Be off now. Good luck Benjen, son of Catherine."

Mama Beth picked up her book and leaned against the post, once more paying the boy no more heed.

He sat for a while rooted to the porch shooting angry looks at Mama Beth, wanting to scorch the paper with his eyes, to catch her attention. Despite his efforts she ignored him. After a time, he stood up and shuffled away from the house.

He'd returned to the beach, angry and defeated.

All he wanted was to go home to bed and wish the night away. Dream of Ariel at the pool, watch her hands drop to the side, her bikini bottom hit the ground. His stomach tightened as he thought of her, his body needed a safe retreat.

He cut through the beach and to the western path when he was intercepted by his friends, led by Jacob.

"I have something for you." Jacob smiled a twinkle in his eyes.

Ben clenched a fist imagining that smile near Ariel. "What?" His voice was harsher than he'd intended.

If Jacob noticed he said nothing as his smile stretched, and he produced a half-drunk bottle of whisky from behind his back.

Ben's eyes widened and as he eyed the bottle. "Where did you get this?"

"I took this from Mama Issy's stash three weeks ago during the ceremony. We don't all stand behind bushes yanking our chains." The boys burst out laughing as Ben cheeks burned.

He shoved Jacob, thanking the heavens it was dark, and jerked the bottle from him. The smooth glass cool in his hand as it gleamed against the moonlight, the alcohol within sloshing around.

"We need to wait till they go to bed." Jacob nodded toward the circle of women still sitting around a small fire.

There was a general nod of agreement.

Ben handed the bottle to Robert. At ten, he was quick and small for his age. "Go bury it by the third rock. Not too deep."

Robert grabbed the bottle and ran off into the darkness, while the rest of the boys played another game. Ben shook off his disappointment and buried himself in the contest, getting lost in the need to conquer his teammates one final time.

Sweat dripped down his back and his legs throbbed as he kicked the ball. It curved around Sebastian and rolled just inside the boundary of the goal. The boys cheered and clapped as he pumped a fist in the air. He was done.

He fell to the ground panting, the boys surrounding him gleeful and raucous.

The group settled down into easy conversation, teasing and laughing as they waited for the last of the women to depart.

When the they left, the boys made their way to the abandoned fire. In the dark night it skirted and danced in the light breeze, a yellow goddess before a black curtain.

Robert returned with the pilfered bottle and the boys licked their lips in anticipation.

Jacob held it as if it was a trophy. He stood before Ben and handed the bottle down to him.

"Now that you're a man you get the first sip."

Although Ben couldn't see all the eyes in the darkness, he felt them. He unscrewed the lid and discarded it onto the fire. The noxious smell of the whisky invaded his senses, he closed his eyes and took a big gulp. The alcohol burned his throat as it went down. He shot up holding back the urge to vomit. His throat on fire, his belly alight and heated. He forced the drink to remain down and wished he'd kept the lid. Now they would have to drink it all.

He looked to the other boys, small smirks painted on some faces, awe on others.

"So how does it taste?"

"Like fire," Ben spat, scrunching his nose.

"But is it good?"

"I wouldn't say that."

"So, is it bad?'

"I'm not really sure."

Jacob gave him an irritated look and stretched his arm out for the bottle. "Well?"

In an effort to cement his manhood Ben took another long sip. The alcohol swam through his veins and settled beneath his skin, warmth rose around his body, veiling him in a cocoon.

He passed the bottle over to Jacob who took a long sip. Jacob's eyes grew wide, his face contorted. He gasped as he handed the bottle over to a boy on his right.

"Horse piss?" Ben jibed at his friend.

"Horse piss!"

The boys laughed.

Ben's head throbbed when he woke up. He pushed himself up and wiped sand from his face. He hadn't planned on falling asleep, but the silence and whisky had taken him in their arms and cradled him into a lull.

Above him the sky changed colour, spewing oranges and reds across the horizon as the sun bloomed. He grimaced at the fiery orb, resenting it as it pulled him into the day he never wanted to arrive, yet found himself wanting nothing more than to etch it all into his memory. Every colour, the slight breeze wafting off the land, the smell of charred wood and burned toast.

Somewhere beyond, a cock crowed and knew his time was running out. He watched the waves crash along the shore and the rising and falling chests of his friends as they lay slumbering on the sand.

He stood up on shaky legs and his stomach lurched, threatening to expel last night's drink. He ran his tongue over his teeth, the furry feeling and rancid smell doing little to improve his temperament.

He should have gone home. But his legs carried him instead to the red door.

Mama Cath sat on the porch. In her hand she held some fresh bread. Her big eyes fell on him as he stepped closer.

Silently she handed him the warm, freshly baked bread.

Ben bit into it grateful for the heaviness that settled in his stomach. But as much as he ate, he could not fill the pit that grew inside him. An emptiness crept from within, its tentacles wound around his neck and ever so slightly began to squeeze.

He sucked in a strangled breath and looked up to the door.

"You can't go in there. Mama Beth made that clear." She tucked away an errant hair that blew across her face in the light breeze.

He tore another mouthful, the doughy bread chewy in his dry mouth. He swallowed hard and set it aside on the wooden step, letting his finger trace the worn wood.

Mama Cath offered a bottle of water which he drank greedily. The water quenching his thirst, alleviating the dryness in his throat, drowning his sorrow.

"We need to go Benjen." Mama Cath looked into his eyes, holding his gaze.

He clenched his jaw and held his mother's gaze.

He saw the pain buried beyond her deep brown eyes and heard the pleading in her voice hidden behind the cracks, he noted the tremor in her hand as she stretched it out to him.

His body ached with tension, his head caught in a vicious battle with his heart. Every muscle taught, resisting the urge to burst through the red door, to go and see Ariel one last time, hear her voice, touch her skin, kiss her lips.

He reached out and took his mother's hand, and with a final wistful look at the door, his body deflated. The battle lost. He was resigned, bleeding and torn, hurting in ways he could not fathom.

Mama Cath laced her fingers in his and led him down the path. With every step he felt the heaviness of manhood settle upon him. These would be his last moments with his mother, on his island home. He didn't dare look back. For if he had, he would have no more strength to resist the need. He would have pulled his bleeding body back up the path and into her arms. He would have risked it all just for her.

He felt his mother's weight on him. This was not his battle alone. He was the last of three sons, she would be all alone. The burden of womanhood suddenly heavier for her to carry. He released his mother and wound an arm around her waist, hers folding across his shoulders. Ben pulled his mother closer until he was no longer sure if she was carrying him or if he was carrying her.

On the shore they were met by the other two families. Mothers and brothers in tears. One boy had a flower wreath around his neck, his younger sister clung to his legs, stretching on her tip toes. The other's face distressed, red with effort and streaked with tears.

In the distance they a boat with two oarsmen approached, steering it to the shore. There were precious few minutes left until they arrived.

He wrapped his arms around his mother. His heart thundered in his chest.

"I love you." He leaned into her and felt the tremor of her chest and the gurgle of breath as her hot tears fell onto his head. There was so much more he wanted to say, words of wisdom and comfort. His pain suddenly tangible as his mother shuddered with sorrow.

He opened his mouth to speak, but then he saw her. Like a wisp in the wind she was flying, bursting from the shrubbery, erupting onto the sand.

Behind him the boat had arrived, low voices of men, curled along the beach.

He smiled. Broad and vast. His heart galloped in his chest as he broke free from his mother and ran.

Their bodies collided. Her face flushed and streaked with tears, her hair wild and face bewildered. Ariel's body shivered beneath his as he wrapped himself around her. Relief washed over him followed instantly by desire and heartache. He didn't want to leave.

A blaring siren sounded across the beach. A final call to board. Only precious minutes, seconds to have her, to hold her, to remember everything. Her skin, her eyes, her laugh, her tears, the feel of them on his face. It would all be over.

He tightened his grip around her. He couldn't let go. Not when there was so much more to say. To do.

To be.

She pushed slightly away from him and looked into his eyes. He didn't expect it when it came. Her soft lips suddenly on his, lingering. He tasted her tears, they seared his dried lips, soothing them with her softness, tenderness.

"I love you too," she whispered in his ear as she broke their embrace.

His chest constricted and his mind reeled. The words seeped into his skin, saturating him, washing over him like a tidal wave. For a split second it was only him and her. He saw all that they could be, and his body whispered to him all that it wanted from her. There were so many words that had to be spoken.

"What are you doing? You must go. Now!" Mama Cath's hand landed on his shoulder. The spell fractured but not broken all together.

Ignoring his mother, he pulled Ariel closer again, and wrapped his arms around her. In that embrace, the world melted away for a single quiet moment.

Without warning, strong arms grabbed his shoulders and yanked at him. He clutched on to Ariel's arms as the foreign hands wrenched him away. Ben clawed at Ariel who tried to hold on to him, his nails dug fresh trails along her forearms as he was finally forced to let her go. Her brown eyes wide, swollen.

"Ariel!" he shrieked as the oarsmen pulled him towards the boat. He fought, twisting his body against the hard muscles that held him, but was no match for their strength. Still, he tried. He struggled. His body slippery against their wet skins. Fingers dug into his skin as their grips tightened around him, then with a swift movement they lifted him into the air.

With a crushing thud that knocked the air from his lungs, he landed against hard wet wood. He rolled to his side and into a briny puddle. Ben sucked in a frayed breath and pushed himself over the lip of the boat.

"Ariel!" he screamed as he watched her sink into the sand. The oarsmen pushed against the sand bank and the boat tilted ever so slightly then dipped as the waves carried it away.

"Ariel," he called for her again. He willed her to look at him, to respond. She sat in silence, her body blurred by distance, denying him her face, her eyes, her voice.

He called for her again.

"Stop now boy," the bigger of the two men growled. His voice sounded like serrated tin, harsh and guttural.

Ignoring him, Ben screamed for her again. "Ariel."

A sudden gush of pain jolted through his back and snaked to his head as he fell face first into the water sloshing at the bottom of the boat. He groaned, muscles twitching as he pushed and slid his back up against the edge of the boat. He searched the horizon, his heart constricted as Inan's golden sand bar lay faint on the horizon.

He gripped the edge of the boat, "Ariel," he howled, his voice broken and hoarse, his throat aching.

A shard of pain exploded in the back of his head as he tumbled over, the sun kissed his face, the blue sky smiled, and the world went black.

7

A salty wave washed over his face. He choked and coughed as the briny water filled his mouth. He rolled onto his side and spat the water out, just as another small wave washed over him.

"Hey, he's not dead," a hoarse voice gibed. It didn't sound relieved.

Ben pushed himself up and leaned against coarse wood, swiping at a rivulet of water that leaked down his face. He grunted as he drained the water from his hair and his fingers skated over an angry lump just behind his ear. He licked his dry lips and took stock of his surroundings, noting five passengers including himself. Given the presence of two unfamiliar boys, he suspected they had made a second stop. He studied the boys which all looked his age and measured himself against them. Two he knew. They had come from Inan with him. He had grown up with them, seen them almost every day.

He examined the newcomers more carefully. One was as white as ghost as if he was fashioned from a cloud. His pale completion pallid, his wispy white hair blowing in the sea breeze and his blue-rimmed eyes seemed pink in the light.

When their eyes connected the ghostly boy turned away, his face a mask of terror.

The other was brown as if moulded from the earth itself. Curled black hair clung to his head and his eyes were deep brown discs floating on a perfect white surface. His frame sagged on a wooden bench, as if he was melting in the harsh sun.

Ben scrubbed a hand over his face and searched the endless blue plane around them. All he could see was water.

The boat lurched forward with the waves, the sensation making his stomach roll. He swallowed hard pushing down the growing unease boiling within him. Taking big long gulps of air, he steadied himself.

Without warning the pale boy pitched his body over the edge of the boat and heaved. The contents of his last meal scarring the water with a long brown and red mark.

The two oarsmen burst into laughter.

"I told you he was going to go first." The younger of the two oarsmen brayed wildly. "You'll have to pay up when we get back."

"Yeah yeah." The thickset man smirked and spat into the water. "This little runt won't make it anyway." He dipped his head towards the ashen boy whose pallor had turned a shade of grey.

"Maybe we should do him a favour and help him out."

"Charity?" The bigger of the two men stepped away from his post and towards the heaving boy.

"A kindness really."

"Save that for the women." He cackled, then, without much effort reached out and grabbed the boy by the neck. The bulky oarsman picked him up as if he was a rag and with a swing of his arm threw him over the edge of the boat.

The boy hit the water with a shrill, savage squeal.

The boat rocked violently as the dark boy bolted up and threw himself against the lip of the boat. His hand skimmed the choppy surface of the water as he reached out and shrieked, "Danny, Danny, hold on." His teary eyes looked to Ben then back to the drowning boy, helplessness carved into his features as he screamed for his friend.

Ben turned to the oarsmen. "Go get him."

"Shut your mouth boy or you'll be next," spat the older of the two.

"Go and get him, now."

The sound of splashing water faded as the screams became more frantic.

"Final warning boy, sit down and shut your mouth."

Ben clenched his fists as the boat drew further away from the flailing boy, whose yelps and screams weakened, his arms and legs thrashing against his blue enemy.

Ben turned to the other boys on the boat. "We have to help him," his voice scratched against his throat, his heart pounding in his chest.

"Get up, jump in. They can't go back with an empty boat."

"Sit down all of you, or you'll all end up like the runt over there." The oarsman's harsh voice threatened, but Ben heard the undercurrent of fear.

He searched the blue horizon until he saw the white head dip beneath the surface then break though again. White hair floated on the water like haunted seaweed. The splashing all but done.

"We need to get in now or he's dead."

Danny's companion was the first to hit the water, like his drowning friend, his body flailed and fought the wet monster.

Without further thought Ben climbed onto the rim of the boat and jumped. The warm water enveloped him like welcoming arms. He broke the surface, gulped for air and scanned over the waves, relieved to find four heads bobbing in the water.

Ben fought against the rippling current which carried

him further away from the boat. It's two remaining occupants red faced and scowling.

The air thickened with shirking and splashing, fear seeped into the water and send a shiver through him.

The boat turned and drifted back towards the boys, the oarsmen plucked them from the water one by one. Steering past Ben, the boat made its way to Danny his motionless body pulled from the water like driftwood. They swept by Danny's dark companion who clutched onto an oar, was yanked into the boat then discarded like his friend.

Ben's head pounded, every cell in his body screamed, his entire body throbbed, as he fought the pounding waves. Salty angry water rushed into his mouth, his head dipped beneath the surface. He came up again and sucked air into his burning lungs. The boat neared him and an oarsman offered Ben no help as he grabbed onto the rim. He clung on, his knuckles blanched with effort. Then, without warning strong hands lifted him up and let him fall into the vessel. Lying on his back he sucked in long shallow breaths, briny water splashing his face with every wave. He turned his head and saw Danny laying against his weeping friend, tears glistening on his ebony skin.

"I thought I had lost you," the boy said to his companion.

"Antoine," Danny whimpered against his friend's broad chest.

Ben looked to the other boys, wet and dishevelled, sprawled across the boat. Despite the pain in his body a grin spread across his face and was shared among the small group.

"Smile all you want boy, but we will be in Dagon soon and all you will understand is pain. Actions do not go unpunished on Dagon."

"And what of your actions?" Ben turned to the man who had threatened him, the older face curling up like a dried prune that has been left too long in the sun.

Before he could retort his companion called out, "Land ahoy."

Ben scrambled to the lip of the boat with the other boys causing it to dip to one side. In the distance he could make out the island of Dagon, the sharp edges and white rock. He swallowed hard, his stomach knotted as he watched his new home draw nearer.

A heavy silence settled over the boat, broken by an occasional sniff and waves lapping against the wood. With each measured paddle of the oars, the blurry outline of the island became more defined, the greenery more vibrant, the earth more solid.

The oarsmen steered the boat towards a long wooden dock that extended from the beach. The waves eased the vessel alongside it, where several men stood to greet them.

Men.

They looked like him. Bigger, broader, taller versions of himself. Yet up until that very moment they were all but a foreign concept. One he didn't know how to embrace.

The older of the two oarsmen threw a long rope to a man with a curled lip that split unevenly down the middle. Without a word he caught the rope and tugged at it, secured it to the cleat, then stood squinting in the mid-day sun.

"Get off," the burly man ordered as he placed his oar down and stretched his back. The five boys stood, swaying gently with the boat. Large hands plucked them one by one from the vessel and in moments Ben landed on the polished wood.

His new home. Where he was likely to remain for the rest of his life. A lump rose to his throat, which he pushed down with a long breath.

They waited on the dock which Ben knew to be perfectly stable, yet, his body felt a disequilibrium he could not explain. He fought the urge to fall to his knees and crawl to the safety in the sand.

"It's called land sickness. It will go away in a few hours," offered a bronzed man who came forward to stand in front of them. He studied each of them in turn then turned his attention to the oarsmen.

"What the hell happened to them? They looked like wet goats."

The oarsmen exchanged a fleeting look, then the younger of the two caught Ben's gaze, holding it as his eyes narrowed

Ben cleared his throat, "A rogue wave."

"A wave you say?" The bronzed man took a step closer to Ben, scrutinising his face.

"Yes, it tipped us over and we all fell in the water. They helped us back into the boat..."

The man advanced toward the oarsmen, and stationed himself between them. He reached over and placed a hand on each man's shoulder. "Tipped over? And somehow these fine gentlemen remained perfectly dry?"

Ben shrugged. "Must have their sea legs or something."

"Mm mm." The man squeezed their shoulders, fingers digging into skin. His eyes flickered to each of the boys, all remained silent, and looked at their feet.

He released the oarsmen with a shove and addressed the boys with a sneer. "My name is Luke son of Mary. For the next few hours I will be your guide. Pay attention and follow me."

Luke swivelled and walked down the dock. Ben hurried to keep pace with his long strides, the other boys followed with unsteady steps. He felt every eye on the island leering at him, judging him, weighing him up. Despite his churning stomach and shaking limbs, he found himself doing the same.

The further away the group walked from the boat, the more Ben fought the compulsion to run back, to dive right off the dock and into the ocean, to swim back to Mama Cath, to Ariel.

To swim home.

Luke turned his head back without stopping. "That feeling will pass too."

Ben tried to push away the thought, and wondered what else this stranger knew about him that he didn't yet know himself.

He looked around the island he had heard so much about, the one that had loomed over his head since the day of his birth. At first look it seemed much like Inan. A white sandy beach encompassed the island as far as he could see in both directions and the village beyond was protected by dense shrubbery that grew up to the sandy beach line.

"We will first stop by the hospital. After that you will be taken to the Keepers where they will assign you a brother."

The boys remained silent, each with their own thoughts as they crossed the beach and broke through the curtain of shrubbery.

Houses littered the sloping mountain side and for a second Ben felt the familiarity of Inan, but on closer inspection he noticed the craggy look of the island and its housing. Instead of the rounder curves of wooden porches and walls there were jagged rocks. The unwelcoming stone houses loomed from the mountain side and were topped with braided thatched roofs. They appeared neither warm nor inviting.

The small group walked further up the path towards a broad building. It extended on both sides far beyond any he had seen so far.

"This way," Luke said as he pushed through the wooden doors and into the building.

Ben followed the man inside and a cold shiver ran up his spine. The stone structure felt cavernous and the temperature plummeted with each step. He wrapped his arms around his torso and shuffled deeper inside.

The group reached an empty room where a row of orange plastic chairs lined the wall

"Sit. I'll go and tell Rob you're here," Luke said, then disappeared behind a secondary door further down the corridor.

Ben's body tightened, the muscles in his legs tensing ready to bolt, to sprint, to help him disappear. His heart pounded in his chest and he pumped his fists to the crazed beat, his toe, tapping the cold ground.

Ready.

He sucked in a sharp breath.

Set.

His knuckled blanched as he gripped the lip of the chair.

Before Ben could bolt from his seat, the ghostly boy whined, tears rolled down his cheeks as he sniffed and sucked wet snot.

"I can't be here. I need to go home, please." The boy's eyes darted from his companion to the door and back again.

"Danny. Danny, look at me." Antoine took his hand and smiled at his friend, seeking his eyes. "We can't go. This is home now. You need to stay calm, so you don't get yourself hurt. I don't know what I would do if you were hurt."

Danny bit his quivering lip and nodded. He allowed Antoine to hold his hand for a second longer before snatching it away and wiping unshed tears from his puffy eyes.

"Danny, son of Annabelle," called a man clad in a white robe, his voice echoed from a doorway down the corridor. Ben caught a wisp of black hair as he disappeared back inside, not waiting for the boy to follow.

Danny stood, his shoulders hunched and gave Antoine a long, desperate look before shuffling down the corridor.

Ben didn't know how long he had waited but being last at anything drove him insane. By the time he was called, his entire body was coiled like a snake ready to strike. The other boys never returned.

He pushed through the door and walked down another corridor. Exposed wall rose on his left built of uneven bricks which rested upon one another unsteadily. A doctor held open a door to what Ben assumed was his exam room.

Inside the cramped room he spotted a single bed and a rock desk that jutted out of the wall. Bright, white light coated the room but didn't warm it. The doctor sat down on an orange plastic chair and rifled through some papers on his makeshift desk.

"Sit on the bed, Benjen, son of Catherine."

Ben followed the doctor's instructions, grounding his teeth.

"Benjen I am Doctor Rob. My job is to make sure you are well enough to stay here in Dagon. It should be quick and painless."

Ben studied the man, he was tall and lanky with long black hair that hung in a braid down to his hips. A fine beard framed his thin face and his piercing blue eyes seemed to smile of their own accord.

The doctor turned back to his papers. "Clothes off please."

Ben felt the heat rise to his cheeks. He peeled off his shirt and pants and resumed his position on the bed.

When Rob stood to face him, he gave a wane smile. "Everything."

Ben sucked in breath and bit his lip then slipped out of his underwear, his hand darting over his groin.

The doctor paid him no heed as he completed the examination, feeling and palpating his arms, throat, neck and legs.

"Open your mouth."

The doctor shoved his fingers inside and felt around Ben fought the urge to vomit as he gagged.

"We're almost done Benjen, but I need you to remove

your hands." He had an air about him that was patient and carefree, yet serious and efficient.

Ben removed them and clenched his fists as hands grabbed his genitals. Foreign hands, hands that were not his… or Ariel's. He scrunched his eyes shut and gritted his teeth.

The doctor gripped, squeezed and palpated, then released him. Ben let out a long shuddering breath.

"Thank you, Benjen. One last test. Please stand with your body towards the bed and bend over."

Swallowing hard, he followed the doctor's orders.

"Now just relax."

Before he could think to do anything, the doctor began to examine him. His body froze at the unwanted intrusion which ended as quickly as It had begun.

"Thank you, Benjen. You may get dressed."

A cold sweat broke along his body cooling him from the unbearable heat he felt a moment ago, Ben snatched his clothing from the floor and yanked them onto his body.

"I have good news for you, Benjen." The doctor smiled broadly. "You may call Dagon home and you'll be assigned a brother. Welcome."

The doctor extended a hand to the boy who looked at it, then reluctantly locked it with his own. He shook then snatched it away burying it behind his back.

The doctor's face broke into an amused smile as he pointed at the door. "Luke will be waiting for you in the main entrance. Good luck Benjen, son of Catherine." The doctor gave him a final smile then turned his back and sat at his desk where he began to write.

Ben opened the door and sprinted back the way he had come. When he burst through the doors, he didn't fail to notice Luke's smirk and the uncomfortable expressions on the other of the boys' faces. All were accounted for but Danny. Luke gestured for the boys to follow him.

Antoine froze in place and asked, "Where is Danny, son of Nora?"

"Where he needs to be I suspect," Luke shrugged.

"What does that mean?"

"It means that it's not up to me to answer your questions."

"I'm not leaving without him."

Luke sighed and ran his hand through his shoulder length hair. Irritation flashed in his emerald green eyes as he stepped towards Antoine and loomed above him.

"Boy, you will come with me whether you like to or not. There are no more mamas here, no one to run home and cry to. No one is going to give you cuddles and wipe away your snot. You will do what you are told or you will be punished. Now, let's go."

Luke pointed at the door where two of the boys stood waiting.

Antoine stood his ground, Ben a step behind him.

Without warning or ceremony, Luke's fist connected with Antoine's face. His head snapped backwards and his legs gave way. He fell to his knees, his lip leaking a rivulet of crimson.

Luke unclenched his fist and gripped Antoine's chin so that he could look directly at his eyes. "The next one won't be as soft." He turned to Ben, "Do you have any questions?"

Ben shook his head.

"Good. Bring your friend, we don't have all day." Luke turned toward the exit and directed the boys to follow him out.

Ben kneeled by Antoine. "I'm sure Danny is fine."

He wrapped Antoine's arm around his shoulder and supported him as he stood. Then helped his new friend to walk.

The sun felt harsh after the time they had spent inside the cool stone structure. They followed Luke down an earthy path that weaved between rocky homes. He pointed out the housing district and food hall, the farms and quarry. Ben paid little attention to the words, lost in his new surroundings.

The group stopped in front of a house that seemed smaller than the others. On the porch sat an old man clad in a purple robe with a long white beard that rested on his lap. A trail of smoke escaped his lips as he sucked on a white rolled up cigarette.

The old man whose skin hung off his bones like wet cloth peered with sharp, keen eyes at the new comers. He turned to Luke. "Go fetch the book."

The hunched man stood up and uncurled with effort as Luke disappeared into the house. "I am the Elder of Dagon, Ethan, son of Gaia. Welcome to your new home. Today I oversee your Keepsaker and it is my honour to witness your arrival."

With his introduction over, he returned to his wooden chair. He flicked his cigarette to the ground, the white tip smouldering as it burned into ash.

Luke returned with a second man. He was clad in a blue robe and held a thick, wide book. Luke set up a portable wooden table where the newcomer dropped the book, it exploded in thud of particles which whirled around in the afternoon sun.

"I am the Keeper G. Once we record your place of birth and date of arrival, I shall assign you a brother. Your brother will be your guardian for the first year of life on Dagon. They will teach you our rules and guide you in the ways of life and in the ways of manhood. They will teach you a trade or, if theirs does not complement your skills, find you a suitable teacher."

Ben swallowed hard. It has been five years since he had seen Logan and another two since he had seen Mason. He wondered what his brothers might look like now.

Logan had always been tall and broad, even as a child his

height had matched their mother's. His fine blonde hair always untamed and his laugh contagious. Ben adored his older brother and the crushing loss alleviated slightly at the thought that they may be reunited shortly.

In contrast, Mason had been caged and broody, with dark circles set under his cool emerald eyes. He clung to their mother on the day they tore him from her. Though never close, the comfort of a possible reunion filled Ben with hope.

A tingle of excitement skittered up his spine as a crowd gathered, closing the group in a half circle. Ben twisted and turned, pushing on his tip toes, searching the sea of foreign faces for any sign of familiarity.

He covered his mouth to stifle the inevitable smile that crept onto his face. He wondered if Logan's laugh had grown with him, if it was now a deep grumble like thunder. If his smile still touched his eyes, if he would remember Ben at all. His smile faltered beneath his palm.

The Keepsaker's voice pierced his thoughts calling each boy in turn, assigning their new brothers.

Ben's hope bloomed as Alex, son of Olivia, was reunited with his older brother. The two collided in a crushing hug, delight splashed across their features as they laughed. Alex's tension melted away from him instantly, his rigid features softened. Alex's brother banded an arm around him and led him away and up the path.

Ben's heart soared.

The next to be called was Ryan, son of Josephine. The Keepsaker called another name, unfamiliar to the Ben. The newcomer stepped out of the crowd and shook Ryan's hand. Ryan fell to his knees, tears streaming down his face.

"I want to go home," he wailed as his body shook like a reed in the wind.

"You are home boy." His brother kneeled by him and pulled him up by the hand. "Come with me, it will be all right."

Ryan sucked in a nose full of snot and scratched the tears from his eyes. Like a reed broken in a squall, his head dropped into his hands and he followed his brother up the path and disappeared.

"Benjen, son of Catherine." The Keepsaker's voice scratched in his throat.

Ben stepped forward his gaze landing on the book that lay open. The old man dragged a long bony finger along the yellowing page. Columns filled with foreign symbols. He came to an abrupt stop, picked up his quill, dipped it in ink then recorded the information that would determine Ben's fate.

He inhaled deeply as the old man placed the quill down and smacked his lips. "Benjen, son of Catherine, meet your brother, Luke, son of Mary."

Ben's lungs emptied and his body shook as if he had received a physical blow. He tried to suck in air but his treacherous lungs refused to fill.

Luke was by his side, a harsh whisper in his ear. "Don't let them see your weakness."

Ben's body froze at the words and he forced the flood of emotion back down. Like lead it sat at the bottom of his stomach, dark and heavy. He sucked in a deep breath and looked to the Keepsaker.

"Thank you." He swallowed the quiver of his voice. "Could you tell me where my brothers are?" He looked to Luke apologetically.

"It's not the way."

"Please?" Ben searched the furrowed face and landed on eyes that were weighed down with wrinkled folds. It felt almost like talking to someone asleep, yet the Keepsaker was quite alert.

His head dipped slightly and gnarled fingers tapped the wooden table before him. With a heavy breath his cragged hand ran along the pages of the book, searching. His lips smacked together and he looked up.

"I was young once. Like you I had brothers."

"Do you know where they are?"

"I do." The old man gave Ben a crooked grin. "But we do not have time for reminiscing."

"Do you know where *my* brothers are?" Ben swallowed the rock in is throat.

"I do." The old man's face split in a melancholy grin. "Mason, son of Catherine, has been shuffled. He resides in the Second Quarter."

Ben exhaled, something akin to relief washing over him. "What about Logan?"

The Keepsaker's eyes skimmed the page and grew wider for a split second. He pushed the book away and turned to Luke. "Time to move on, I am yet to finish recording."

He turned his head to Antoine, who stood alone waiting to hear his fate.

Ben's heart skipped, then pounded. "What about Logan?" he called to the old man who paid him no heed. "Please. What about Logan?"

A heavy hand landed on his shoulder and tugged. "Time to go brother."

When he didn't move, the hand turned his body with force and guided him away from the Keepsaker.

8

Despite himself, Ben put one foot in front of the other and trudged up the path behind his new brother. A whimper escaped him and he felt tears pool in his eyes. He swiped them away pretending his heart was not ripping at the seams, breaking and bleeding, that his hope had not just been violently torn away.

"Are you listening?"

Ben mumbled a reply. He continued to stare at his feet as he followed the older man around, catching only fragments of words. His brothers were gone. Any hope for meeting them again vanished with a swirl of white smoke and a crooked smile.

"We're here."

Still in a daze, Ben walked straight into Luke's solid mass and stumbled backwards.

"Here?"

"Your new home."

He looked around for the first time. They had ascended the mountain of Dagon. The island splayed beneath him. The village sprawled about like a lazy octopus and the blue ocean sparkled beyond. He scanned the empty plot and raised his face to Luke.

"There's nothing here."

"There's land."

"But it's empty."

"Yes."

"So where is my house?"

"You must build it."

"I don't know how." Hearing the quiver in his voice, he cleared his throat.

"Well lucky for you, your brother does." He flashed him a smile and punched him playfully on the arm.

The punch hurt more than it should have and Ben sucked in a long breath and rubbed his arm while surveying the plot of brown earth, his mind erecting a palace.

"How long will it take to build?"

"Three to four months."

"Three to four months?!" He choked back the tears that were on the verge of spilling. "Where am I meant to live until then?"

"Here." Luke gestured to the empty plot.

"But... there's *nothing* here."

Luke sat down and gestured for the boy to follow him. They sat in silence for a while and gazed at the sun stretching towards the horizon.

"This is your home now. If you do not claim it someone else will. Once you lose your claim it will be difficult for you to regain it."

Ben face furrowed, "I'm not sure I understand,"

"It's okay. We've all been there."

He sniffled as anxiety wound tight inside him, suffocating him. He was grateful for the show of empathy, despite it being so short.

"Look." Luke pointed to the Village. "Dagon is divided by

three invisible lines. Stay within your line and you'll be all right."

Luke drew two invisible lines with his hands. "The Western District is for the families where those with blood ties live. They have a camaraderie only real brothers share, one many of us no longer get to enjoy."

"But some brothers come years apart?"

"Yes, but they live there in the hopes of a sibling joining them. If no one arrives they are moved to another district."

"What about this one?" Ben pointed to the right side of the island.

"The Eastern District." Luke's face hardened. "The men on that side of the island are singles, like me and you. No blood relation of any kind."

His pensive voice tugged at Ben's heart.

"What of the last area?"

Luke cleared his throat and shifted slightly. "The Central District. That is where the eldest amongst us live. They will remain there until they are picked as Watchers or until they die. They ensure the rules are upheld and that Dagon remains trouble free."

"How do they do that?"

"You ask too many questions kid."

"But—"

"That's for another day." Luke stood up and brushed the dirt from his pants. "Let's go get something to eat and then we will get you settled."

Ben followed Luke to the mess hall. Raucous laughter and hearty conversation filled the air as they approached. Unlike on Inan, this mess hall was packed, and full of displays of power and prowess.

He followed Luke to the service area where they each received a plate of fish and vegetables. His gaze drifted across the room as he trailed him to find a seat and crashed into a human wall, his dinner spilling from his plate and onto the chest of an unfamiliar boy. Blazing blue eyes set in an angry scowl crashed into his. The bigger boy stepped back allowing the food to fall away from his body.

"Watch where you're going pretty boy."

"Sorry, I'm—"

"You should be sorry." The boy closed the distance between them, his chest expanding like peacock feathers.

"Back off, Liam. He said he was sorry. Didn't your mummy teach you any manners?" Luke growled.

Liam grunted and shot a lingering look over at Luke then stepped back. "Sleep with one eye open pretty boy, your brother isn't always going to be around..." He walked away and joined a group of men sitting at a table.

"Don't worry about Liam." Luke jutted his chin towards the group. "He's all talk."

Ben studied the boy then his dinner as it lay wasted on the floor.

"Don't worry about that either, go get another plate."

"But..."

"There are plenty of fish in the ocean, they repopulate faster than we do. It's what we trade for other commodities. Go get another plate."

He retrieved a fresh dinner plate and found Luke seated with a group of other men. He ignored their amused expressions as he wolfed down his meal. He didn't realise how hungry he was until the food reached his stomach and it growled with appreciation.

Once they had eaten Luke led Ben to a house that loomed over the others.

"Stay here."

He disappeared inside and returned a moment later with a pillow and blanket as well as a rolled-up tent.

"Come on."

Ben followed the older boy. His legs heavy, his eyes bleary, his heart weighed down with emotion.

"Was that your house?"

"Yes."

"But it's so much bigger than the others."

"That's what she said." Luke burst into laughter as the setting sun cast his face into shadow.

Ben tilted his head. "I don't understand. Why is it bigger?"

"Cause I built it." He turned and winked then resumed his long powerful stride.

By the time they pitched the tent, the sea had turned black and a white streak of moonlight sliced across its swelling waves.

Luke threw the pillow and blanket into the tent and gave Ben a final look. "You'll be okay here tonight. They usually leave the newcomers alone on their first night." He put a sturdy hand on Ben's shoulder and looked to his eyes, then nodded stiffly. His hand fell away and he turned to leave.

"Them? Who? What are you talking about?" His heart pounded, the blood slamming through his veins like a rogue wave.

Ben sat by the fiery torch he'd been given, haunted by Luke's chuckle as he'd descended back to his home. It was not a cold night but the warmth from the fire felt somehow comforting.

He sat looking at the ocean, the black swells shining in the moonlight, and felt the hot tears as they streaked unchecked across his cheeks, leaving trails of anger and grief. The warmth of the fire could not halt the shudders that ran through his fragile frame. His heart filled with emptiness as the seams of a life he could no longer hold on to snapped.

With hitched breath and a heaving chest he drew his knees up until he was nothing but a ball of flesh and bone on the dirt.

Ben woke with a heaviness he could not contain. The air around him felt suffocating, crushing. The sun was yet to rise and his fire was nothing more than a sunken pile of charred sticks. He rubbed sleep from his eyes, his body and heart aching. He stood, scanned his bare patch of earth then took a step away from it. Then another. With every step his body felt lighter. His heart fuller. He knew where he had to go. The one place that would make him feel better again.

Home.

Purple tendrils inked the sky. The sun would not be far behind. He sprinted.

His breath came in short sharp gasps as he fought exhaustion, his muscles burned as they pumped, faster and harder. The ocean called to him like a siren and he reached for her. Ben scampered into the shrubbery, his body heaving, sucking in breath, filling his lungs with oxygen.

He spotted the boat as it bobbed in the calm waves, thudding gently against the wooden dock.

He scanned the beach.

Empty.

He sprinted from the cover of the greenery and headed for the boat, battling the sandy beach. He leapt onto the dock, his bare feet slapping against the polished wood as he raced to freedom.

Ben reached the boat and stumbled over the wooden lip, his face met the bottom with a cold splash. The boat jolted and rocked wildly, then settled into a soothing lullaby as the waves lapped gently upon it. Ben sat up, swept the water away from his eyes and scoured the vessel. His head swung madly like a deranged pendulum. He sucked in a long breath pushing down the rising tide of panic and spotted the cargo container. His stomach knotted and churned as he tucked his body into the small space. He shut his eyes and attempted to ease the fire in his lungs. The boat would set off for its daily trade, by the time they discovered him, he would be home.

From his hiding place he heard the village come to life. Bird song and voices sounded across the island. His heart stammered in his chest. He curled up tighter into the hole, the sun baking the heavy tarp that covered him. Sweat dripped down his face as he waited.

Two voices grew closer. Ben's heart smashed in his chest as the boat shook with heavy steps, his fists tightened around the tarp, fearing the entire vessel would topple over as it sloshed around.

"Did you fix the net?" the first voice asked.

Ben's stomach coiled.

"Why bother?"

"Oh come on Simon, we need to bring something back or they'll replace us and then—"

"Okay, no need to get yourself all twisted up about it. Let's put some distance between us and them and I ca—"

"Simon, Ian." The hair on Ben's body stiffened at the sound of Luke's voice. "How are you on this fine morning?"

"What the do you want?" Simon grumbled.

"Not enough whisky in your coffee this morning?"

"Not enough whisky on this island to get him to be more charming." Ian's voice held a note of mirth and was greeted with a grunt.

"Smells like he's already drunk all of it." Luke and Ian burst into laughter while Simon grumbled under his breath.

When the laughter died down Simon asked, "What are you doing here? You know we need to cast off for the day. Island isn't going to feed itself now is it?"

"Before you go, I need to check your boat."

"What for?" Simon's surly voice held a note of irritation.

"Seems I've misplaced my brother."

"Misplaced you say?"

"Lucky you. I've been stuck with mine for the last twenty years." Ian chimed in.

"Yes, well you do seem to be suffering."

"Why do you think I drink so much?"

Another bout of laughter rocked the boat.

"So, you think this brother of yours has been misplaced on this boat?" Simon grumbled.

"I'm sure that he is far too intelligent to think he could sneak onto your boat and be taken back to an island he has no business being on." Luke's voice edged closer as the boat rocked.

"Yes well," Ian huffed, "he wouldn't be the first, would he now?"

Luke didn't respond.

The boat rocked once more then sunlight seared Ben's eyes as the tarp was ripped from above him. Ben rubbed his dazed eyes then looked up to see Luke looming over him.

"Is this where you got to? Your new home not comfortable enough for you?"

Ben remained silent as he wedged himself tighter into the small hole. Luke squatted so that he could meet Ben's eyes. "Time to get up now and let these fine gentlemen start their day."

Ben bit the inside of his lip, holding Luke's gaze.

"Look, one way or another you're coming with me. I would much prefer if it was your decision."

Motionless, his skin prickled with anticipation. Ben squeezed his eyes shut and ground his teeth. His heart thudded dully in his chest and his expression emptied.

Luke sighed and made to stand when Ben uncurled himself and wiggled out of the nook. His brother smiled and offered him a hand up.

Ben scanned the scene, taking in the two sullen oarsmen, Luke's troubled face and three men he'd never seen before standing on the dock. When Luke gestured for him to follow, his eyes swung to the ocean and back to Luke.

"Don't." Luke's mouth tightened in a thin line as Ben's weight shifted.

He jumped onto the bench and with a swift motion launched himself off the boat and into the water.

Ben heard the voices behind him as he swam. His arms ploughed through the water with force, putting distance between him and this strange place, sweeping him closer to home, to Mama Cath, to Ariel.

The voices and shouts faded behind him and he chanced a quick look back. A row of men stood along the dock, their eyes solely focused on him. His veins flooded with determination as he continued to fight the waves and thrust through the water towards freedom.

His arms grew weary and his muscles throbbed with pain. He searched the vast, blue emptiness spread before him and knew would get no further. He could swim back to his new home and face his fate or let the ocean swallow him whole.

Ben flipped onto his back and allowed the current to carry him as he drowned beneath a slew of thoughts. He looked to the shore, to the men waiting as if they knew. He realised that the longer he was out in the ocean the greater the punishment would be, but this small taste of freedom, of rebellion, lit a warm flame inside of him.

Like a lazy mirage the boat appeared through the fog of his thoughts. The two oarsmen watched as he slapped at the water with sloppy chops of his arms, his strength all but sunk to the ocean floor.

Simon shook his head, his jaw set while Ian barked a coarse laugh. "Are you done yet boy? Or do you want us all put before the Elder?"

Ben's gaze landed on the man's face. Beyond the sun beaten skin and windswept hair were two eyes as deep and blue as the ocean, endless wells of compassionate woe.

Hands grabbed at him and plucked him from the water. He lay wasted and drenched on the bottom of the boat where his fists pounded the wood as it steered back towards the shore.

Simon breached the silence as they drew nearer to Dagon. "Don't fight boy, accept."

Ben coughed and sucked in humid air. "I can't."

"Then you will suffer."

"I'll suffer anyway."

The man grunted and turned his attention to the beach where the waiting party waded into the water as if to welcome him home.

Ben's knuckles blanched as he grabbed the lip of the boat, splinters shredded his palms as strong arms tore him from the vessel. The men pulled him towards the shore, his feet dragging in the water as a violent shudder tore through him.

They didn't stop as they passed Luke, his arms locked across his chest, disappointment floated across his features like a dark cloud.

Fingers dug into his skin as his feet dragged along the soft sand, slicing a path to the waiting crowd. His stomach knitted and sank, like an anvil into the depths of the ocean, as the hands released him and he dropped to his knees in the centre of the gathered crowd.

Ben scanned the men, noting their tense jaws and ashen expressions. The silence fed the gnawing fear that brewed inside him. The crowd parted as a man dressed in purple garb stepped forward and came to a stop before him, his hazel eyes sunk deep into the cavern of his face.

"Stand Benjen, son of Catherine, for no man in Dagon will be judged on their knees. Peace is not possible when we are not all equal."

His legs wobbled beneath him as he stood to his full height, he squared his shoulders and sucked in a galvanising breath, searching the crowd for a friendly face. He found none.

"I am the Elder Rohan, son of Willow, and Dagon has been left in my charge." He tipped his head and continued, "Conflict is not the natural human state, but often times a result of circumstance that pits brother against brother. There is always a cause. Do you agree, Benjen?"

Ben remained silent as the Elder's gaze bore into him.

"What caused you, Benjen, son of Catherine, to bring about discord and chaos to Dagon?"

He shuffled his feet through the sand then studied the long, thin ravines they left behind.

"Do you have shelter and food? Do you have water? Were you assigned a brother to look out for you?"

"Yes." Ben's hoarse reply hung in the humid air.

"So why would you disrupt a morning's routine for the pursuit of selfishness and conflict? Do our rules not apply to you? Do you fail to understand that Dagon is now your home and that by creating unrest you are putting us all in danger?"

"Danger? I went for a swim."

The Elder scoffed. "Do not play me for a fool Benjen, for the consequences will be dire."

He locked eyes with the older man who signalled, with a tip of his head, to the two men who still stood by Ben's side.

"Dagon is your home, and all in it are your brothers. When you jeopardise yourself and challenge our ways, you endanger all of us. Do you understand Benjen?"

"I do," he said as the two flanking men grabbed his arms and pushed him back onto his knees.

"To remember this, I order thirty lashes."

A murmur went up from the gathering crowd yet no one protested, not one man came forward.

"What?" Ben tried to jump to his feet as powerful hands held him down. "You can't!"

"Remember Benjen, the pursuit of peace is always safer and less dramatic then the pursuit of conflict."

"No! Wait! I'm sorry! I won't—" His screams fell on deaf ears as the Elder turned to the crowd.

"Bear witness for your brother, for you are all bound by the same order."

A crude hand pulled his shirt over his head, and a light breeze kissed his wet back. The whistle swept by Ben's ear a second before the whip cracked along his back. He yelped as the afflicted area turned momentarily numb. The numbness dissolved into a crawling itch that burned and stung his back and spread like branches beneath his skin. Before he could settle into the sensation, another lash swept his back, followed by yet another. Each strike jarred and sent his ridged frame jutting forward. He thrashed against the men holding him, but not avail. His knuckles blanched, his jaw set and clogged with tears and foam and broken words.

Ben gritted his teeth as tears cleaved his cheeks. He'd lost count of the lashes as the deluge of pain rained across his back, each blow softening his flesh, until his entire body burned as if set on fire. He smelt his blood as it oozed down his back, stinging the freshly torn skin.

Fog clouded his senses and he felt the world about to slip away when everything stilled.

"Release him."

The hands released their grip and Ben collapsed, his face swallowed by the sand.

"Luke, son of Mary, take your brother to Doctor Rob."

Ben flinched when Luke touched his shoulders. "Can you stand?"

"No," he whispered through gritted teeth and choked breath. Sand lodged in his mouth like the screams trapped in his throat.

His body jarred and a hollow whimper fell from him as

Luke lifted him from the sand, his skin ripped and pulled with the movement. "It's okay little brother, I have you."

"I have you too." Antoine appeared from the dispersed crowd and slipped his hand beneath Ben's other arm in support.

He screamed gripped by pain. The world blurred and blackened, his muscles cramped and squeezed as though his insides were in a vice. Sweat poured in rivulets down his face and an uncontrolled shudder crawled beneath his skin.

Sounds pounded against the mist in his head, voices, familiar and soothing. He sucked in frayed breaths and pushed through the throbbing agony that tore his body apart.

"Almost there," the voice said. "Hang on."

The world burned. White, cold pain skittered across his skin. He lifted his head to better study his surroundings, the movement ripping a cry from him.

"Shhhh, Benjen." Doctor Rob's smiling eyes dimmed. "It's all going to be better now."

"What…?"

"It's a balm. It will help heal the broken skin, but it's best if you lay still."

Ben ground his teeth. His tongue swept the inside of his cheeks, finding them swollen and raw.

"How long?"

"Today. You will still have pain tomorrow, and for a while yet, but the wounds will start to heal and close."

He nodded, tears pooling in his eyes while his body shivered with agony. "Can you give me something for the pain?"

Doctor Rob scrubbed a hand over his face. "I'm sorry Benjen, your punishment does not permit me to give you anything."

Ben whimpered as he moved. "Please..."

"Rest. Or better yet, sleep." The doctor pushed away from the bed.

"The pain..." Ben's voice cracked, his chest heaving.

"Once it gets unbearable, rest will come." With that, he left the room.

Ben stared at the white wall wishing his body would surrender to the pain.

⁂

"It's been three days. If I let you take one more off, I will be the next to be lashed." Luke loomed over him, hands folded across his chest, the compassion long erased from his features. "Get up. Get dressed."

"Everything hurts."

"It was self-inflicted. You were warned."

Ben swallowed the anger and resentment that brewed inside him. "Doctor Rob told me not to let the scab dry out."

"You'll sweat enough today and after work you can go wash yourself in the ocean."

"But—"

"Enough! Get up or they'll be back to give you another thirty."

Ben scrambled to his feet, grabbed a shirt and pulled it over his raw back with Luke's help. He followed the older man up the winding path that snaked around the side of the mountain.

A white rock face greeted him as he rounded the corner, a gaping jagged mouth that had been carved away like flesh. The rough ivory expanse stretched along the side of the mountain and disappeared beyond the round horizon, like an ocean of rock into the sun.

The murmur of men milling around died down at the sight of them.

Luke looked over them and his face tightened. "Get to work."

Without further instruction, the men turned away and grabbed their tools from a pile gathered by a small wooden shed tucked into the rock face.

Luke turned to Ben and his chin jutted towards the pile. "Go ahead. It's time to work."

He looked from Luke to the pile of tools and back again.

Luke sighed as if that was all the answer he should have needed. "You will learn best on the job. Have a look at the stone."

Ben turned and studied the rock again, noticing for the first time the thin trenches etched into the stone.

"Grab a pickaxe, carve along the trenches once the grooves are deep enough, we start to dig vertically till we form bricks, which we remove."

"That's my job?" His body trembled with exhaustion.

"No, you will be a mason, like me."

"So... why?"

"These limestone bricks you carve, they will be a foundation for your home and for the homes of your brothers. Picking at the rock you will learn all about its nature, where to find its weaknesses, discover its strengths, learn where the fissures and cracks lay, and how, with patience, you can release the internal rock stress."

Ben stared at the white rock face. The task seemingly impossible.

"Can't stand around all day, Ben."

"I..."

"One chip at a time. By tonight we will have enough rocks to mark out the foundation to your new home."

"My—"

"Go! Now! You're wasting my time and yours." Luke walked towards the rock face already screaming with the impact of axes upon its flesh.

Ben sucked in a steeling breath and ambled over to the pile of tools. He grabbed a pickaxe, the weight tugged at his shoulders and stretched his wounded back. He hissed at the sudden pain and took hesitant steps toward the scarred mountain. The clanging of metal on rock rang in his ears.

He climbed the makeshift stairs and found an abandoned trench, the beginning of a brick peeking out from the white rock. His torso twisted as he lifted the pickaxe above his head and slammed it into the rock. His back flared in searing pain as his hand vibrated with the brutal smash. The sound sending shudders across his body, as if he too had been struck.

He dropped the tool, his chest squeezing. He fought to regained control of himself.

"You okay boy?"

He looked up to find a man peering down at him. White dust lay in the creases of his skin and sweat carved rivers into his dusty face.

"Yeah... I think so..."

"Doesn't give you much ol' Luke, does he?"

Ben shrugged, unsure how to answer.

"Aiden, son of Gwen." He stuck his hand out to shake.

He grabbed it and shook. "Be—"

"I know who you are. Listen, you are not cutting a tree, but breaking rock. It will not succumb to violence, you must be gentle and slow."

"I don't understand."

"Like this." The man grabbed the pickaxe and chipped at the rock, small yet powerful movements that over time dug and broke the stone, carving a deep, long fissure. "Do you see?"

"Yes."

"Like much else in front of us, we think that brute strength will get the job done, but I can assure you, chipping slowly at it will always be more effective."

The man dropped the pick axe and made to leave.

"Thank you, Aiden."

He scoffed. "See if you thank me by lunch time."

Ben's arms burned and his body screamed as he chipped away at the rock along with his time, and pain, and heart ache. Dagon was his new home and he was building himself a foundation.

Maybe if he kept chipping away, one day, he would believe that.

9

4 years later

"Oi, are you still sleeping?" The fuzzy voice filtered its way through his dream.

He was happy. He was by the pool, with Ariel. Her bikini top on the ground, her nipples like ripe raspberries. Her eyes dark, her mouth soft. He wanted to touch her but, as usual she was just out of reach. She smiled at him then, her lips pouted, glossy red, pillowy soft...

"Oi." The voice sliced through the dream.

She disappeared again and all that was left was the throbbing in his swollen groin.

"I'm awake." His voice was groggy with sleep.

"Sure you are. Better get your ass up and to the quarry before Luke gets there." Jacob's voice was full of mirth but carried with it the harsh warning Ben needed.

He shot out of bed and rushed to his bathroom, the straining in his pants painful. The dreams had become more frequent. Thoughts of Ariel plagued him day and night. His body reacted in the only way it knew how, harder, tighter, tougher. He would have to deal with that problem later.

Even after four years with Luke he couldn't wake up on time. Ben splashed cold water on his face and stuffed himself into a pair of pants then flew out the door, running towards the quarry.

His long powerful strides made up for his sleep in and he caught up with Jacob as he entered the quarry.

"You made it." his friend jested.

"Thank you, again."

Jacob slapped him across his back. "No problem man, but one day I'll find a way for you to repay me."

"I thought I already did. Your house is almost as big as mine."

"Almost." Jacob winked at his friend and they both burst out laughing.

"Slacking already?" Luke appeared behind them trying to hide an amused expression.

"Slacking? That's harsh. Someone had to keep this place going while you were away enjoying yourself."

A sly grin crossed Luke's face. "Repopulating the earth is hard work boys." He winked at them. "Get to work." The brash young expression disappeared as his eyes fell to the tools which lay unattended.

The boys reached for their picks and hacked away at the limestone.

Ben's shoulders ached with the effort as he raised the pick again and again. Sweat covered his body as the hot sun beat upon it.

He liked the hard work. The bite of his muscles as they flexed and churned with every hit, the burning of tendons and flesh as his body screamed. But mostly he delighted in the fact that it took his mind off all that lay beneath him, all that lay behind him, and all that was yet to come.

He gulped greedily at his water flask and surveyed the

rock face. In four years of labour they had hardly made a dent in the looming crag yet, they had built almost twenty new homes.

He heaved in a breath and continued beating at the white rock, clearing his mind blow by blow.

"Time," Luke called out. The ringing of metal against rock faded as tools were dropped to the ground, the clang echoing against the precipice.

"Move it, we don't have all day." Luke glared at them.

Ben and Jacob exchanged a look and rolled their eyes. Jacob shook his head and positioned the wheelbarrow near the cluttered pile of bricks, where both boys begun to fill it.

Breathless, they checked over the wheelbarrow. Jacob raised a brow as his eyes flickered between Ben and the over-loaded cart. "I reckon we can fit at least two more."

"No, it's full enough."

"Oh come on, if we just add a few more we won't have to do as many loads." He jabbed Ben with a sharp elbow.

Ben stepped away from him. "No! it will topple over like last week and we will have to spend ages reloading, and Luke warned us there would be a consequence." He fingered the long scar that rounded his hip, the ridge thick and swollen with the heat.

Jacob shrugged. "Fine." He grabbed the pilot bar. "But I'm leading."

"Sure thing," Ben didn't argue. He lifted the weight off the ground. His body screamed for relief, his arms buckling against the weight. He grunted and pushed, his feet digging into the white particles of powdered rock that lay like snow on the ground.

They had come to rest in a shady spot where a pile of broken stones waited. Ben slumped to the ground. Jacob unloaded the barrow while he took the drink bottle and emptied its contents on his face. The cool stream relieving the searing pain.

"Work's not done yet, kid." Luke's shadow hung above him and he craned his neck against the sun to meet his eyes.

"Just catching my breath." He forced himself up and helped Jacob with the last of the bricks.

They meandered back up the hill, Ben's steps light as Jacob pushed the empty barrow.

Reload.

Descend.

Climb.

Reload.

Descend.

Climb.

Busy hands.

Empty mind.

The sun streaked the lazy water with orange and yellow as it kissed the horizon good night. Ben shovelled the rest of his dried meat into his mouth and pushed himself up from the sand, his muscles protesting. He knew the water wouldn't be cold enough to ease the dull ache, still, he ploughed his way through the white sand and splashed into the sea. Chest covered by water, he fell backwards and allowed the waves to wash over him, lulling and cradling his exhausted body. He revelled in the silence.

He felt weight on his chest and instinctively closed his eyes and sucked in a lung full of air before his body was plunged under with a violent shove. He grabbed at the hand and pushed it off as he planted his feet on the ocean floor and stood up.

Jacob's laugh washed over him as he broke the surface. "Looks like you needed to cool off," he screeched between heavy bouts of laughter.

"You're an idiot." He raked the water from his hair then waded through the water and onto the beach.

"Hey, wait up. I was only kidding." Jacob's hand landed on his shoulder with a wet slap.

Ben shrugged him off and made his way to where a group of his friends sat in a line watching the last of the light over the ocean.

He had accumulated them like lost thoughts. They'd appeared at random and stuck. Antoine never really recovered from Danny's loss and sought comfort, despite his initial fear that his secret would be spilt, he grew to trust Ben and confided in him often.

Oliver arrived three months after them and had an empathetic nature that compelled him to help Ben whenever he was injured.

Lucas first appeared arrogant and fearsome until the night he'd discovered him cowering in the trees shedding tears for the mother he would never see again.

Jacob arrived two years prior. A scared and lost thing, like a used rag, his 'brother' had polished and spat him out. Ben found him sleeping on his porch, curled like the babe he still was.

He'd taken them all in, broken boys who needed to be loved, who needed someone to look up to, a mentor, a brother among brothers. They were like a collection of shells on the beach. Each unique and beautiful and flawed from the waves of life that had broken against them.

He hadn't minded the task. The long confessions, the giving of trust, yet he remained a closed thing. A rock. No hammer or pick could break against him, no cracks showed on his exterior. Luke had taught him well. He would never show weakness or fear. He would never give them a weapon to turn against him.

He fell to the sand, the fine particles sticking to his body like a second skin. The boys gathered around him, laughing and chirping. Then a hush fell and a whisper went around the circle.

Ben sat up. His skin prickling. His eyebrows gathered in a V over his suspicious eyes. "What's going on?"

"Surprise," the boys whispered in unison.

Oliver hoisted a full bottle of whisky in the air. He placed it back onto the sand and covered it with his limbs.

"Where did you get that?" Ben's voice was full of apprehension and appreciation.

"I pilfered it from Old Henson's house. He's blind and senile."

"What's the occasion?"

"Your birthday is in two days." The boys nearest to him clapped him on the back.

"And we all know what that means." Jacob leered as some of the other boys cheered and whistled.

Ben nodded, a tired smile on his face.

"Why so serious?" Oliver asked as he pulled the cork from the bottle.

"He's worried that his girlfriend forgot about him." Jacob leered.

Ben's blazing eyes shot to Jacob's face, his fists clenched by his side.

"His girlfriend?" a few boys asked in unison.

"Who?"

"What's her name?"

"Who is she?"

The shouts went around the circle.

Ben's nostrils flared as his eyes stabbed at Jacob.

"Your Mama's." He suddenly burst out laughing. "All your mamas'."

"Oh, Jacob, you're gross." Antoine flicked him in the back of the head, much to the delight of the other boys.

"He's probably more worried he won't be able to get it up..."

"Or know where to stick it…"

"Or what it does…"

As the boys burst into laughter, Ben's heartbeat settled against his chest. He grabbed the bottle from Oliver and sucked at it, swallowing a generous mouthful.

"Shut up, the lot of you." His voice croaked and he coughed as the hot liquid burned his throat.

More laughter followed as he handed the bottle to Jacob who took a long sip, his face contorting as the bitter alcohol coated his tongue.

"It still tastes like horse piss," he whispered to Ben.

He nodded. "Horse piss."

I t wasn't a long shower. The water coursed over his body and washed away the last of his youth. Ben rinsed his hair one final time, stepped out of the stream and grabbed a towel. He sat on the edge of his bed with his head in his palms, his elbows resting on his knees. He stared at the empty space between his toes, the golden polished wood contrasting with his bland, white rock walls.

Ben imagined Ariel. What her day might be like. Rosalie helping her bathe. Mama Beth frowning and arranging, then rearranging, her dress and makeup. She would walk down to the water and the wind would catch on her white dress. Her nipples would pinch in the sea breeze. She'd hate it and be uncomfortable and cover herself. He wondered if she'd look over the water and search for him. Wish for him to put a hand across her shoulder and comfort her, make her laugh.

He shook the image from his mind and stood up. The familiar words of the women of Inan sending vessels across the seas, rang in his ears and echoed across his room.

He found the white shorts that Luke delivered earlier and slipped them on. The material light, almost translucent, revealed plainly all it was meant to hide, so that he questioned its purpose. Ben studied himself and felt the heat rise to his cheeks at the blatant show of his body. Guilt washed over him at the thought of the women in Inan, their own abashment as their bodies were displayed for all to see. He swallowed down the bitter taste in his mouth and joined Luke in the living area.

He found Luke on the floor dressed in his own white ceremonial shorts. Ben didn't dare look down instead, he focused on his broad smile.

"Sit brother." Luke invited him with a gesture to the floor, where a bottle of whisky and two shot glasses awaited.

He did as he was asked, the cool stone frigid against his warm skin.

Luke poured the whisky and set the bottle back down. As he looked at Ben, his beaming face seemed more of a proud father than an adopted brother.

"Brother, tonight you will join the league of men who have come before you, to sow our women, and fulfill your duty. Tonight, you will land on Ishmin and you will be tasked in finding yourself a vessel, a mate, who will bare your children."

Ben's heart pounded in his ears.

"There are rules on Ishmin as there are on Dagon."

Ben's fingers shot to his back, the ragged skin a constant reminder.

"The Watchers observe, they see and hear everything. You must obey *their* law on *their* island, for you are their guest. You are never to strike or force yourself upon any woman and remember that they in turn must obey by the same rules. No man can proceed with the mating unless the woman has agreed wholeheartedly. Once mating has commenced you must ensure your seed does not spill nor waste. *All* occupants of the island *must* choose at least one mate before their seventh day, although trust me brother, once you have tasted their flesh you will be like a hound unleashed, seeking them all out." Luke chuckled at his own words.

Ben bit the inside of his cheek. He didn't want them all. Just one.

"The seventh day is for judgement and play. Women who do not mate willingly will be given a mate, they will have no choice but to copulate, this is not seen as forceful. It is part of the law for the Takers to take. Any man who has committed a misdeed will be punished and branded an abomination. He will not be welcomed back to Ishmin." Luke's face darkened.

"Finally, all mates must be recorded by the seventh day to ensure no inbreeding. Watchers will intercept if inbreeding is suspected. Although, I find it better to report back daily, it's too easy to forget." Luke chuckled to himself.

Ben's lips curled into an uneasy smile, his stomach coiled.

"Do you have any questions brother?"

He shook his head, not trusting his voice.

"Excellent, let us drink to your manhood and to salvation of the human race." Luke passed the shot glass to Ben, who took it with an unsteady hand. The glasses clinked and both men downed their drinks, their faces curling at the biting alcohol.

Luke pushed up from the floor, extended a hand then yanked him from the ground and slapped him across the shoulder, the sound ringing in the near empty room.

"See you soon, brother." Luke's knowing grin spread wide across his face. "Oh, and put some underwear on, you're falling out everywhere." He winked and left the house.

Ben stood alone, heat burning his cheeks.

His feet felt heavy as he meandered down to the beach. Anticipation hung in the air like evening mist off the ocean. Ben waded through it.

Men gathered on the beach, bodies clad in white shorts, torsos on display. His stomach clenched and throat squeezed as he neared the water. The pounding of his heart drowning out the talk and laughter.

An arm wound around him and he looked up to see Luke's beaming face. He led Ben to the forefront of the gathered crowd while oarsmen pushed their way through the crowd and walked towards the waiting boats. A cheer rose up as they began their final preparation before departure.

As if on cue the men all took a step forward, grouped like a bunch of salmon about to swim upstream.

Rohan stepped out of the gathered group and raised his hands for silence. Ben's fingers twitched as he fought the urge to run them across his back. A hush fell across the beach.

"Step forth new Sowers."

"Go little brother," Luke nudged him forwards.

Ben took a few steps and joined four other boys, Sowers to join a man's world and pursue their way of life.

Rohan looked to the five young men. He glared at each of them in turn and spoke softly.

> *"We offer you to the sea full of vigour and vitality.*
> *Go forth, preform your deed, lay inside the womb*
>   *your seed.*
> *Become a man, honourable and kind*
> *Give to her your all, body, spirit and mind.*
> *Create a life, bring forth the child.*
> *Like a sea of flowers plant many to grow wild. "*

A cheer went up as Rohan completed the incantation. Without further ceremony the men marched to the dock, feet thumping like drums on the wood below.

Luke tugged at his arm leading him to one of the boats. It swayed against the dock as the men boarded it. Laughter and chatter closed in around him and drowned out the thundering of his heart. Like a chain of pearls, white pants lined the benches as row after row of masculinity and testosterone filled the long vessel.

Ben looked to his left and his right. Naked chests stared at him, some with a splattering of hair, others with smooth canvasses. A medley of strong bodies, muscular arms, facial hair and set jaws. Each one of those men was his brother. His competition. His enemy.

A sonorous siren drenched the island of Dagon and the men on the boat took up another jovial cheer. The oarsmen pushed away from the dock and soon they belonged to the sea. Lolling and teetering with the waves as they drew closer to Ishmin.

Ben's stomach coiled and revolted. The hot sun beat against his damp skin. A heavy hand landed on his back, the slap stinging. Luke's dazzling smile stretched across his face, anticipation dripping from every fibre.

"Relax kid. Here, have a drink." He handed over a bottle of whisky. The amber contents sloshed inside.

Ben watched the amber waves then took a sip, regretting it the minute it hit his stomach. He felt eager eyes on him. The wait. The men surrounding him wanted the liquid to tumble back up, a laugh at his expense.

Ben forced a smile, drew in breath trough gritted teeth and passed the bottle back. Luke's face fell and a soft moan of disappointed washed across the boat.

Laughter broke toward the back and then a cheer went up as one man bent over the side and emptied his innards.

"We got one,"

"There he goes!"

"There's always one."

Ben remained still, shut his eyes and concentrated on the falling and rising of his chest, his deep breaths settling the discomfort in his body. He opened his eyes as the cries and laughter fell away and the man fell into a quiet lull of conversation.

The sun crawled over the horizon and the calm sea dragged their boat towards Ishmin. His mind spiralled into exhaustion, as anxiety spun thin webs of doubt around his stomach and tugged. If he stayed perfectly still and looked at the space between his knees, he could control the creeping nausea. The constant companion who threatened to show itself should he lose control. He grew weary of his fight, unsure he could hold it at bay much longer.

One of the men shot up from his seat. "Boats!"

The rest got to their feet almost as one rocking the boat violently. Lean, strong bodies pushed against one another, trying to get a glimpse of the other boats as they appeared on the horizon.

His agony momentarily forgotten, Ben spotted five other long boats carrying blurry shapes. There were hundreds of men.

His heart squeezed in his chest. How could he compete? Would he have to?

He scanned the horizon and spotted Ishmin. The curved dip of the land as it sloped away from the mountain top.

The oarsmen docked against a rickety wooden dock, and the men clambered off, running and pushing to get to the sand. Like excited children they elbowed and jeered and clapped and ran to The Keepersakes, who waited by the water's edge. The gate keepers, men of time and patience.

Words and laughter fell away as one by one, the men were sorted by The Keepsakers.

Ben's feet wobbled as he reached the sand at last. The sensation comforting and reassuring. He waited in line studying the men around him, men who had been here before, that knew secrete pleasures he could only dare to imagine.

He arrived at the sorting table. A pair of sharp green eyes

scrutinised him through spectacles that perched high on his long nose. A wiry smile touched his lips.

"Name and age please."

"Benjen, son of Catharine of the Island of Inan. I am eighteen years of age." His voice choked and hollow.

The green eyes seemed to focus more keenly, the smile spreading slightly. He recorded the information in his book. His neat writing steady and composed.

"Benjen, son of Catherine," the old man didn't look up as he spoke, "you will be sleeping to the right. Blue tent. Number 31."

"Thank you."

The Keepsaker looked up with something akin to surprise. His smile stretched across his face as he looked at Ben once more. "You are most welcome, Benjen." His head sank again as he returned to his pages. "Do not forget to come register your mates each morning."

The Keepsaker did not look up again so he stepped away and into the belly of Ishmin.

He found his tent easily. The three other bunk beds that lined the walls taken. Oliver, Lucas and Antoine all looked up as he walked in. He saw the anxiety fall from their face as they saw his.

The four men exchanged awkward smiles then each returned to their own thoughts.

Ben's bunk sank with his weight. He felt the sand beneath him and questioned the point of the fabric that separated him from the earth. His feet dangled off the edge, his back flat against the ground, his head rested on an arm. He stared into the light blue fabric above him, waiting for sunset. His body tensed at the thought.

Luke's head popped into the tent. "Let's go boys." His head seemed suspended in mid-air as a wild smile crossed his face. "The wait is almost over."

Once outside the boys followed Luke toward a dune.

When they rounded it, an open plain spread before them. The mountain side had been carved in a semi-circle and kissed the dune at its edges, which had been piled high. The large walls protected the crowd from the elements. Stairs had been carved into the sides of the dune that were used as seating. Polished wooden planks covered the levelled sand bank.

Luke led the boys to the bar which was positioned along the back end of the arena. He grabbed five pints and handed each boy a drink in turn, saving one for himself. While handing out the drinks he dipped his head towards two men clad in brown robes. They walked around the arena setting the torches alight.

With a suddenness he was not prepared for, the sun disappeared behind the horizon and the black sky spread its wings above Ishmin. "Who are they?" he whispered to Luke.

"The infertile, they are too old or could never have children, or that ability was taken from them."

"Why?"

"They were deemed faulty or an abomination. To avoid spreading their bad seeds they will never multiply." Luke shrugged.

Before he could ask anything more, Luke raised his glass.

"To seeding many vessels!" His eyes locked with Ben's before he tipped his glass and downed its contents.

Ben sucked on the honeyed ale. The cool drink tingling away at his senses, softening the tension in his body, calming the anxiety. He took a larger gulp. Yellow light flickered along excited faces that were hungry, needy, eager. Ben scanned the thirsty crowd.

A siren sounded over the island, it started low than grew louder, drowning any doubt that Mating Season had begun.

It died down and was replaced by the beating of drums. A rhythmic pulsating sound that beckoned all to come, one that required movement.

Ben sensed the testosterone as it leaked from the men in

the arena. Wide eyes, open mouths, wet tongues, they waited in silence.

He heard the blood gushing through his veins, the thrumming of his heart as it crashed against his rib cage. He gulped the last of his drink.

A wild cheer rose among the men as women clad in white dresses poured into the arena and spread throughout the men.

The faint smell of flowers, the sight of red lips, the feel of soft bodies. He had forgotten what they were like. Instantly he was ravenous. His eyes devoured them all.

He leaned against the bar and wiped his palms against his pants, his eyes scanning faces, bodies, lips, hair.

Searching.

Would she recognise him? Would she want to? Would she be there?

Ben stuck his heels into the sand, his hands wrapping around the lip of bar as he leaned against it.

"Hello handsome." She smelt like vanilla. It was deep and sweet like her smile. Her eyes sparkled, slick blond hair coming to a rest at her shoulders. "I'm Mika, daughter of Agas." Her smile widened as her eyes travelled the length and breadth of him, landing on his lips.

"Benjen, son of Catherine." He scoured her body, then averted his eyes wishing he hadn't.

"Is this your first time? I think I would remember you if you were here last time." She trailed a finger up his arm and purred.

He flinched away.

If she noticed his reaction, she said nothing. She grabbed a drink and sipped at it delicately. "Well?'

"Yes. First time."

"Mmmm."

The low vibration sent a shiver up Ben's spine. He looked

to the dance floor. Like the ocean, it moved in waves of people, undulating and wild.

"Do you want to take me down to the beach?" Mika shifted closer, her hips easing slowly against Ben's.

He cleared his throat and stepped away. "I'm just..." He looked around, helpless, foolish. And then he saw her.

Ariel.

She broke away from the dancefloor. Ben's heart caught in his chest his mouth falling open.

She didn't look his way as she reached the bar and grabbed an ale. He watched her sip the drink. It was still the same beautiful face. Just a little longer. Her hair brushed back, pinned up on one side, a large red flower tucked at the back.

She took another long sip, her ruby red lips glistened against the glass, shining in the torchlight. Ben swallowed hard as he took a step around Mika and closer to Ariel. Her jaw set, her long fingers pulled and tugged her dress away from her body.

His breath hitched in his throat as he scanned the length of her. In the flickering torchlight he could see she had become a woman in his absence. Heat coursed beneath his skin flushed, engulfing him as Ariel drained the contents of her glass.

He watched in growing fascination as she grabbed a second, draining it in half the time it took her to drain the first.

A tug of disappointment grabbed at his heart as he closed the distance between them. She didn't seem to be looking for him. He shook the thought away.

With a galvanising breath he leaned on the bar once more. "I didn't take you for a drinker." He rolled his eyes at himself and waited for her to turn to him.

"I'm not." Eyes remaining forward she slammed her glass on the bar.

"I see." He chuckled, her temperament just as fiery as he remembered.

"I don't usually drink at all." She reached for a third pint. "But maybe tonight is a good time to start."

His fascination grew to concern. "And you've had how many?"

"This would be my third."

"And it's going to be your last if you have it." Ben tried to sound nonchalant, fighting every urge in his body to knock the drink from her hand.

"Is that right?'

He gritted his teeth. "Yes, the drinks tonight are made extra strong, if you don't usually drink, you won't fare well."

Glass half-way to her mouth, Ariel stopped and put it down. Ale spilled across the bar. Her expression fell. "I don't feel so well."

"Here, let me get you out of here." He extended his hand to her.

"Not interested." She slapped it away.

"Of getting out of here?"

"Of being your mate."

"That's not what I offered." He swallowed hard.

"Oh." Her shoulders slumped and crimson coloured her cheeks.

He took her by the arm, ignoring the warmth of her skin against his, her smell, her sullen expression, and marched them away from the bar and dance area.

The sand felt safe beneath him. The dune like a barrier between them and the others. He spotted a rug, strewn on the sand like a desert island.

Ariel's weight shifted. She wasn't walking so much as shuffling.

Ben pointed at the rug. "Sit."

"No thanks."

He shook his head and released his grip. "Okay, suit yourself." He walked over and sat down by himself then looked over as she tumbled to the ground. For a moment he thought of helping her again. Taking a long breath he let the feeling pass. Instead, he watched in fascination as she crawled to the rug then lay panting on its edge.

"I don't feel so good." Her voice strained.

"You don't look great either."

"Who do you think you are?" She looked up for the first time and met his eyes.

He could see the slight frown that crossed her face, then the line smoothing out as her eyes grew wide and her mouth fell slightly open. His breathing accelerated.

"Ben?" As she uttered the word, vomit erupted from her mouth. Thick sticky honey ale covered the rug and most of his legs.

"Nice to see you too, Ariel." He grimaced at the smell and watched it trickle between his thighs.

"Oh god, I'm so sorry."

"Don't worry about it." He gave her comforting smile, his heart racing. "Now if you don't mind," He pointed to his legs and groin and stood up, "I'm going to go clean up."

Vomit leaked down to his feet as he made his way towards the sea. He shuddered, then proceeded to remove his pants. He felt her eyes on him and his face broke into a smile as he ran into the ocean, allowing the water to swallow him up. He scrubbed himself in the waves washing away the sticky liquid, wishing he could wipe clean this memory. Wishing she was in the water with him. He sank under the waves hoping to settle the turmoil in his body.

When he emerged, he noticed Ariel had stood up and was swaying towards the water line. Even in her state there was something beautiful about her. Feminine in a way he could have never imagined. Her hips swayed with every step, her hair fell like silk across her shoulder.

Ben waded out of the water and walked towards her. He

knew Ariel. Stubborn. Fiery. Independent. If he offered to help, she would push him aside.

"For a moment there I thought you were going to join me." He stopped in front of her. Waiting for her to look up.

She paused, wide eyed, as she stared momentarily at his manhood. "Get that thing out of my face."

He ran a hand across his face trying to hide his smile.

"I'd love to, but you puked on my only pair of pants so unless you plan on giving me your dress to cover up with, I guess you're stuck with this." He clenched his jaw. If he laughed now, he would lose her.

"That's not happening."

"Why? I showed you mine." He winked at her, face splitting into a lopsided grin.

"And it still isn't much to look at." Ariel huffed.

"Oh? So you've thought of what it used to look like?" His grin widened but his heart raced, the question more than just humorous.

"No! I didn't say... that's not what I mea..." She hissed, threw her arms up the air and turned her back to him, walking away without another word.

Ben bit down on his hand, supressing his laughter. He'd seen her interest. Her words had no real conviction. His heart soared. She *had* thought of him.

Ben grabbed his pants from the sand and ran after Ariel, catching her with ease. He cleared his throat. "Accommodation is the other way."

"Yeah, I know. I just wanted some fresh air." Ariel's eyes flickered across his body then landed on his.

"You're still a shit liar, Ariel." he scoffed.

"I wasn't lying. I have a headache and I want to go lie down."

"And miss the party? It's the first night." His eyebrows furrowed in a distinct V.

"So? Who's stopping you from enjoying it then?"

"You!"

"Me?"

"Yes, you." He folded his arms across his chest.

"How?"

He raised an eyebrow. "Are you really asking me that?"

"Sorry I puked all over you. Now go find more pants, or not, and enjoy the party. I'm a big girl now. I can look after myself."

"I've been waiting for you." He studied her face.

She tore her eyes away from him. "No one asked you to."

He winced at her words. "I've been waiting for you for five years. I really didn't think that after all this time it would be like this..." He shook his head, grinding his molars.

"Like I said, no one asked you to." Her voice wavered and she tugged on her dress.

"Ariel."

"Just go to the party, find a mate and have fun. Leave me alone." She took a step back.

"Ariel." He reached for her but she flinched away.

"Just go."

A heaviness settled over him as he watched her march off. The stab of pain seared his insides. He took a steadying breath and then another, ran his hand through his hair then trudged up towards the accommodation tents. This was not over.

He could still make out her figure as he took long, fast strides in the cooling sand. His eyes locked on her. A figure appeared from the shadows and the newcomer fell into step beside Ariel. Ben froze for a second, his fists clinching his soggy clothes. He hastened his steps and was soon close enough to hear the man's honeyed voice followed by Ariel's harsh one. Ben allowed himself a small smile, his fists relaxing slightly. She wasn't interested.

His smile fell away as he saw the man following Ariel into her tent. He froze. He recognised the profile, the arrogant slant of the shoulders, the moonlight could not disguise Liam's form. A blazing furnace lit itself in Ben's belly.

His muscles contracted with tension, blood raged through his veins, he approached the flap, his fists clenched, eyes locked on the light blue material. Close enough to touch, he took a deep breath, willing his fists to relax, the charged muscle to unwind. He turned away. Then immediately turned back again. He fought an endless battle with his body. His thoughts pierced him like thorns. All he wanted was to pry Liam off Ariel, wash away the past and make her his. Every muscle stood on edge as he clenched his teeth. But what if…

He heard the howl. It punctured the night like a thunderstorm.

Without thinking he ran into the tent, tripping over his own feet. He stumbled then righted himself.

"Are you okay?" His eyes swept the room. They flickered from Ariel's agitated face to Liam's body which lay curled like a foetus at her feet. The other man whimpered.

"What are *you* doing here?" Ariel snapped.

"Well, that's no way to thank your rescuer." His lip curled slightly as he noticed Ariel's eyes sweep over his body.

Her brows knitted in a frown as her eyes found his. "Does it look like I need to be rescued?"

"You bitch!" Liam hissed from the floor. His breath coming in short sharp intakes.

"Watch your mouth, Liam." Ben resisted the urge to kick him.

"Mind your own business." Liam pushed himself up to a seated position while his knees remained firmly tucked to his chest.

"Make me." His chest swelled, shoulders rolling back as he straightened his spine. He met Liam's heated stare.

"Ben!" Ariel's eyes levelled him with a glowering look. "Get out! I don't need your help. And you," She turned her stare on Liam, "go with him. I said no, and I meant it. All I want is to sleep and I've been doing that all my life, so I don't need either of you to show me how."

His face cracked into a wide smile while Liam's folded in a snarl.

Liam pushed himself to his feet and hobbled out, still hunched over.

He waited for Liam to exit then stood and watched Ariel. She unpicked the flower from her hair and let it fall across her shoulders like a wave. "So, are you really going to bed now?"

Ariel turned to him and closed the distance between them. Her warm hand landed on his chest, his breath quickened, his pulse hammered in his veins. She shoved him backwards. Her hand lingered on his flesh, her heat searing him.

Ben could have grabbed her hand, could have stepped forward and pressed his body against hers. He should have. Instead he allowed her to unglue her eyes from his and turn to her cot.

"Goodnight, Ben." Ariel lay on her cot and turned her back to him.

He stood at the door, waiting. When Ariel made no other move, he pursed his lips and stepped out of her tent.

He trudged away, stopped and retraced his steps to her tent. He stood outside with his fists clenched in mid-air then turned around once more and stormed off.

At the end of the tented area he stopped. As he stomped back to her tent he shook his head, jaw clenched. By the flap once more, he exhaled deeply, his eyes burning holes though the blue. He raked a hand through his hair and turned to leave, only to find himself right back where he started. He ran both hands down his face and grunted.

Defeated, Ben sat down. He wasn't finished talking, and he wasn't leaving until he said all that he had waited to say. Longed to say.

Music and moaning surrounded him, soothing the anger and disappointment that swept through his body. His twisted muscles softened and he lay on his back. He threw his wet pants over himself and watched the starts as they danced to the night music.

A foreign touch stroked his abdomen, swift and subtle, followed by a soft thud. Still half asleep he groaned softly and fell back into the dream, warm and tender.

The blow to his arm came out of nowhere.

He shot up. "Ow! What was that for?" Ben rubbed his arm and looked around for the source of the blow. He met Ariel's glowering face, caked in sand and anger and burst into laughter.

"What the hell, Ben?" Her hair was wild and her eyes slits of annoyance.

"What?"

"What are you doing here?"

"I was just—"

"Making sure no one else came in?" She finished the sentence for him.

He shrugged.

Ariel stood up. "I told you I don't need any help."

"I know, but I was hoping we could at least have some breakfast? You know, catch up?" He gave her his most charming smile.

"Fine." She huffed. "But not till you put that thing away."

He turned his face away biting his lower lip. He had noticed the shift of her eyes, the wonder on her face. He patted the sand around him and located his pants. He stood up with his back to her. His face parted in a wide grin as he pulled his pants over himself.

He turned back, a hand rubbing his face to rid himself of the sand and his lingering smirk.

riel's melancholy expression tore at him from the inside. When they were kids, he knew all he had to do was band an arm around her. She would lean her head into his shoulder and he would promise her everything would be all right. But they were not children anymore and he didn't know if she wanted comfort from him, or friendship, or all that he wanted from her.

He gulped down his coffee, the taste as bitter as his feelings.

A Brown Robe placed Ben's breakfast in front of him and he begun shovelling the meal into his mouth.

"Sorry about last night." She was still glaring into her cup. He wished for a second that she would look at him as longingly as she looked at her coffee,

"Don't be." He shrugged and continued eating.

"But you didn't get to... you know..."

"Mate?" He put his fork down and stared at Ariel. She hadn't touched her food.

"Yeah." Crimson leaked into her cheeks.

"I have a week, Ariel. I'm sure I'll be fine."

"I'm sure you will," she mumbled into her coffee.

The silence stretched between them. All he had to do was show her she could trust him.

"So, I was thinking—"

"I hope you didn't hurt yourself."

And there she was. His friend, the girl who knew him, the one who teased him but looked at him like he mattered. He smirked. "Did you just? Really?" Ben shook his head, amused. "As I was saying. *I was thinking*—" He paused. When she said nothing, he cleared his throat, "How about we go explore the island after breakfast?"

"Explore?"

"Yeah, like we used to back home, you know."

"Home? Inan hasn't been your home in years."

"Inan will always be my home." The words come out as a mere whisper.

"Wouldn't you rather..." She gestured vaguely at the crowd. "You know?"

"I already told you I have a week, and let's be honest, I don't think I'll have any trouble finding a mate." He waved and winked at a circle of women who were eyeing him off, giggling. "See? Now, are you in or are you out?"

"Isn't that your job?"

They both burst out laughing.

Ben wasn't really watching where they were going. He knew about the path leading up the mountain. Luke told him about it one night after a return from Ishmin. Instead he watched Ariel, her face full of excitement, her stride full of purpose and her eyes wide with wonder. She was mesmerising. He studied her while her gaze swept the length of the green border along the sandbank.

Being with her like this, felt like the most natural place for him to be.

"So, what do you do on Dagon?" Ariel broke their silence.

"Well, mainly the same thing as you, but no kids or babies to run around after. We hunt and fish. The daily boatload goes over to Inan and some of the other islands in the Quarter, as you know. When I was younger, when I'd just arrived, I tried to sneak on one of the boats so I could come and see you and my mum again. Turned out I wasn't very good at hiding though." He snickered to himself.

She chuckled, her eyes flickering over his body.

"I was a kid…I wasn't always this big…" He gestured awkwardly to his own body.

"No, but you've always been this goofy."

"Hey." He shoved her with his shoulder, pushing her aside.

Ariel was quiet for a moment. "Is that how you got those?" She pointed to his back.

His smile vanished and his lips pursed in a thin line, his fingers trailed the familiar scars. "There's always a price to pay." He didn't elaborate.

When he cleared his throat, Ariel pried her eyes away. "So, what do you to do then?"

"I'm a builder. Turned out hunting and gathering wasn't my thing, I was more a giver of shelter and protection."

"You sound like a great catch." She smirked.

"What's wrong with building a shelter?"

'Nothing. I'm sure it would be a beautiful place to starve in." Her grin widened.

"I won't starve." He pushed a branch from his path as they continued walking.

"How's that?"

"I'll have you bringing all the fish home." His heart skipped a beat waiting for her response.

"Will you now?"

He stopped in his tracks, anchoring all his attention on Ariel. "Your mom is the Elder. She can always appoint you a fisherwoman."

"I guess she could."

"Well, I don't see the problem then." He shrugged as if he had won the argument.

"And who would look after the kids while I'm out fishing all day?" She played along, her mouth spread wide in a mischievous grin.

"Kids? So we're having more than one?" He bit his lower lip and raised an eyebrow.

She laughed and shook her head then continued walking. "*We* are having none. Pretty sure I've told you that you aren't coming anywhere near me with that monstrosity between your legs."

"Oh, so it's a monster now?" he teased. "It might be big, but it's not very scary."

"Pretty sure you have it the wrong way around." She bolted ahead.

"Hey!" he called after her a wide grin cracking his face.

He gave chase, catching her easily, and tackled her to the ground. Ariel squealed. Their bodies tangled as they rolled onto the soft sand. Tucked beneath his wider, bigger body, her squirming didn't budge him.

"Let me go," she shrieked, her body fighting fits of giggles.

Ben grabbed her hands, forcing them over her head. His heart thundering. "Surrender." He laughed a hoarse raspy sound, his body shaking with hers.

"Never," she called through locks of hair which covered her face in a frenzy.

He sniggered at her effort to blow it away then pushed her down, holding her body in place.

The laughter faded. "Surrender," he whispered into her ear, his lips grazing her delicate cheek as he pulled away, inhaling the flowery perfume that rose from her skin. Her body stilled beneath him, as he stroked the hair from her face. Her eyes wide and locked on his. He swallowed hard, his body alight.

Ben's wild hair tickled his forehead as he pressed himself to her, his lips inches from hers. He felt her rapid breaths mimicking his own as his heart hammered. His body reacted, tightening, hardening, swelling.

He knew the moment she felt it. Her eyes fell from his and her body bucked. A silent request which he granted immediately. Ben rolled off her, laying in the sand, his chest rising and falling in a frenzy.

Ariel shot up and shook the sand from her body. "Coming?" she asked in a raspy voice.

"Not now, I guess," he mumbled under his breath.

"What's that?"

He shook his head and sucked in a long steeling breath. His tight, hard body rigid and uncomfortable. He scrubbed a hand over his face and studied Ariel as she turned away.

"Come on." She pointed to a break in the greenery and headed for the opening

He adjusted himself as best as he could and followed her, his uneven gait awkward and slow.

They ascended in silence.

Ben fought the image of her lips so close to his. Tried to forget the scent and delicate softness of her skin. He had to change the subject.

"How is Rosalie?"

"She's not the same." Her face curled into a grimace. "She has two boys."

"Oh." His heart constricted with pain, for Rosalie's inevitable loss, for her boy's inevitable pain.

"She's come to terms with it." Ariel increased her pace and stared dead ahead as she led the way.

Ben broadened his steps and soon overtook her. Ariel caught up again, jabbed him with an elbow then moved ahead. He winced at the sharp blow and growled. Increasing his speed once more he shoved into her shoulder as he gained ground.

By the time they reached the cavern entrance they were breathless and giggling, a comfortable and familiar rivalry egging them on. The pair stepped inside, loose pebbles crunching underfoot.

"Shhh." Ben halted, and blocked Ariel's advance with an extended arm.

"Ben, what—"

"Shhh." He held up a finger to his lips and jutted his chin. Her face shifted when she registered the sound. A scuffling in the rock as if it was being scratched from inside.

He looked into her eyes and saw the challenge, his lip curled into a smirk. As one, they stepped forward and rounded the wall.

Ben froze, his mouth falling slightly ajar. The man leaned on the wall his torso exposed, his hands laced through a woman's thick black hair. She rested on her knees before him, his hands guiding her head.

The man's eyes shot open. "What the hell, man? Can we get some privacy please?" The man leaned back against the rock wall. Despite the interruption, the couple didn't stop.

Ariel bolted from the tunnel. Ben took a deep breath, settling his face, and followed.

She waited by the exit her face flushed pink. He grinned, "Don't like to watch?"

"Do you? Maybe you need lessons?"

"I don't need lessons from anyone." He squared his shoulders and straightened his spine.

Ariel's head tilted. "Oh?" With two strides she closed the distance between them and pushed Ben, forcing his back against the cold wall. Her eyes locked on his, intent and unwavering, as she traced his face with a delicate touch, her body pressed against him.

His heart galloped, he swallowed hard and leaned down to meet her face which was a hairsbreadth away from his. She grazed his lips with hers, not quite a kiss. His entire body came alive. Heat rose from within as his breath hitched, his body once again his enemy.

"You know," she whispered in his ear, her voice husky, "I may not know much, but I am fairly sure, that that, was the wrong hole..." Ariel stepped back, the warmth of her body falling away, a smirk painted on her face.

Ben remained against the wall gulping in calming breaths, before his face broke into a wild grin.

He followed her to the edge of the cliff which gave them a view of the main foreshore of Ishmin. They had a front seat to all its goings on. He noticed the colour stain her cheeks as they spotted couple after couple, spread out behind bushes, in bungalows, hidden behind tree trunks and happily out in the open.

He swallowed away his own desires.

"Do you miss your mum?" she asked quietly.

The thought of Mama Cath sent his heart reeling. "Sometimes." He ground his teeth to stop himself taking back the lie.

"I can send her a message if you want."

His heart jolted. "You'd do that?"

"Of course." Her soft gaze met his.

There was too much to tell, not enough words to convey how much he missed her every day, how he needed her comfort and guidance. How he missed her voice. He shook his head. "What would I even tell her? I haven't seen her in five years."

"I'll just tell her you said hi and you miss her. I think she'd like that."

"I think she would too." He swallowed the lump that wedged itself in his throat and sighed, he considered telling her about Mason and Logan but decided against it.

"Tell me more about your home."

"Not much to tell."

"Ben."

He gave a sour chuckle. "It's different than how I remember Inan being. There's less... softness."

"What does that mean?"

Ben gazed over the horizon as if looking for something lost. "There are less words and more actions."

"Like now?"

A smile tugged at his lips and he sighed, resigned. "Do you remember that one time when we hid in the orchard and ate those oranges?"

"Oh yes, they were so juicy." Her mouth split open at the memory and the tip of her tongue traced her lower lip.

"And do you remember when Mama Cass caught us?"

Ariel's mouth twisted at the memory. "Yeah..."

"She pulled us by the ears all the way to Mama Beth." An amused expression painted Ben's face.

Ariel grimaced, "Mama Beth was so angry."

Ben laughed. "She turned so red yelling at us."

"And you kept telling her I didn't eat any."

"And she pointed out the orange juice stain on your shirt and chin."

At that Ariel's lips twitched. "She never misses a thing."

"But then that was it. She shouted a whole lot, explained a bunch of stuff, gave us extra chores and that was that."

"For you. I still had to go home that night." She elbowed him lightly as he nodded.

The humour drained from his face. "Well, Dagon is different. There's no shouting and explaining. There are rules. It's all black and white without any grey in the middle. There's no need for talking or explanation. It's clear cut. Practical, logical. No emotion weighing down on it."

"And that's the right way? Emotionless?"

"I didn't say that. I just said it was different."

"What about anger?

"What about it?"

"That's an emotion."

"Ariel…" He raked his fingers through his hair and sighed. "I didn't mean there's no emotion on Dagon, just less talk. Things are calculated, straightforward. Everyone knows the rules, and if you break them you get punished." His fingers automatically found the length of scar across his hip and traced the damaged skin. When he noticed her gaze following his fingers, he clasped his hands firmly in front of him and shifted slightly, shielding her view of his back.

They sat there for a while longer. Ben watched as Ariel studied the island. Her eyes widening with wonder or horror depending on what she saw.

"I'm getting hot. Let's head down for a swim." He didn't wait for her to answer but simply stood up and retraced his steps towards the cave. He didn't want her to see him like this, needy and flushed.

He was halfway through the cavern when Ariel side-stepped around him and ran ahead, the hollow nook that was previously occupied now empty. Ben chased her all the way to the beach, drowning in her shrieks of delight and gleeful giggles as he allowed her to win.

Panting, they stood at the water's edge.

His heart galloped and he wasn't sure if the run had anything to do with it. "I'm going in. Are you coming?"

"Think I'll sit out." Ariel retreated.

"Why?"

"Because…" She bit her lip and wrapped her arms around her waist. "I just don't want to." She gestured at her body.

His brow furrowed. "But you're beautiful, Ariel."

Ariel's eyes avoided his. "I've never been beautiful."

"You've never stopped." The muscles in his cheeks flexed and he ran a hand through his hair. "What if I hold your hand and look straight ahead? I won't peek. Also, if anyone does look this way, they'll see us and think we're together. They won't bother you."

"But if they think we're together then—"

"I know." He shifted his weight on the sand.

"But then you won't get to—"

"I still could. With as many as I wanted to." His heart pinched at the words knowing he didn't want anyone else.

"Ben. I don't want to be your mate. I don't think I'm ready to mate with anyone." She wrung her hands.

"Then I'll wait for you. Like I have been."

"Ben—"

"Will you just come swimming with me already?" He threw his hands up, his mind torn at the prospect of more rejection, his body seeking relief, exhausted at fighting itself.

"Fine." She frowned. "But keep that water snake away from me."

"Oh, so he's a snake now?" He wiggled his eyebrows, his face lit up in a boyish grin.

"Shut up." She giggled.

Ben removed his shorts, then stepped behind Ariel to help her with her clasp.

"You will look straight ahead?" Her voice quivered.

"Promise."

Ben unclasped the ring of Ariel's dress and watched the soft fabric cascade down her tanned body. The curves like tumbling waves, perfect. He gasped. Being this close to her all he wanted was to reach for her, touch her, comfort her. Instead, he forced himself to look ahead as promised and allowed her to lace her fingers into his. She tugged at his arm and led them in a sprint into the water.

When she released him he dove under a wave, letting the water cool his skin. Coming up for air, Ben studied her. Droplets fell from her brown hair as it stuck to her face. Her dimples dipped as she smiled at him. Her long neck protruded from the water and his fingers itched to trace it down to her navel. He noticed the swell of her breasts and their pink tips that stood erect just below the water.

The splash came out of nowhere. Salty water rushed into his mouth and across his face.

"Stop staring or your eyes will fall out." She laughed.

"That's an old wives' tale." He wiped water from his eyes.

"No such thing."

"What?"

"An old wife. Any wife, really."

He frowned, trying to understand her meaning as another splash sprayed across his body.

"What was that for?"

"That one was because I can," she teased.

"Well, you get those two for free, but once more, and there is no telling what this water snake will do."

"It would have to catch me first." She giggled and took two steps away from him, as if preparing to flee.

He knew there was no beating her in the water, so he stood to his full height and headed to shore.

"Hey, where are you going?"

"Think I've cooled down enough, anyway, I promised not to look on the way in. We never said anything about the way out." He gave her a wicked grin then trudged through the swelling waves.

"Ben! Ben, you come back here!" Panic rose in her voice.

He chuckled, satisfied when he heard the rush of water behind him as she struggled to catch up. He sucked on his bottom lip to hold back his laughter. He felt her step for step, just behind him, as he walked to their clothes that laid carelessly on the sand.

He could have turned around. Could have seen all of her, instead he resisted. His muscles ached with effort, an inferno raging inside him. If she was ever going to be his, she needed to want him just as much as he wanted her. This was not for him to take but for her to give.

He slipped into his pants and tried to sound casual.

"There will be another party tonight, and the night after that. Are you going to stay in your tent the whole time?"

"What else is there to do?"

"Come dance with me."

Ariel moved in front of him, a frown on her face. Without a word she turned around, indicating that he should clasp her dress back up.

He brushed his fingers along her shoulder, the bronzed skin breaking into goose bumps. He bit his lip and pulled the dress shut. He inched closer to her, his mouth by her ear and whispered, "Everyone will think we're together. I told you, you can have fun, worry free. No other guy will make a move as long as you're with me."

"But what about you?" She spun out of his reach.

"I told you, I'll be fine." He sucked in a long breath.

"You've already wasted a whole day with me."

"When will you realise, Ariel, that time with you isn't wasted? Not where I'm concerned."

"Okay." It was a whispered agreement. Ariel gave him a wane smile, her hands fell to her sides. "When the drums start to beat, I'll come find you. One dance and one drink."

"Are you sure you should have any?'

"Oh, shut up." She walked by him shoving her shoulder against his chest. He gave a gruff laugh and followed her up the beach.

When they arrived at Ariel's tent, Ben leaned into the cool blue structure and arched a sly brow. "Do I need to take my nap outside your tent again?"

"I'm pretty sure I can take care of myself!"

"You know what? I'm pretty sure you can too." He winked and walked away. As he strolled towards his own accommodation, he felt a glimmer of hope rise in his chest.

Ben's foot twitched, his body churned, tension gushing through his veins. The drums beat in a wild rhythm and bodies moved on the dance floor.

He smiled at the blonde girl. She licked her lower lip and smiled back. Her hair was smoothed back making her forehead look too big. The other blonde looked like her sister, the same piercing green eyes, same stocky build and high-pitched voice. They both giggled at his joke then shared a short, whispered conversation.

He scanned the entrance to the arena and the dance floor for what felt like the hundredth time. His jaw tensed when he still hadn't spotted Ariel.

The sisters were talking at him again, he nodded not listening to their words. The urge to run away from them grew. The heated look in their eyes unnerving. They inched closer. The shorter of the two raised a brow and licked her upper lip. Her fingers brushed Ben's forearm. He gritted his teeth in a forced smile.

He spotted Ariel and his heart squeezed in his chest. Her hair gathered to one side accentuated her long neck, her full lips glistened in the torchlight. He excused himself from the sisters and moved towards her, his face splitting in a roguish grin.

"Didn't think you were coming," he shouted over the music.

"The music just started. Anyway, I have been here for ages. It's you that's been otherwise occupied."

"With them?" He thumbed behind him at the blondes who were now arm in arm with two new men. "Just kept myself entertained till my real date showed."

"And by 'entertained' you mean?"

"Do you really want to know?" He wiggled his eyebrows wildly.

"Oh, shut up." She giggled, the sound searing his skin. "So, are you going to get me a drink?"

"After last night's performance? I think not."

"Ppfft." She pushed past him and grabbed a pint of honey ale from the bar.

He watched her as she sipped. A smile crept across his face, he admired her tenacity. "Take it easy now."

"Yes, Mother." Ariel gulped the rest of the drink, smacking the glass down on the bar as she finished.

"Or not." He shrugged wanting to wrap himself around her, protect her, even from herself. "Dance?"

"Sure." Her eyes sparkled. Ariel laced her fingers through his and led them through the mass of bodies and onto the surging dance floor.

Bodies crashed into them like waves on the rocks, the heat rising around them drenching them in sweat. Ariel's dress clung to her body, revealing all that lay beneath.

Ben swallowed hard and pried his eyes away. His hands clenched on her hips as he drew her closer, fingers digging into her flesh.

She wrapped her hands around him, his skin quivered with her touch. Her eyes locked on his, filled with hunger and desire that matched his own. Ariel drew closer still, her hips swaying, leading.

Ben felt the drums beat through him, the rhythm of his heart at fever pitch. He slid his hand along her slick back as the frenzied crowd closed around them, swelling like an undulating ocean, pressing against one another like a pent-up tempest, until there was nowhere to go but into one another. His face was only inches from hers. Not thinking, not waiting, he brushed his lips with hers. The warmth sent shivers down his spine.

Ariel gasped. Her eyes searched the depth of his as she jerked her head back.

Ben did not release her, instead, weaved a hand through

her hair, pulling her closer, clutching her tighter. He was lost in her, with her. He wanted her, despite knowing that if he kissed her, truly kissed her, it would mark the beginning of unavoidable heartbreak. His body warred with indecision when without warning, she pushed herself to him and their lips collided. Hungry and urgent they kissed. Like a flood smashing through the barriers, their kiss smothered everything in its path, drowning and sweeping, obliterating his senses, leaving him wrecked and yet fully intact.

He was intoxicated, drunk by her promise of more, her velvety skin, the taste of honey that hung from her breath, her soft lips and hungry mouth.

Ariel broke away. Her gaze roamed his face, his eyes, his lips, then she turned away and carved her way through the throng of bodies, disappearing.

Dazed, he stood, heart thudding in his chest. He called to her, his voice lost in the crowd. Ben pushed his way between slick bodies, he slipped out of the dance area and spotted Ariel running out of the arena. He sprinted and caught up with her before she reached her tent, grabbed her arm and yanked, so that she spun around to face him.

He sucked in a long breath and his eyes darted over her. Her hair wild, tears brimming in her eyes. "What was that?"

"A mistake."

"That wasn't a mistake." His voice hoarse and breathy.

"It can't happen again."

"What the hell, Ariel? Don't tell me you don't feel it too." The cords of his neck stretched taut.

"We can't. I just can't." Ariel spun around and marched away.

Ben scrubbed a hand over his face, inhaled a long breath then chased her down and blocked her path. "Why? What's so wrong with me? With us?"

"Everything." She sighed "We can't. I won't."

"Just tell me why and I'll leave you alone." Torment twisted his features. "I won't hurt you, Ariel."

"Can't you see? That is exactly what you'll be doing."

He shook his head. "What are you talking about?"

"I don't want to end up like Rosalie."

"I don't understand." He reached for her arm, but she flinched away. Ben looked to her eyes swollen with unshed tears, to the lips that he'd tasted, now clamped together.

"Ariel?" He tried again, taking her hand in his. It remained limp.

"If we do this, I will lose you all over again," she whimpered.

"No." His voice clipped. "Ariel, we can—"

"No!" she snatched her hand away. "We can't." Without another word she turned away and raced back to her tent.

He watched her go. His legs rooted to the ground, his body feeling a heaviness he could not shake. Anguish surged inside him. He pushed it down and instead, allowed the simmering anger beneath to rise. He kept the hurt and pain locked away, untouched, unfelt. He loved her, he wanted her, but he needed to protect himself. Maybe that meant keeping his distance. He turned away and returned to the party. Grateful that the alcohol on Ishmin didn't taste like piss.

A ll he had to do was drink less. Or maybe all he had to do was drink more. His throat burned dry. The alcohol gave him temporary sanctuary from his thoughts, but with the sun, rose sour disappointment and anger.

Ben rolled over onto his back and rubbed the sleep from his eyes. He was not in his tent. He shot up and looked around, his body retaliating against the sharp movement.

He scanned his surroundings. The sun just beginning to rise, a spattering of purple diffusing against the blue. He lay on the beach, a golden sandbar that stretched out as far as he could see, wrapping itself against the mountain. The view interrupted only by the temporary tent village that was set up along its east coast.

His body ached. The feeling of being caught up in a surging swell and spat out again washed over him. Ben tucked his knees to his chest, wrapping them with an arm. He rested his chin on a knee and turned his head to the left.

In the distance, torches were snuffed around tents and bodies fell out to begin their day.

He turned to the right.

A naked woman lay on her side. Her hips sunk into the

sand, her full blonde hair swept back from her long milky shoulders.

Ben drew a sharp breath and choked, gasped then looked down at himself. Relief and confusion flooded him when he found he was still dressed in his shorts. He examined the blonde again and noticed the hand curled up in her hair. He blew out a shuddering breath and tilted his head further.

"Like what you see?" The voice was full of sleep and mirth. "I told you last night that you could have joined in."

The blonde stirred as Luke pulled his hand away from her hair and sat up. He winked at Ben, his face cracking in a roguish smile. He traced his fingers over her body. The delicate touch began at the shoulders, followed the swell of her breast then trailed along the grooves of her ribs and into the dip of her hip. He continued along her slender leg, then retraced his journey, waiting for her to wake.

She moaned softly and stirred as he continued. Ben stared. His gaze following the progress of Luke's fingers. The stare was unintentional, fascination and confusion fogged his thoughts, as if a part of his brain stalled for a moment and needed to be restarted.

"You can touch her if you like." His grin cracked open to reveal a row of teeth. "She won't mind."

Ben recoiled and turned his head away. Luke broke into a fit of laughter.

"Good morning." Her voice was mousy and high pitched.

"Good morning indeed."

Luke and the woman giggled as she turned into him. They shared a murmured conversation.

"Oh, hey man, we're going to go... You know..." Luke stepped into Ben's periphery. "You should come, she has some friends."

Ben forced a smile and shook his head. "Have fun, I'm still a bit groggy from last night."

"Yeah, I'm not surprised kid, you were throwing those

ales back like they were water. To be honest I'm not sure how you managed to stay upright for as long as you did."

Ben frowned and turned to look at him. "How did I get out here?"

Luke's eyes flickered to the waiting woman. "Look, stick around. I'll be back in a bit and I'll tell you everything. I'll even bring back some friends, but right now..." He shot another long hungry look at the woman. "The earth isn't going to populate itself." He slapped Ben across the shoulder then walked away. Leaving a heated mark and shrieks of laughter in his wake.

He rubbed his shoulder and batted the image of Luke and the woman from his head. His clearer mind allowed Ariel's words to echo and swirl inside him. He clenched his fists and shook his head.

Ben stood up and stripped off his shorts then wadded into the sea. His heavy head and leaden body felt weightless as he floated atop the waves, allowing them to lap over him. His brain wracked with confusion, he wondered what he did the previous night. Not knowing gnawed at him, tugging at his spirit like a heavy anchor.

T rue to his word Luke returned. The blonde and a gaggle of her friends trailed behind him.

Ben and Luke lay on the sand facing the ocean. The women surrounded them like a flock of birds, cooing and warbling among themselves. The blonde from earlier mounted Luke's back and massaged it gently. Resting his head on his crossed arms, he sighed.

Ben turned his head from the girl to his brother. "Tell me about last night."

"Not much to tell."

"Luke." Exasperation filled his voice.

He chuckled. "Relax kid." Then purred in pleasure as the blonde rubbed his back. "I found you by the bar. You mumbled something about striking out. You were really beat up about the whole thing. Guess you're not all you thought you were going to be." Luke snickered.

"You were downing ale like it was all for you. Analise here tried to introduce you to some of her friends. In fact, I think that Rose over there came with us to the beach." He pointed at a woman with curly red hair. She turned to meet Ben's eyes at the sound of her name. Her glossy lips parted in a captivating smile.

"You could barely walk by the time we got down here. You fell on your face. Rose over there tried to resurrect you a few times but you were out cold." Luke was howling with laughter as heat rose to Ben's face.

When his laughter died down, he signalled Analise, she rose and he flipped onto his back then turned to Ben. "Don't worry. Today is a new day and I'm sure Rose would be more than happy to take anything you want you give her."

Ben stiffened at an unexpected touch. Rose slid up next to him then melded her body into his as if that was where it belonged.

"Hi." It was a deep, breathy sound. "Nice to see you up and about."

"Hi." He cleared his throat as she raked fingers through his hair, purring with the movement. He swallowed hard as she leaned into him. Her breath sweet like her name. His pulse hammered as he thought of Ariel's words, of the feel of her velvety skin, the taste of desire and the heat of her kiss.

Rose leaned in. He turned his face away, her lips falling on his bristled jaw.

She pulled up and looked at Ben's face, her own turning a shade of red as deep as her hair. Rose bit her lower lip and allowed her hair to fall across her eyes.

Ben pushed himself up on a single elbow and reached for

her. He tucked the long locks behind her ear and truly looked at her. She was lovely, her moss green eyes welling with a film of moisture. He saw the confusion there, her urge to remain poised, the desire to get angry, the need to run and hide, the inclination to sit and endure humiliation.

He pressed his lips into a tight line and smiled apologetically. "I'm sorry," he mouthed.

She flinched away from him, her eyes narrow slits. She got up and re-joined the group of other women.

Luke gave him a sidelong glance, his trademark smile back across his face. "Well, kid, guess red isn't your colour."

"Guess not." Ben inhaled deeply and stood up. "See you later," he called to no one in particular as he shuffled back to his tent.

H e woke to the slow gnawing pain of hunger. He allowed it to growl and snarl at him from the depths of his body and wondered how much of the emptiness was to do with hunger.

Ben shuffled to the mess hall under the blazing midday sun. He was yet to see Ariel, and the weight of her words still pushed down on him. The searing heat of her rejection burned deep and angry.

The lunch table lay stacked with juicy meat, fresh fruit, breads and sweet biscuits heaped on wooden platters. The smells made his stomach churn. He reached for a coffee and a slice of bread when he spotted Ariel. His body tightened at the sight of her, the air rushed from his lungs.

He allowed himself a minute to steady his emotions while he studied her long, drawn face, her ashen expression. She said that they wouldn't be together, not that they couldn't be friends. He took a few tentative steps and sat by her side.

"Why so glum?" He ripped a chunk of bread with his teeth.

"Who's glum? I'm having the time of my life, just like everyone said I would be."

"I can see that. You have 'party' written all over your face."

"And you have saliva all over yours." Her face crinkled in a sharp frown.

His heart skipped a beat. "Jealous?" Hope clung to his question.

"Of those girls? No."

He ran a jittery hand through his hair to cover his nerves. "Oh, but you are jealous. How many girls did you see?"

"Shouldn't you be behind a bush somewhere sticking that sausage in someone?"

"So, we're at food items now? Does that mean you'd like a taste?"

At his words she finally looked at his direction, a scowl marring her face. "I've told you a hundred times, I don't want that thing anywhere near me and certainly nowhere near my mouth."

"Who said anything about putting it in your mouth? But if you want to, I won't stop you..." When Ariel got up and walked away, Ben scrubbed a hand over his face then jumped up and followed her.

"Hey, I was just joking." His tone soothing.

"I know." She didn't stop.

"I didn't do anything with any of them."

"It's none of my business."

"It could be." Ben overtook her with two long strides, pivoted, then blocked her way forcing her to stop.

"I thought I made myself clear." She tried to push by him, but he sidestepped into her path.

"I guess *I* haven't made myself clear yet." Ben stood to his full height his jaw clenched, his eyes marred by creases. "Why do you think this is only about you, and what you want? I know it's your body, but it will be growing my child, or someone's child." His face grew taut. "Do you have any idea of the enormity and weight that bears? I know you know what life is like without a father, but do you understand how painful it is at thirteen to lose your mother as well?" His voice clipped as a devastating ache seared his chest.

"Oh, Ben." Ariel approached him, but he stepped back, his face twisting in anguish.

"Why do *I* have to give a part of me to any of these women? They will forever take that piece away and I will have nothing to do with it. You have no idea how many nights I stayed up crying, missing my mom. Brought up by strangers with different rules, different hierarchies. A man's world is unlike yours." His voice strained as he choked back tears, a finger tracing his familiar scar.

"Turns out my mom liked to have fun." He sneered. "It was a costly exercise for me to find out all of my mother's mates. It took three years to compile all that information. When I did find the potential candidate, I discovered he was Shuffled four years before my arrival. Records show he died a year later in the Second Quarter. The man who had brought me into the world, gone - and I know nothing about him except that he was a good swimmer, and I am not, and that he probably died alone and surrounded by strangers. I will die never knowing if I have anything in common with him, and I will die never seeing my mother again."

Ben sucked a frayed breath and ran his hands down his pained face, pulling at the taut skin. "Why would I want to bring a child into this world knowing I would never see their face or hold their hand? Never teach him or her how to swim or dance or build a fire. Never tell them how beautiful their mother is and that I have loved her since the first day I saw her."

Ariel winced, her bleak eyes searched his face, at that, his rant softened, his harsh tone lowering to a whisper.

He stalked forward and took Ariel's hand, placing it on his chest, the soft flesh warming the emptiness. "If I give a piece of me to someone, I'd rather it be my heart, and you already took that with you many years ago on that mountain in Inan."

Ben hooked a hand around her slim waist and pulled her against him, the other stroked her chin, then meandered to the back of her head where he gathered a handful of hair, gently tugging, forcing her to look into his eyes.

They stood frozen, suspended in each other's arms. His mouth a hairsbreadth from hers, his heart thrashing in his chest as he felt her warmth around him. He inhaled the sweet smell of her, sunlight shinning in her glistening eyes.

Ariel pushed on her tiptoes and closed the distance between them, slamming her lips into his.

Heat seeped inside him, her mouth on his, her lips achingly soft obliterating his every thought. Ben groaned, his hold tightened around her, and he drew her closer, hands delving in her hair as he deepened the kiss. His tongue slid beyond the barriers of her sweet lips tasting hers.

Like the flow of a silver river, they twisted and turned, electric and delicious. His chest heaved, a low growl rumbled deep in his throat, as the gushing torrent of desire flowed between them.

When at last he released her, his breath came in ragged rasps and his heart raced as he looked into Ariel's eyes, wild and frenzied, he instantly missed her velvety touch.

"We can't, not if we both feel this way." Her voice carried her hopelessness.

"How can you say that?" Ben's fists clenched by his side.

Tears welled in her eyes. "Doing this will only bring us pain. You will break me. This will bring us only sorrow."

"No." His heart pounded in his chest.

"Yes, if I fall pregnant—"

"So don't."

"Ben…"

He pushed his hair out of his face and rubbed his jaw. "Maybe we can, but not really?"

"What do you mean?"

Ben sat down on the hot sand, a clear and terrifying thought saturating him. He tapped the sand at his side and waited for Ariel to sit. Her warm body sagged against his and he wrapped his arm around her, enjoying the feel of her head on his bare chest.

"We can pretend," he whispered, his heart galloping even as the words left his lips.

"Pretend what?"

"We can pretend that we are mates. We can fake it, and then we can be together."

Ariel pushed away from him, her eyes searching his face. "How?"

He felt the heat rise to his ears. "We can work out the," he cleared his throat, "logistics later. But the important thing is that if you don't fall pregnant, you'll have to come back. We both will. You have five rounds before you are deemed barren."

"And you won't try to…?"

"I would never hurt you, Ariel, not now, not ever. We would only ever do what you want. You have the power, remember?"

"Do I now?" A quirky smile spread across her face. She wiggled her eyebrows before she pushed Ben onto the sand and mounted him.

His heart threatened to break through his rib cage, his stomach knotted. "Seems to me as if you're in total control," Hiding his reaction, Ben bucked, forcing Ariel to lose her balance. In a swift, agile movement, he flipped her onto her back then blanketed her body with his, his face inches from hers.

"Total control," he whispered into her ear and peppered soft kisses up her long neck, then trailed along her jawline and came to a stop at her lips.

It was then that Ben saw a pair of feet not a metre away from them. Looking up, he saw an old silver-haired man, whose hazel eyes were creased at the corners.

"Good," the old man said, nodded, then walked away.

When he was out of earshot Ben whispered, "See, we're doing it already."

"Doing what?"

"Fooling everyone."

"They're watching us," he whispered, his lips pressed against her cheek. The sensation sending a ripple of heat through his body.

"I know."

"It's 'cause neither of us—"

"I know."

"So, we have to pretend to—"

"I know, I know." Ariel sighed.

"Where do you want to go?" He wanted to help lift the burden that sat so heavily on her. He hoped that giving her control would help.

"I don't know."

"Well, that's unusual, isn't it?"

She threw a kernel of corn in his direction and finished chewing. "How about the caves?"

"The caves? They are pretty far and very dark."

"Exactly." The tautness in her face giving just a little. "They are dark and isolated. It will be harder to see, harder for them to be certain."

Ben thought for a moment letting the idea settle around

him. "Okay, but we'll have to head out soon. We'll have to spend the night there, it won't be safe to climb back down once night falls."

Elated with the prospect of spending the night with her, he left her with instructions. She needed to collect a blanket and some food, he would grab the rest and meet her by the entrance to the arena.

Ben caught a glimpse of Ariel as he marched to meet her. The slight breeze playing with the hem of her dress and the tips of her hair, which she gathered in her hand and flipped over her shoulder.

A tall man intercepted her path, his broad shoulders loomed over her. Ben quickened his pace, trudging through the sand and over the dune.

When he reached her, the man turned away and pushed by Ben mumbling to himself, his face a mask of disappointment.

Ben's lungs burned with exertion and he sucked in a deep breath. "He seemed to like you."

"It wasn't mutual."

"Lucky me."

"Famous last words."

Ben burst into laughter. "Come on, we better get moving." Bound by uncertainty, he fought the urge to take her by the hand. There were still so many rules to set.

His nervousness mounted with each step up the unused path. His attempts at conversation fell at his feet as she shot him short answers. Her stiff walk and tight jaw testaments to her own nervousness. He had no idea how to soothe her, how to ease her pain and fear and make them melt away into the sea. His torment constricted his chest, where his heart thudded like a rock.

When they arrived, he lit her torch, the hay bursting into a hot flame. He touched his torch to hers. The fire kissed the hay and engulfed it in heat and light.

"Wait here," Ben ordered then took a tentative step into the cave. He scanned the makeshift rooms, burning light into dark crevices and hidden corners.

"It's empty," he called out to her.

"Good." Her voice echoed in the empty chamber.

Ariel rounded the corner, her face lit by the glow of her torch. She set her bag on the floor and emptied its contents, setting the blanket on the hard floor. Ben left the cave in search of firewood. He gathered a handful of kindling and larger sticks then returned to the cave. He built a small pyre then lit it. The fire crackled in the deep silence that resonated between them.

"Can I ask you something?" Ben raked his hands through his hair and locked eyes with her.

"Sure." A tight smile tugged at her lips.

"Why do you keep saying you don't want to end up like Rosalie? What happened to her?"

Ariel sighed. Her eyes focused somewhere beyond the yellow flames. He listened intently as she told him Rosalie's story; her heart break and grief and all her pain yet to come.

He watched Ariel's face, the torment that she held for her sister, the love that she carried for her and the helplessness she felt. He wondered if she saw those feelings stretch across his face too. He swept a hand across his chin trying to erase any trace of sadness. "I can't imagine Rosalie sad."

"It's heart-breaking to watch. She isn't who she used to be."

"And if we do this, will you be the same?"

Ariel didn't answer, choosing instead to watch the fire. She lay down on the blanket, her eyes sweeping over him.

At her invitation, he made his way to her, lay down and wrapped his arm around her, his bulky body encompassing hers. He felt the momentary stiffness and then she allowed herself to sink into familiarity. They had done this many times before.

But this wasn't like before.

Ariel turned into him, taking his face in her hands, her touch sending a shiver down his spine. She trailed a finger, like a soft feather hovering just on the edge of his skin, his body responded, heat rushing from his core and spreading outwards. She traced his strong jaw, the length of his neck, his broad shoulders and taut torso, pausing for a moment over his heart, then, retraced her path.

His body ached and tightened. His need desperate and painful. He clenched his teeth, her touch an agonising bliss. "Stop."

"But I like touching you."

He held her hand, cupping it in his own. "Please stop. I don't think I can take it."

"This was your idea," Ariel teased.

He fell onto his back and wrenched a hand through his hair. "I know. I just didn't know it would be so hard."

Ariel sucked in a quivering breath. "You can touch me, but do not attempt to get under my clothes."

Ben swallowed the rock that had lodged itself in his throat. He rolled to face her, his heart thumping violently in his chest. Hand quivering, he traced the shape of her, taking his time, allowing his fingers to absorb her warmth as they touched all that hid beneath the fabric of her dress. Her soft curves yielded to his increasingly firm touch.

Ariel moaned softly. Her heated eyes falling on his lips.

The kiss was warm and soft, like her curves and dips. He curled his fingers around her hair and pulled her closer. The kiss growing deeper, desperate.

Breaking away from him, she peppered kisses along his skin. His breath stalled as she kissed his chest and arms, her lips exploring every inch of exposed skin. His arousal mounted, the pleasure agonising.

"We need to stop," she whispered.

"We need to finish." His voice rasped through clenched teeth.

"I don't understand. You promised." He didn't miss the note of fear in her voice.

Pushing himself away from her, he scowled. "Don't look at me like that. I've already told you I'll never hurt you."

"I know... I'm sorry."

He blew out a strained breath and rested on his elbow. "I know you think we may be alone, but we are being watched. We have to make it look like...." His faced strained, willing her to understand.

Pursing her lips, she nodded and settled on her back.

He blanked her body with his, every nerve ending screaming. He put on just enough of a show, anyone watching would have thought he removed himself from his pants. He adjusted and looked into her eyes. "I'm sorry, Ariel. I'll try and make it quick."

He shut his eyes. Shutting out his uncertainty and his fear, then began rocking against her.

Her body tightened and shivered beneath his. His need grew and his confusion mounted as he focussed on the thin layer of fabric that separated them.

He found her mouth, urgent and needy as his and when he pulled away, her eyes seared him with heat and desperation. Her hair lay beneath her in a cascade of mahogany, her body shimmering with sweat.

It was his undoing. For a fraction of a second the world shattered and he felt as if he was underwater, floating but breathless. Pleasure splintered through him. Ecstasy and agony wracked his body as he groaned into Ariel's neck. The scent of her soaking into him as he spilled himself between them.

He pinned his forehead to hers and sucked in a ragged breath, his body recovering. "I'm sorry." He fell off her in a heap. Satisfaction and confusion coursed through him. He scrubbed a hand along his face. "I'm not sure how to feel right now."

"What do you mean?"

"I mean, I have been waiting for this moment for five years and it was nothing like how I hoped it would be." Guilt gripped his stomach as she flinched, disappointment washing across her features.

"Sorry I can't be more for you." She turned away from him.

"You never need to be more, Ariel. You're already everything." He kissed her shoulder, but she did not turn back to him.

He wrapped an arm around her, resisting the urge to pull her close, to mould his body to hers, to touch every inch of her skin. He feigned sleep. His thoughts pinched by regret and torment, confusion and desire.

Ben fell asleep listening to her shallow breathing, holding her quivering body.

He wrenched himself away from Ariel and watched her mouth move while she spoke. Her plump, pink lips inviting, he paid no heed to the words that spilled from her. He nodded and stared until she burst into laughter and walked away, leaving him with her scent and her promises.

Ben strolled to the beach, his heart set in a tug of war suspended between fear and joy, between light-heartedness and a bleak heaviness.

The waves grabbed at his feet as he revisited images of the night before, his body tightened and shivered.

He spotted a figure. The man sat alone watching the

ocean, his long legs pulled up to his chest and his face glistening with tears.

"Antoine?"

He jerked at the sound of his name then turned his wet face away, running a hand over it.

Ben approached, sat down next to his friend and eyed the waves as they churned along the shore, the sea as restless as his mood.

He waited in silence, the sun pricked his face with its angry hot rays. He wiped away a layer of sweat that hung across his forehead.

"Danny is here," Antoine whispered. "He is alive."

Ben's body seized for a single moment, before a hesitant smile tugged at his lips. He studied Antoine's tear streaked face and his elation melted away into concern.

"Antoine?"

More tears erupted from the darker boy as his body shook.

Ben placed a hand on his shoulder, stared a head and waited, watching the waves burst from the ocean.

When Antoine opened his mouth to speak, his voice faltered. "He is a Brown Robe."

"An infertile?" Ben's mouth stretched in a grim line as Antoine's breath shuddered and a fresh stream of tears rolled fiercely down his cheeks. He sucked in a long hollow breath then wrapped his arm around his friend. Antoine's body quaked. Ben held him close, understanding his pain.

When Antoine pulled away, he wiped at his cheeks, his face contorted with embarrassment and grief.

"I'm sorry," he said, his voice cracking around the edges. "I don't know how to feel. All this time I thought I had lost him and now he is here... a Brown Robe..."

"Be happy."

"How can I be happy? We've lost so many years, so much time, and now—"

"Now? Now you know he's alive."

Antoine's eyes grew wide, glistening. He looked to Ben and a ghost of a smile crept along his otherwise broken features. "Yes, my Danny is alive."

Ben had no choice but to be satisfied with giving Ariel long lingering looks while he spent time with her. Their friendship setting deep hooks into his already claimed heart. Besotted with her laughter and her shyness. She was enthralling.

He enjoyed her company in public, but he savoured his time with her when they were alone, hidden from all but The Watchers.

The warm sand cradled his tired body. They lay side by side beneath the shade watching the sea chase the horizon.

"Tell me about Luke."

"Not much to know. He's a jerk." Ben chuckled and shrugged.

"So, what you are saying is that he is an incredible specimen and I should take time to get to know him?"

Ben growled from somewhere deep inside him and pulled himself onto an elbow, his eyes locking with Ariel's. "If you know what's good for you, you'll stay away from him."

"Worried he has something you don't?"

Ben huffed.

"I thought so." Ariel's face split in a sly smile. She laced her fingers through Ben's. "Tell me."

Ben looked at the endless horizon and let her hand drop. "He was assigned to me." He gave a joyless chuckle. "At first, I was a chore for him, but over the years he has become like a real brother. He's gotten me out trouble more times than I deserved." He grunted at some unshared memory.

"Does he have any real brothers?"

"No. He has a sister. He said that he met her here three years ago, I think." He frowned as he searched the recesses of his mind. Coming up empty, he shrugged. "He hasn't seen her since so he thinks he might be an uncle." Ben's face split into a natural smile which fell again with his next words, "Or you know..." He bit his lower lip and swallowed the words.

Ben cleared his throat and continued. "He taught me to build, the satisfaction of seeing something through, of completing a job."

"I'd love to see the house you built someday."

He found her face and sighed, his body aching with longing. "I'd rather build you a new one. Someplace we can grow a family..."

"Ben... Don't." Ariel took his hand again forcing him to look into her eyes. She gave him a reassuring smile that shattered his aching heart.

His weak smile tinged with desperation. "Luke sets me straight when I misbehave. He's taught me everything I know about being a man."

"Everything?" Her eyebrow shot up.

Ben prowled above her and cradled her face in his hand. "Not everything." Ben's mouth brushed against hers. He pressed their lips together, soft and comforting, enjoying the feel of her body melting into his. He pulled away, her eyes dazed and heated. "Not everything," he repeated as his lips found hers once more.

The sound of a horn woke him. It resonated across the island. Ben groaned. Sleeping next to Ariel tortured his body in ways he was willing to endure for the rest of his life. He rolled off the too small cot and onto the sandy floor.

"What's that?" His voice groggy with sleep, he cleared his throat.

She stood from the bed and brushed down her dress, "I'm not sure."

Ben swept fingers through his hair, tucked strands behind his ears, then rubbed the sleep from his eyes. He stood to his full height and stretched his aching limbs, sensing her eyes on him.

"Like what you see?" he teased.

"Meh."

"Meh? Meh?" He stalked towards her, a menacing grin on his face. Ariel stepped back and shrieked. "I'll show you meh." He dived. Ariel sidestepped him, giggling, his fingers brushed her skin. He pivoted, his face a mask of delight, his eyes hungry, focussed.

Before he had another chance to pounce, the horn sounded once more, its heavy forlorn sound falling across Ishmin like a thick fog.

"We better go." All mirth ebbed from his features when he opened the flap of the tent and peered outside. "We are being summoned."

"We?" Fear drained the colour from her face.

"Everyone," he corrected and held out his hand to her.

Ben led them toward the gathering area. The makeshift arena had been transformed once again, the bar gone, and in its place, a raised platform awaited. The Watchers filed onto the stage, led by a man and a woman. Ariel's body stiffened beside him.

The woman introduced herself as The Watcher Tay and

began to speak of judgements and witnesses. With each word the dread sank deeper into his veins. Luke had told him about this. He winced knowing the spectacle awaiting them.

He ground his molars watching Ariel's pallor change as Tay imparted her judgement. The colour leeched from her as the screams carried over the crowd. Next to him, her muscles seized and her jaw clenched. Ben inched his hand to hers, brushing the edge of a finger with his own offering comfort in the only way he could. Her eyes flickered to his, her eyebrows gathered in a severe V over her bleak enraged eyes. Her attention returned to the stage, cries of The Taken seeped under his skin and tormented him with a deep agony.

"A feast shall await you all tonight as a farewell. We thank you for performing your duties and look forward to hosting you once more. You have seven hours left to enjoy one another on our shores. Do so at your pleasure. All duties have been fulfilled." The Watcher had brought her show to a close and the subdued crowd began to disperse.

Ariel's hand trembled in his when he led them away from the stage, her brow wrinkled, and eyes pooled with tears.

They had reached the tree line when she pushed away from him and collapsed on her knees. Vomit erupted from her in harsh violent waves. He clutched her hair, holding it away from her face and waited for her to finish. She rose on unsteady feet a sheen of sweat across her brow.

"That could have been us," her voice scratched.

Ben pulled her to him and kissed her sweaty forehead, then whispered in her ear. "But it wasn't."

"But—"

"It wasn't."

"They know—" Her voice held icy shards of fear.

He tucked an errant hair behind her ear. "If they knew, we wouldn't be here."

They sank to the sand, her face buried in his chest. Ben held her as she sobbed. Her tears leaked down his torso, her body shivered, fingers digging furrows into his arms. Her pain wrenched through him. He drew her closer, rocking gently, soothing her pain the only way he knew how.

The undulating sea mocked them as they sat at its feet. They watched the sun vanish beyond the horizon and take with it their last minutes.

The thought of not seeing Ariel for three more months strangled him as he kissed her a final goodbye.

They embraced, and he held her as if he was about to break and she was the glue that kept him in one piece. His lips on hers were like words that didn't need to be spoken.

Ben watched her as she walked away, each step leaving behind a footprint that would soon be erased by the rising tide. She did not look back and he was grateful, for if she had, he may not have been able to let her ago again.

His body ached for her as she disappeared into the swarm of women all heading for the boats. Soon she was nothing but a black speck, bobbing away on an endless ocean.

At the second signal he stood up in a daze, his legs aching with the weight of his body and forced himself to his boat. The hard wood beneath him wet and splintered, worn with age and kissed by the sea. The boat rocked with the waves and with the bodies of men as they piled back into the vessel. Boasting and laughter surrounded him. He searched the darkness for torch light but found none. She would be halfway home and soon he would be back at his, feeling more alone than ever.

B en descended the boat and walked by Antoine who fell into step behind him. Ben's thoughts streamed through his head all leading to Ariel. They had parted in the best way they possibly could have, and yet, he felt empty and alone as he strolled up the path to his home.

A hand came out of nowhere and wrapped itself around his shoulder then slithered loosely across his neck, half pulling, half choking. "So? How was it brother? Did you repopulate the earth?" Jacob's smile split his face in excitement and curiosity.

Ben shook off the hand and gave him a weary smile. "Sure thing."

"You should have seen him!" Luke's thundering voice boomed from behind them. "The girls love fresh meat and he is as fresh as they get."

"If you're talking about his breath, you're not wrong." The two boys laughed as Ben continued to trudge up the path, Antoine still silent behind him.

"Hey, what's wrong?" Jacob chided.

"He's got the Ishmin blues."

"The Ishmin Blues?"

Ben's steps faltered and he strained to listen to Luke.

"Yeah, everyone gets it after their first time."

"What is it?" Jacob's voice laced with curiosity.

"It's missing a warm body of the female persuasion." Luke chuckled and continued. "See, after you've been solo all your life and get a taste of what it feels like to be with a woman... it changes how you feel about things. It makes it harder knowing you won't indulge again for another three months."

Jacob nodded while Ben shook his head.

"Gives you something to wait for, to look forward to, but it also drains you in a weird way, makes you ache for something, leaves you a little empty, you know?"

Jacob looked at Luke blankly.

Luke sighed and swept a hand over his stubble. "Ishmin rips off your band aid. You have no time for fear or qualms, you have no time for asking yourself the questions you wonder about, about yourself, about them. You just do what nature made you for." He shrugs. "After the relief of that first time, there comes the intense overwhelm and the internal questions you ask yourself in secret. You compare your imagination to the real thing, knowing that you never even came close. And once you've pushed all those feelings aside and dealt with them, you realise that you've just broken a seal that can never be replaced and you crave it endlessly. The warmth, the sensation, the beauty and intensity of it all."

Jacob looked at Luke's face, glazed eyes searching for a lost memory. He shook it off and nudged his chin towards Ben. "Give him a few days, he will process and deal with it, then I am sure he won't shut up about all his seedings, of course they'll all be lies." He chuckled. "He was probably flimsy and confused and had no idea what he was doing or where anything goes." Luke's laughter grew as he pushed by the two boys and playfully ruffled a hand through Ben's hair.

"Don't worry little brother," he called over his shoulder as he marched away. "It gets better."

"Do you wanna—"

"I'm tired, I'm going home." He shared a silent look with Antoine then turned away and trudged up the mountain. His stomach in knots and his body stiff as Luke's words continued to wash over him.

He did suffer from longing and desire, but for none of the reasons Luke mentioned.

Ben's skin prickled. He scanned the dance floor for the tenth time and still found no trace of Ariel. His heart stumbled as he took a sip of the strong ale then pushed away from the bar and meandered through the crowd and toward the exit.

He spotted her then and every nerve in his body tensed and strained like distressed wood about to snap. She stood with another man. His body pinned against hers, pushing her into the wall of the dune.

Ben edged closer.

"Liam, if you do not get away from me now, the next kick I give you will ensure you will never mate again, because there's no way you'll be getting that thing up ever again."

Ben's body warmed as Ariel's words drifted to him. She had always been a fighter, strong and bull-headed, she knew how to stand her ground. Still, anger flowed inside him like an undercurrent. He knew Liam's intentions. He ground his teeth and edged closer.

"I *will* have you looking up at me one day."

"That will never happen."

"Am I interrupting something?" Ben interjected and his gaze fell on Ariel's face, where he found delight and relief.

"No." Ariel ducked under Liam's arm and rushed to Ben. Her body fell against his, her soft lips tenderly meeting his for a second.

"Hi." Her face broke into a wild smile.

"Hi." He returned the gesture.

"I see," growled Liam as he pushed by them, ensuring his shoulder struck Ben's chest. "Ben," his voice dripped acid.

"Liam." Ben smirked at the man whose wounded ego saw him walking straight to the bar.

"How long were you standing there?" Ariel scrutinised his face.

"Long enough to see you hadn't changed your mind about me."

"So, you saw him harassing me?" Her eyes narrowed.

"Yes."

"And you didn't come to rescue me?"

"I'm pretty sure you made it clear last time the three of us shared the same space that you don't need rescuing. And after seeing what you did to that man in your tent, I was taking no chances." He covered his groin took a step back.

She giggled and elbowed him playfully. "I don't *need* to be rescued, but it would have been nice, anyway."

"Didn't want to take any chances…"

"Oh, shut up already."

"Make me."

Ariel pushed herself on her tiptoes, slamming her lips into his. His entire body responded to her. A momentary stillness of the muscles, an intake of breath, and then he melted into her, his tongue dancing wildly with hers. His strong arms closed around her, pulling her closer as if he wanted to be a part of her.

Their lips broke apart. Ben's arms tightened around her and he inhaled, drew her nearer, then released her.

"I thought you weren't here."

"Nothing will keep me away from you."

"Would you like to get out of here?" his husky voice strained.

"I thought we had a deal."

"We do, but I haven't seen you in three months and I want you all to myself, just for a while."

Ariel smiled at his candour, at his tenderness and slid her hand into his, leading him away from the chaos and noise and towards the quieter beach.

They walked in silence until the the cool water licked at his toes.

"How did your mum take it?"

"Not good." Ariel sighed. "She doesn't hide disappointment well."

Ben nodded, a grin splitting his face. "I remember. What about Rosalie?"

"I think she suspects the way I feel, but I haven't said a thing. My mum thinks I need to take on other mates."

"Does she now?" His fists curled at his side as he tipped his chin slightly, eyebrows rising.

"She seems to think the one that I have chosen is not good enough or I would have been back with her grandchild."

"Is that right?" He sucked in a long breath through clenched teeth.

"She seems to think that I need to do *it* more often, with more men," she teased as he got more agitated.

His nerves wound beyond their limits. He swept Ariel's feet from beneath her, catching her before she fell, then laid her into the sand. He straddled her, pinning her down, his breath frayed and ragged.

His mouth crashed onto hers. His lips devouring hers, his hunger insatiable, restless hands scoured her body, fingers digging into hidden flesh.

"Hey." She broke away and took his face in her hands, looking into his eyes. "I was only joking."

"I know." His heart pounded as he loosened his grip on her. "I just don't ever want to think about that."

He buried himself in her neck, her flesh breaking out in goose bumps when his lips left a gentle heat trail on her skin. His hand travelled up to the clasp behind her neck and he stopped, his eyes looking at her questioningly.

Her teeth skated over her lower lip and she drew in a sharp breath before nodding. His lips grazed hers and her body stiffened as his clumsy fingers grabbed at the plastic ring and unclipped her dress, the fabric falling around her shoulders. His lips travelled the length of her jaw, peppering a trail of kisses along her neck and shoulders. He searched her face once more, asking for permission. It came in the form of silence.

Ben tugged on the dress, teasing the fabric from her body, revealing her bosom. Her shaking breath forcing her chest to heave and her breasts to rise. No longer the flat-chested girl he remembered, her flesh rounded and white, the pink nipples hard and splendid.

He gasped at the sight of her, his eyes locked on her exposed torso.

At that, Ariel bucked and pushed him off her, her hand flew to her breasts providing cover. "Stop."

"Ariel, I…" He ran a hand through his hair. "You're just so beautiful. I'm sorry, I didn't mean to — "

She swallowed his apology with a soft, tender kiss, her bare chest pressed against his. "I know, I'm just… not ready, not yet… I'm sorry." She cast her eyes down, a flush crept across her cheeks.

Ben swallowed, his mouth too dry, his lip pressed in a tight line. "Should we…" He cleared his throat. "Finish the show?" His warm whisper sent shivers down her spine.

Ariel clenched her jaw, nodding.

When it was done, he reached for the folds of her dress and reset the clasp, then fell back into the sand. His brow netted together, his thoughts clouded in confusion. Desire and disappointment fused inside of him.

"I'm sorry." She covered her face in her hands, her knees pulled tightly to her chest.

"Don't be." His voice a raspy whisper as he tried to regain his senses. "Take all the time you need." He exhaled deeply.

She responded with silence.

"Come lie with me. Please." He waited, until slowly, she uncurled, allowing her frigid body to melt and tangle in his.

"I need to go clean up. This stain will show in the morning." She rose to her feet.

"Do you need help?"

"I think you've helped enough." She winked at him and left him where he lay.

He already missed her heat, the sensation of her body against his. Too soon he was getting used to the feel of her, to the idea of having her, belonging to her. Everything about Ariel made him feel in ways that both exhilarated and scared him. Each taste set his entire being alight leaving him to crave more. Her lips shaped to fit his perfectly. The way in which her body relaxed and relented, melting into his.

He rolled onto his back and stared at the moon as it brushed the beach in dim light, mocking him. Ariel's words echoed in his head. *'She seems to think the one that I have chosen is not good enough or I would have been back with her grandchild.'* He clenched his fists and they met the sand with a muted thud. He would not allow those thoughts to consume him. Instead he removed his clothes and ploughed into the water, cleansing himself, preparing himself for Ariel, for her softness, her comfort.

He dried and waited.

When she did not return after a time, fear rose inside him

like a current. He searched for her in the growing darkness, only the moon accompanying him.

When he could not find her in the shower cubicle, he scoured the path as he made his way to her tent. He strained to listen and heard a soft whimpering that emanated from within.

"Ariel?" Ben pushed through the tent flap to see her curled onto her cot, shaking. Tears streamed down her face.

"Ariel!" he stepped further into the tent. "Are you okay? Did I hurt you?" She looked up at him and his heart panged at the terror etched across her face.

"No. It wasn't you." Her voice cracked.

Relief flooded through him for an instant, replaced by a cold fear that clasped around his throat. He took small steps approaching her. "What happened? Did someone—"

"Why is this place so cruel? Why is there so much misery here?"

"Ariel, did someone hurt you?" he ground the words through clenched teeth.

She sucked in a shaky breath. "Not me." Her voice shook.

Ben wound an arm around her shoulder, drawing her into his chest, allowing her tears to sting his skin with their despair.

"This entire place is built on a lie. It brings nothing but anguish."

His stomach clenched at her words, but he knew she spoke from a place where bottomless pain lived. A hopeless place.

He tried to pull her out. "It could be worse."

Ariel pushed away from him and sneered, snot and tears running down her face. "How?" She sniffed. "How could it possibly be worse? You are not a woman. You couldn't possibly understand. The invasion, the fear, the shame..."

He sighed and his shoulders slumped. "You're right, I'll

never understand those things in the same way that you do." He pinched the bridge of his nose, his eyes clamped together, then stood up, his decision made. "Wipe your tears away, there's something I want to show you."

"Ben, I—"

"I *need* to show you something." He stood resolute, towering above the bed and stretched out his hand for her. "Come on."

Ariel placed her hand in his and he yanked her off the cot and into his arms. He wiped the tears from her eyes and kissed the top of her head. "Come on," he whispered and led the way out of the tent.

The moonlight tinged the tented landscape in shades of white and grey, as if all the colour had drained away with Ariel's hope. They walked serenaded by the sounds of the night, crashing waves, rustling leaves and the choir of humanity as it rang and resonated in the midst of it all. They were in the male territory now. Her hand tightened in his as they crossed an invisible line drawn by the Keepers of Ishmin. Ariel's steps got smaller, unsure, the deeper they ventured into the male side of the island.

They meandered through the ocean of tents until Ben came to a stop at a blue one identical to hers. He released her hand. "Stand here, don't go anywhere."

Her face contorted, seized with terror. "Ben—"

"Just wait. Don't go anywhere."

He turned away from her and pushed his way into the tent where three bodies occupied three of the four cots, their chests rising and falling in their sleep. He crept up to Antoine and shook him gently. The slender boy mumbled and turned on his side. He shook harder. "Antoine, get up," he whispered.

Antoine opened his eyes and slowly focused on Ben, then shot up. "What's happened?" his groggy voice croaked as he rubbed sleep from his eyes, his body stiffening.

"I need something from you." They exchanged a look until Antoine's shoulders slumped, not in defeat, but in understanding, as if always expecting this day to come.

"Outside. Hurry." Ben pushed through the tent flaps and found Ariel. Despite the warm night she hugged herself, arms wrapped tightly around her chest, her gaze swinging from left to right in a petrified pendulum.

"Ben." Relief slackened the tight muscled of her jaw and shoulders. She clutched onto him when the large dark boy appeared behind him.

"Ben—" she stammered.

"Shhh, it's ok. Let's go."

Ben led them away from the tents and into the fringes of the forest. Hidden by the palm trees and shrubbery, the trio sat down in the sand, a tense silence shrouding them.

"Ariel, I want you to meet Antoine."

The boy frowned as Ariel nodded an uncertain hello.

"What are we doing here, Ben?" Antoine's voice held an edge of pain, of uncertainty.

"Ariel has lost all hope, and I want you to show her that even in the bleakest of moments, there is always some to be found."

Antoine grimaced and nodded, his hands digging into the sand.

Ben placed a hand on his friend's arm. "It is your secret to share, and so I am asking you to make a choice. You don't owe me anything—"

"I owe you everything."

"No. You don't. But Ariel — "

"Is your Danny?"

Ben nodded, biting his lower lip, his toes digging furrows into the sand.

The two boys shared a long knowing look. Antoine sucked in a long breath and turned to Ariel who had been watching the scene unfold, clutching her knees to her chest as she rocked in the sand.

"My name is Antoine, son of Claudette, I come from the island of Unenet, now shuffled to Dagon. I came over with another boy. Danny, son of Nora." He rubbed his arm as if searching for comfort within his own skin. "That boy is the man I love."

Ariel swallowed her gasp as Antoine continued to talk. "He's always given me comfort and love and I cannot imagine life without him. The disease that makes his hair white and eyes pink and his skin burn in the sun has made him unworthy in their eyes. An abomination." He spat the word as if it bit his tongue. "Danny is gentle and caring and just being around him conjures so much joy within me." A small smile tugged at his lips.

Ariel's mouth fell open but before words could spill out, Ben squeezed her knee, imploring her to listen.

"On our arrival to Dagon, we were separated. He walked into a room and never walked out and I was certain he was… That I would never see him again." He sucked in a shaky breath. "For the last five years I have been walking around with a heavy heart, empty, barely feeling a thing. The loss too great to bear. Ben here helped me through the darkest times. Although I've told him more than once that he should have just let us both drown."

Ariel's gaze shifted to Ben. "What is he talking about?"

"Nothing." He turned to his friend. "Just tell her…"

Antoine nodded. "I have always dreaded Ishmin. I may look like a man, but I do not have the urge to be with women. My heart belongs to Danny." He sucked in a long breath.

"When I arrived here on my first cycle, all I felt was despair, and trepidation. The thought of being with another and a woman no less… It all felt unbearable. But then a miracle happened." Antoine's face filled with delight, "I was sitting for my breakfast when a Brown Robe served me a meal, his hand landed on mine and our eyes met."

"Danny?" Ariel gasped, unable to hide her excitement.

"Yes." Antoine shot her a warm smile. "Not only is he alive, he has been here all this time, hoping. Waiting for me. Of course, we could not talk or touch. Not just then, but I was washed with relief—with joy—for the man I loved was alive and here, with me... Near me."

Ariel edged closer to Antoine as if his rapture was a warm fire.

Antoine bit his lip. "I have yearned for Danny for so long, have spilt so many tears for our lost love. I was alone and confused and a little broken knowing he was here, knowing ours is a forbidden love. Being here, with him, is almost twice as painful as thinking he was dead, because when I thought he was dead, I was free. Now, my heart is locked with his and my body and mind must be used in the confines of our rules. It brings me so much sorrow that I want to tear my heart out of my body so that is stops hurting all the time."

Ariel locked eyes with Ben. A thousand words exchanged in their silence.

Antoine sighed and flicked a hand in the air as if batting away his thoughts. "At the end of the first day I was a desperate mess. I had women chasing me and a body that would not function. It wanted something else. *Someone* else. In truth I was confused. I was afraid and relieved and desperate and more than anything, I was alone. But you know, hope lives in the darkest of places." His smile broadened.

"I found Ben, and you know what he's like, always brooding over something..."

Ariel cocked her head and an eyebrow shot up. "Always?"

Antoine chuckled. "Always. Maybe now I know why." He winked at her.

"I'm right here you know," Ben interjected.

They ignored him.

"Ben saved my life. More than once. Has he told you?"

"No." She shook her head and it swivelled to Ben, her eyes trying to see right through him, to find the answers to all her questions.

"Ben has saved me many times over and so I knew without a doubt I could entrust him with my secret. Even today when he needed me, he didn't force me, he asked. So let me tell you the end, let me give the hope you seek." Antoine exhaled deeply and continued. "I told Ben that I found Danny, that he was right here, with me, but so far from me. That I needed to see him, touch him, talk to him… Your Ben—"

"He's not *my* Ben," Ariel cut him off. Ben's insides constricted at her words.

Antoine's brow arched and he chuckled. "That is your loss then." He shrugged and continued. "Ben, as always, reassured me, and promised me that Danny would be in my arms once more. It was like he was speaking of his own heart when he said he knew the agony of distance, the power of ache, the longing…" Antoine studied Ariel over a long silence. "I can never thank my friend enough. He endangers himself for others, for their sake, for their happiness. He brought Danny to me under guise and we shared a few precious hours together. He is of course maimed as a Brown Robe, but I still found comfort in his arms, against his skin, wiping away his tears with my kisses." He ground his teeth, his face hovering between sadness and acrimony.

"Danny gave me permission to live. He told me I must be with women and spread my seed so that I could keep returning to him, until one day I am old enough to be a Watcher. Until I can win my way back into his arms when we can grow old together."

"But you are both in prison, you can never truly be—"

"But it is a prison of my own choosing. Don't you see,

Ariel? Even with the distance and longing, he is *alive*, and that gives me hope. As long as Danny is here, and safe, I can keep going because I get to see him live, to be closer to him than I thought possible, even when that means being away from him. But most of all, I know that he loves me and that one day we will reunite, and that is enough."

"And this gives you hope?"

"What else is there? The man I love is here, and he loves me too, he waits for me."

Ariel's eyes brimmed with tears and she bolted from the sand and wrapped herself around Antoine. She cradled him like a cherished friend, until his stiffened body sagged against her and he too enveloped her in his arms.

"Your Ben is a beacon of hope for all of us. Hold on to that, to him, and you too will survive this place," he whispered in her ear then broke away from her embrace. His mouth split into a wide smile as he got up. "I must return to bed now. I must look my best for breakfast tomorrow."

"Thank you." Ben tipped his head toward his friend who returned the gesture before turning away.

They sat watching Antoine go, and listened to the night fade away into silence.

Ben stood up and offered his hand to Ariel. "Come on, let me take you to your tent."

She placed her hand in his and stood up, her forehead furrowed. "He really loves you."

"He's a good friend."

"You saved his life?"

Ben shrugged it away not wanting to dwell on the past.

"He called you a beacon of light and hope."

Ben stopped and pulled Ariel into his arms, her breath stalled as he gazed into her eyes, his lips mere inches from her own, his heart ricocheted in his chest as he grazed her lips with his. "Do I give you hope?"

"More than you'll know."

Their kiss was fragile and hesitant at first, until her lips simmered and burned through him, heating his blood and flooding his veins. He tore away from her, raked with regret, his body close to breaking.

His teeth clamped and he felt like a brute above her, putting on another show, his body burning, aching, longing for what he denied himself. Full of chagrin and contrition, he released himself above her, wishing he could have all of her.

His sweaty head fell to her chest and he regained his breath, her fingers weaved through his hair.

"It wasn't always like this," Ariel said, her voice piercing his wounded thoughts.

"What?"

"The way we live. Mating Season."

"Wasn't it?" He tilted his head toward her.

"No, there was a time when there was a thing called marriage."

"I've never heard that term before. Is it a good thing?"

"I don't know, but I think it's better than this."

His hand tightened around her. "What is it, then? This Marriage?"

"I read about it in that book I found. I asked Mama Beth what it was, she said it was a myth."

"But *what* is it?"

"It's a promise."

"Of what?"

"It's a promise people used to make one another, sometimes even before they had kids." Ariel's gaze latched onto his. "They promised to stay together and raise their children together. They would share a house, share chores, and share the child-rearing."

Ben brushed his hands over his face and let her words sink in.

"They promised to only be with one another, not other mates." Ariel bit her lip before continuing. "They promised to love one another until death."

Ben remained silent, mulling over all she had said.

"Where is this book, Ariel?"

"My mother burned it when I questioned her about it. Don't you remember?"

He stared up at the dark sky, his fingers absently tracing the lines of Ariel's back. "So, there was a time that people stayed together? All the time?"

"Yes."

"And they, a man and a woman, would raise children? Together? Watch them grow? On the same island?"

"Yes. But it was from before the islands."

Ben shook his head at her words. His heart twanged with hope, almost too painful to bear. He pushed himself off the sand and turned to look at her. He hesitated, uncertain. "Is that something you would want to do? With me?"

"More than anything in the world." Ariel answered with a wan smile, her eyes dropping to her feet. "But I don't think we will ever be allowed to. You know what the rules are. You know what the living arrangements are. How are we going to be able to do this?"

"There has to be a way."

"How?"

"I don't know, but I have to believe that there will come a

time when we can be together. There has to be a way I don't have to wait three months just to see you for a week, to wait that long to be able to feel your body underneath mine, to be able to feel your warmth, your lips, your touch."

His words fell away.

Ariel pulled away from his body and sat up, looking at the ocean. "I want to believe that, too. That there could be a way for us, but I just don't see it happening."

"We can run away. Just float around the ocean until we find our own island."

"And if we don't find an island?"

"Then we'll be on a boat, together."

She snorted at the idea as Ben grasped at weak straws.

"Okay, so let's say that somehow I will let you talk me into your boat. What about our families? Rosalie? Her boys?"

"Mama Beth?" He raised an eyebrow.

"We can leave her behind." Ariel's face curved into a sly grin.

His head fell back into the sand and he stared into the vast blackness above them, "I don't have a family, not really, but if you come with me, we can make a new kind of family. One where we have a child and he can enjoy both of us, his entire life. *Our* entire lives."

"He?"

"Or she."

"Ben." She gave him a pained look. "Don't do this…"

"We could. Just you and me and them." His jaw ticked as he clutched at her arm.

"I don't want to live on your imaginary boat! Why have kids deprived of knowing their grandmother and aunt and nephews? You didn't get to have a family, so having gone through that, why would you want to deny your future children a chance of being raised by those who love them?"

"But *I* would love them. If only I'd be given a chance."

"Ben." Her voice laced with sadness.

"No!" Bitterness tinged his voice as he hissed his harsh words. "Why should that child be robbed of the opportunity of loving *me*? Why can't they have a father and a mother? Why should I lose at every possible turn?"

Tears pricked his eyes as his festering feelings bubbled to the surface. His pain and anguish nicked at his heart as they peeled away the scars, exposing his open wound to the world, his deprivation, his desperation.

Ariel's arms closed around him, and he sank into her softness, his tears soaking through her white dress.

"What if we just ask?" Her soft voice pierced through his anguish.

"Ask?" He raised his head, and their eyes locked.

"Yes. What if we ask? We can go to The Watchers, tell them that we want to be together, stay together. They cannot keep us apart. I won't let them keep me away from you forever." She stroked his face, wiping away his tears.

"That's madness, Ariel. You know what they could do to us." His breath caught in his throat at the prospect of losing her.

She ground her teeth, deep in thought. "What about my mum? Let me talk to Mama Beth first. Let me see what she says. Maybe she will help."

"Mama Beth? Help us?" His head cocked to the side, his voice sardonic.

"I think you underestimate what my mother is willing to do for her daughter, and for her grandchild, born or unborn."

"Ariel, what if she reports us?"

"It's a risk we must take."

"I can't watch you be taken by another."

"She won't let it come to that."

"But—"

Her lips landed on his, delicate and sweet, dragging away the last edges of doubt and fear.

"*I* won't let it come to that," she whispered as she fell into his fierce embrace. Their lips locked in desperation and she lay on the soft sand beneath him, anguish giving way to desire.

He wrenched himself away from her, and rolled onto the sand, his body tight with pain. Ariel placed her head on his chest, her breath whispering along his skin, stealing his away.

"You seem to have a tent peg problem."

His lips parted in a strained smile. "That I do. Would you like to help me with that?"

"I'm still enduring the joy of the last time I helped you with that." She grimaced at her moist dress.

He exaggerated a sigh and flashed her a set of white teeth, then let his head fall back into his hands.

Ben watched in pain as Ariel boarded her boat. His senses frayed, his mind crushed.

Antoine's deep-set voice pierced his brooding. "It's just another three months and you'll see her again."

Ben nodded, his skin already feverish with longing.

"What's wrong with him now?" Jacob exchanged a look with Luke. "You said the blues only affect you on the first round."

"He must be a special case."

"Yes, our Ben is very special, and so sensitive."

Luke and Jacob continued talking around him. About him. Prodding at his resolve. Ben ignored them, hacking at the rock as if it was his heart. The harder he hit against it, the further he carved, the more pain he unleashed. The pickaxe grew heavy in his arms that missed the softness of Ariel's flesh.

He threw his body into his work, erasing minutes and hours without her, until every muscle ached and each tendon cried with burning agony. Still he hacked the rock face, making it pay for all his frustrations and anger, all of his desires and boundaries. They were both prisoners of circumstance and as much as his mind churned to find a way to free them, he came up blank.

Days dripped away, trampling his spirit. His frustration grew, rising like the tide. She would talk to Mama Beth and while he waited to see her again, only fear and uncertainty consumed him.

⟡

Ben hacked the rock, his palms growing tender and numb. If he worked harder, his mind would fall into a mindless hollow where he would be momentarily at peace.

"Ben." His name pierced the ringing clangs and he looked up to see Luke. "Come with me."

"Where are we going?"

"You have been requested."

"Requested?" His heart squeezed in his chest and the sheen of sweat coating his body turned icy. "By whom?"

"Let's go. I can't hear myself think with all this noise." Luke climbed down the rock face and waited.

Ben dropped his pickaxe and followed.

"Who summoned me? Where are we going?" the strength drained from his legs and they threatened to buckle beneath him.

"You're needed on a boat."

"A boat?" Uncertainty rippled inside him.

"They're a man short today and the job cannot be done by one man."

"But why me? Why not Oli—"

"I don't know." Luke halted and spun to face him. "All I know is that Simon asked for you, by name, and you alone, and so you'll go. You'll help and you will do what you're told."

Luke spun back around and continued trudging down the mountain.

"Why are you so—"

"Because," he swivelled back towards Ben, white dust exploding from his clothing, "it means something. I don't know what, and that worries me, as it should worry you."

Ben's face erupted into a grin. "Oh. You care about me."

"Really? I tell you something is't right and that's what you got out of it?'

"Maybe even love me? Like a brother?"

"I'm serious."

"So am I," jested Ben, his face beaming.

"Ben—"

"Luke." Ben mimicked his brother's deep growl.

He scrubbed a hand across his face, swivelled and marched on. He slowed, turned his head. "Maybe." He turned back and continued walking.

Warmth gripped Ben's heart as if it had been touched by the sun.

They didn't say anything more as they made their way to the dock. Whatever fate awaited him it was already decided and there would be nothing either man could do about it.

They reached the dock in silence and walked toward the boat where Simon stood, his craggy face set in a scowl. "You took your time."

"There is an entire mountain between you and the quarry."

He shrugged and tipped his chin to Ben. "Get in. We're already late."

Ben looked to Luke, his pulse strumming as a fog of emotion clouded inside him. Luke's hand gripped the back of his neck and he drew him close, held him for a second then released him, the moment awkward and raw in equal measures.

"What the hell are you two doing? Get in the boat, he'll be home before lunch time then you can hold each other's hands all you want."

The shared a tight smile before Ben hopped into the boat. It rocked beneath him and he grabbed the lip, his knuckles blanched against the rough wood.

Simon pushed away from the dock then swiped the water with his oar, moving them away from Dagon. Ben's gaze remained on Luke until he was nothing more than a speck. He turned his attention to Simon.

The older man ignored him, steering the vessel against the light waves and further into the blanket of blue sea. When he was satisfied with their position, Simon grabbed an anchor and threw it overboard, the splash rearing against the boat.

Waves churned around them in the unsettling endless blue. Ben sat, nausea clawing its way up his throat and met Simon's scrutinising gaze.

"What am I doing here?"

Simon ignored the question. "Grab the net boy."

Ben swivelled around to find a cast net set behind him. He passed it to Simon who secured the rope, gathered the net in his arms and with a practiced twist of the wrist, cast the net across the blue expanse. It floated for a mere second before descending under the water.

Simon bent down, the boat jolted with his movements. Ben sucked in a breath and stabilised himself as Simon produced a whisky bottle. He sucked in a few mouthfuls then hissed in pleasure.

"Drink boy?"

"Stop calling me boy. You know my name."

"How could I ever forget? You've always been more trouble than you're worth and now, once again your existence affects mine." He slugged another sip of whisky and set the bottle inside a rope cocoon as if it was a baby.

"I've done nothing."

Simon huffed then stood and pulled on the line, dragging the net back into the boat. He spun towards Ben. "Don't just sit, come help."

Ben swayed with the boat and reached for the rope. The rough strands weaved through his hands as Simon coiled the slack around his forearm. They heaved the net into the boat and Simon released the catch onto the wooden floor. Fish twitched and danced in the pooled water, Ben watched their scales gleam and their mouths beg for breath.

"In the buckets! Quick."

Ben grabbed a bucket and his hand grasped at the fish who slid and slipped out of his hands, their slick, slippery bodies fighting.

Simon clicked his tongue and rolled his eyes. "Can't do anything right boy, can you?"

Ben glared at him. "I told you not to call me boy."

The men locked eyes. Ben's nostrils flared, his lip curled up. Simon chuckled and looked away, then chased his fish and threw them into the bucket easily, searing the edge of Ben's irritation.

Simon cast the net out for a second time and looked over the ocean.

"Why do you hate me so much?" Ben swiped a hand over his sweaty brow.

Simon made a sound akin to a chuckle and snapped his eyes towards Ben. "Tell me, why can you not conform? Why can you not do what you're told? Let the runts drown, don't run away, don't hide, catch the fish."

Ben chewed on the inside of his cheek, digesting the question. He pinched the bridge of his nose then stood up and grabbed the rope. They hauled the net into the boat and secured the second load.

"If I did all those things I'd be just like these fish, trying to catch my breath in a world that suffocated me."

Simon nodded, the creases around his eyes softening for a moment. "Here." He reached into his faded shorts and grabbed a shard of paper no bigger than a thumb nail. "Read it and throw it into the ocean."

"What is it?"

Simon shrugged. "The trade I made was for a delivery, not for information. Whatever that is, I doubt it was the worth the price I charged."

A shudder ran over his neck and down his spine as he noticed the glint of malevolence in Simon's eye. He grabbed the shard of paper and unfolded it. He read the simple message and his heart flooded with hope so dense it hitched his breath and wrung the air from his lugs.

He read the message again and again looking over the meticulous round writing.

'I told you so'

The words tumbled from the page and into his heart. They echoed in his head and a smile tugged at his lips.

"Get rid of it. We need to finish, then my trade is complete."

"Can I send something back?"

Simon chuckled, his eyes traced the length of Ben's body. "You're pretty all right but you have nothing I want."

A shudder crawled underneath Ben's skin as Simon cast the net out once more.

"You know Benjen," Ben's head jerked towards Simon at the use of his full name, "I believe that unlike me, you are a good man. And in fact, I owe you a favour for keeping your mouth shut."

Ben opened his mouth to talk but Simon batted his words away with a flick of his wrist. "I didn't forget, nor would I, so I do owe you a favour. However, before you ask me to deliver words consider this: One day you'll do great things, and there will come a time when you might feel like a fish out of water. It might be useful to have someone like me around to catch you."

The two men remained stoic, Simon's bargain floated between them like a mischievous wind. Ben grabbed the back of his neck then nodded. A silent agreement.

Simon turned his attention back to the net and dragged the heavy saturated rope back into the boat. Ben stepped up to help, keeping his mouth shut, fighting the silent battle of emotions that raged inside him. With the fish in the buckets and the net cast out once more, he read over Ariel's message a final time then allowed the paper to fly from his hands. It fell onto the water like a broken butterfly, water teased the edges then stained the shard, it grew heavy then sank and disappeared beneath the surface.

A warmth settled inside of him. Ariel had given him hope and he would cling to it with two raw desperate hands until he saw her again.

Ben raced to the boat, eager to visit Ishmin once more. Ignoring the jeers and sneers of the other men and the sickness that rose within, he clung to the ragged lip and allowed his thoughts to drift to Ariel, her exquisite smile, the fruity scent of her freshly washed hair, the feel of her fingers laced through his. His body hardened and knotted with anticipation.

Ben endured the welcome procession, signing his name into the record book and being assigned his tent. He couldn't help the chugging of his heart or the smile that crept across his face at the prospect of seeing her.

At the sound of the horn every nerve ending scratched at the surface of his skin. His body twitched and ached from waiting, from wanting. He leaned over the bar counter and watched the entrance to the dance floor.

Music and women poured in, bodies and alcohol flowed around him. His body tensed and coiled when he didn't see her. Cold panic set in like a blade ripping slowly along his spine. He pushed away from the bar and made his way through the throng of moving bodies on the dance floor, searching for a single familiar face.

He ran, ignoring reaching hands and soft suggestive voices. He found Ariel's tent and ploughed through the flaps.

Deserted.

He sucked in a breath attempting to settle his nerves and turned toward the beach. He searched behind bushes and along the shoreline, and still he could not find her.

Ben fell to the sand, his heart hammering in his chest. He tried to push away the settling dread that, like a fog, begun to shroud his every thought.

He sucked in a galvanising breath and returned to the dance area hoping he may have missed her. Again, he scoured the faces of the crowd, seeking her out. His heart plummeted into a gaping hole of darkness that opened into his stomach. Ariel wasn't there.

His body coiled and fear whispered along his skin as the implications of her absence painted grotesque pictures in his mind. He knotted his arms in front of his stomach, his heart slammed in his chest suffocating under its own beat.

"Hello."

Ben looked up at the woman who smiled serenely at him. Flickering hazel eyes met his own and her glossy lips turned up in a saccharine smile. Her flowing black hair slicked to the back held together by a single red flower.

"Rosalie?" his voice stammered as his mouth remained slightly ajar.

"I see what she means."

"Rosalie?"

"Hi Ben." her smile broadened, her lips shining in the flickering flames.

"What are you doing here? Where's Ariel?"

"Not here."

"Where is she? What happened? Is she okay?"

"Why are you so concerned with someone that isn't here when you have a sea of women to choose from?" Her smile didn't falter.

A stab of uncertainty rose inside him. "Rosalie whe—"

"What about that one? She's cute." Rosalie pointed to a slim redhaired woman whose dress clung to her body showing off her curves.

Ben turned away, heat rising to his face. "Rosalie, where is she?"

"Drink?" Rosalie held two glasses of ale and pressed one towards Ben.

He grabbed it reluctantly and she raised her glass towards him. "To Mating Season." She made no effort to disguise the bitterness behind her sweet voice. Rosalie tipped the glass to her lips and took a long sip.

Ben nipped at the drink.

"You're not what I expected." He brushed his hands over his face and took Rosalie in. "Ariel made you out to be different…"

"Well not everything she says is true you know." At that her façade faltered and regret seeped through her ugly mask. She recovered quickly and continued. "Anyway, she isn't here, and what happens on Ishmin stays on Ishmin, right? So, go ahead, go have fun. It'll stay between us."

Ben slammed his drink onto the bar, the amber liquid sloshing across the wooden surface. He stared at Rosalie who smiled at him unperturbed, then stormed off, a wild storm smashing inside him. Dark clouds filled his thoughts and trepidation set in, as his entire body wound and coiled around Rosalie's words and actions.

He found himself at the edge of the water, the waves snapping at his toes, luring him in.

The warm water parted for him as he carved a path into the waiting sea. It cradled his searing body, the saltwater stinging his wounded heart. He lay on his back, the lulling waves carrying him, comforting him, as he stared at the mocking moon and wondered if Ariel shared the same sky.

B en's body ached and his mind wondered, his night full of nightmares and restlessness.

He spotted Rosalie in the mess hall having her breakfast surrounded by a group of men each more leery than the one before. Competitive in their nature, aggressive in their pursuit, yet she remained proud and astute, letting none penetrate the sheer wall she had built herself. Like a perfect puppet master, she played with their strings, steering them along with a smile or a flick of the hair, with a scorching look, or a bite of her lips. They ate out of her hands like hungry pups.

When she spotted Ben, she rose, her breakfast half eaten, and walked out of the mess hall. When the other men stood up to follow, Rosalie raised her hand and whispered to them across the table. They smiled, nodded, and remained seated.

Ben followed in her wake.

"Good morning, Ben." Her face remained neutral.

"Rosalie, where's Ariel?"

Rosalie huffed. "Are you still going on about her?" She turned and walked away.

Ben grabbed her by the elbow, swivelling her around. "Stop this now. Whatever *this* is." He released her, his hand plunging into his hair. "Tell me where Ariel is, tell me if she's okay. What happened?"

Rosalie sighed then walked off, Ben trudged behind her.

"Rosalie!" he cried after her, but she didn't turn around. She stopped near a gaggle of women, whose giggles and conversation fell silent when they approached.

"Hi ladies," Rosalie started in a honeyed voice, "this is my friend, Ben." She shot them a warm, mischievous grin.

As one, the women turned to look at him like they would a coveted treasure. Heat rose to his ears and he took a small step backwards.

"Hi Ben," the women said as one, as if they were a singular being, a multi-headed sea serpent, inviting and deadly all at once.

He shot Rosalie a scowl. "I have to go," he mumbled and turned away, anger bubbling inside him like an underwater volcano.

He spent the rest of the day brooding, pacing around his tent and searching for Rosalie, who seemed to have vanished. His body quaked and clenched with apprehension, with each passing hour. His obligations on Ishmin loomed above him like a noose.

The evening breeze blew forcefully. Waves leapt from the ocean and crashed onto the sand, mimicking the turmoil of his mind. Ben stared at the undulating, hypnotic sea wanting to disappear beneath it. Uncertainty clawed at him like an angry monster

"What's wrong brother? You seem as angry as these waves." Luke sat by his side, materialising from nowhere.

"Nothing."

"Lady trouble?"

Ben shrugged.

"Well, she is a looker. You sure know how to pick 'em." Luke chuckled as Ben cringed at the image. "But you know, pursuing a single mate is unhealthy, it breeds the wrong intention and doesn't help with actual breeding." He elbowed him playfully.

"It's not like that. I'm just… I don't feel very well."

"Ah yes, women will do that to you. The trick is not to let them into your head, or worse into your heart." His voice faltered a little and he fell silent.

"No chance of that happening."

"Best that way anyway." He shrugged. "Seems like your lady is fond of a more mature flavour anyway."

"What are you talking about?"

Luke pointed back towards the mainland. He spotted

Rosalie standing with a silver haired Watcher, one that seemed too familiar. He wrapped his arm around her shoulders and led her away. Ben swallowed hard, his forehead crinkling.

"A Watcher?"

Luke chuckled. "So it seems."

"I thought they were beyond mating…."

"Only the women." Luke shrugged. "Their body stops making children after a while and I guess if they cannot be a vessel, they are no longer useful."

"You talk of women as if they were objects."

"You must learn to do so too," Luke snapped.

"But they are people."

"You cannot see them like that."

"Why?'

"Because…" His eyes glazed over for a second and his shoulders slumped. "This place gives us entitlement to engage in behaviours that bare no consequences. The minute you see them as anything other than a vessel, you understand their humanity, their vulnerability, and you open yourself up to neediness and desperation. You understand then, that every minute spent with them is too precious and too delicate, and you will find yourself investing in them. Investing emotions you shouldn't be feeling, investing time you don't have to waste." Luke scrubbed a hand over his face. "They make to borrow your heart, but they never return it."

Luke fell silent then cleared his throat. The callousness returned. "They are nothing but vessels and we are nothing but the seeds we plant inside them. If you want anything other than that, find a man to remain your friend."

"What was her name?"

Luke's body stiffened for a microsecond, his mouth formed a thin line that twisted with tortured emotion. "Be careful Ben, protect yourself. Do what needs to be done." Luke pushed himself up and brushed the sand from his legs.

He looked out into the ocean watching the waves crash against one another, "Anastasia, daughter of Tatiana."

"Where is she now?"

"Gone." He let the words be carried away by the bruising wind then turned on his heel and left Ben with his thoughts.

O n the fifth day Ben's desperation had bloomed into a field of despair.

Trepidation took hold and his body protested the inevitable consequences that would be bestowed on him should he not mate. Stifling fury and anxiety twisted in his stomach as he plucked at empty solutions, none of which would end in his favour.

A shadow fell across his table as he used his fork to push food around on his plate, his appetite diminishing with each day. Ben looked up to see Rosalie standing above him.

"Can I sit down?"

"Suit yourself." He shrugged, not hiding his disdain.

"Don't be like that, Ben."

"What do you want?" he hissed at Rosalie through clenched teeth.

"I just wanted to know how your week has been. Have you managed to find a mate?"

His voice fell to a sharp whisper. "No. I. Have. Not. Mated."

"You must have been lonely."

Ben ground his teeth, wanting the conversation to be over.

"Ben, look at me." He lifted his gaze to meet hers. "Why haven't you found a mate? Are you not afraid to be Taken?"

They looked at each other for a long time. Ben raked a hand through his hair then exhaled, defeated. "I can't break my promise to Ariel and if that means being taken by force then..." He clenched his jaw. "Then I guess I will be on that stage in two days. I've made my decision."

Her hand slipped over his and he flinched away as if she had bitten him. "You have nothing to prove."

"Is that what you think this is? Some kind of game?"

"Isn't it?"

Ben pushed away from the table, the bench wobbling with the force. He gave Rosalie a heated look then turned around and stormed out of the mess hall.

He ignored her calls. Hot anger rushed through his veins like scalding lava.

"Ben, slow down. Wait!"

Ben ground his teeth, slowed, released a breath then stopped. He waited for Rosalie to approach. His fists clenched by his side, the nails biting into his skin. "What else do you want, Rosalie? How many more ways would you like to try and hurt me? Why will you not tell me what's happened to Ariel? She told me you had changed, but I never imaged it would be into this cruel thing that you are."

Her face twitched, faltered, then corrected. "I guess I deserved that, and now you deserve this."

Rosalie reached for him and he flinched away. "Don't touch me."

A sad smile crept along her face. "Open your hand. I have a gift for you."

"A gift?" He arched a brow.

"We don't have much time."

Ben extended his hand holding his palm upwards. Rosalie dropped a small green pill into it. "What is this?" Uncertainty twisted his insides.

"This is how you get to go see Ariel."

His eyes bore into Rosalie. "I don't understand."

"Follow me, we don't have much time."

"Rosalie—"

"Come on."

She led him past the accommodation tents, beyond the rocky edge of the beach where the old supply docks lined the island.

"Take the pill now."

Ben examined the pellet. Green leaves mashed up and encrusted in a translucent coating. His nose wrinkled as he brought it to his mouth. He swallowed the bitter tablet, an acrid aftertaste lingered on his tongue and burned his throat.

"Through here."

He followed her into one of the mating bungalows peppered sporadically along the beach, dread rose inside him, "Rosalie—"

"Just listen now." She went over to the bed. "In about a minute you are going to fall violently ill. As ill as Ariel has been."

"She's been sick?" His voice clipped. "How bad? Is she okay?"

"I'm sure by now she is…" Her hand came to his face and she cupped his chin, a bittersweet smile touched her lips. "She is lucky to have you."

Ben grunted and doubled over, his face contorting in pain as he fell to his knees.

Rosalie bent over him. "This is your gift from Mama Beth." She placed a gentle kiss on his cheek. "Soon, you'll be granted sick leave. You'll be taken away and won't return for the rest of this cycle. When they take you, do nothing, say nothing, or it'll be the death of us all."

With that she ran out of the bungalow screaming for help.

Pain tore through his abdomen, as if he had swallowed a fist which wrapped itself around his entrails and squeezed and pulled, ripping him to shreds from the inside. His mind fogged over, his thoughts falling into one another, incomplete. His body curled into the foetal position as the agony spread slowly throughout his body burning and radiating in all directions until agonised screams tore from his lips.

"Hold on." A voice cut through the torment. "It won't last long. You're going home."

Home. The word echoed in his mind as his body twisted and coiled. Arms grabbed at him and he felt weightless for a moment before he fell with a thud onto a hard surface, his face and body saturated as he lay in a puddle.

His body lulled around, water doused his face and body.

He lost track of time. The pain ebbed away with the lull of the waves and he opened his eyes, uncurled, then looked about him.

In the moonlight he found the solitary shape of the oarsman as he sat at the hull, his oar moving slightly right or left as he navigated by the stars.

"You're awake."

"Yes." He rasped.

"There's water for you." The silhouetted shape pointed at a small box tied with rope to the edge of the boat. Ben's body protested the movement as he reached for it. He yanked the water skin from inside and emptied the contents into his burning throat.

"Where are we?"

"Almost there."

Ben pulled himself up and looked to the horizon. In the distance, he thought he could make out the tiny embers of fires burning in homes or on a beach. And then a familiar shape. One that he had not seen in almost six years.

"Is that—"

"Inan? Yes."

Ben's heart leaped and smashed against his chest. "How?"

"I don't know who you know, or what business you have here, but someone has taken an interest in you, someone who matters."

Ben didn't answer, instead, his gaze focussed on Inan, the place he still considered his home. His breath stalled as his eyes brimmed with tears.

The boat neared the island, and Ben knew soon they would reach the break water. "This is as far as I go." The husky voice of the oarsman carried to him. "You must take yourself the rest of the way."

"How will I get back?"

"Tomorrow I'll meet you on the beach as I prepare to collect the daily trade. When the moon is at its highest. If you're late, you'll be left here to meet your fate."

"Thank you."

"Just go, before I'm spotted."

Ben dived into the water, his trembling arms propelled him forwards with each stroke, his heart pounded with the rhythm of the waves. As soon as his feet reached the sand-bank, he sprinted through the water and onto the beach. When his feet reached dry sand, he collapsed into it, tears ran down his face and mixed with the salty seawater. His heart cramped with happiness so intense his entire body shuddered.

Finally.

He was home.

He did not take the time to indulge, later he would allow himself to feel the enormity of this moment. He pushed himself up and ran into the shrubbery seeking shelter.

Ben studied his home. Not much seemed to have changed in his absence. Several new, dilapidated buildings scattered the mountain's edge, but it *felt* the same. The breeze touched his face and carried with it the familiar smell of the mess hall as the sounds of crying babies rolled down the mountain and collided with the cackle of old women.

Elation saturated his senses and rendered him almost paralysed. He pushed through the wall of overwhelm and crept along the path, hiding in shrubbery and gluing his back against walls as he ascended toward Ariel's house.

When he glimpsed the red door, his heart stalled. He had arrived at the footsteps of her door, in the only place he knew to be home. His eyes searched the darkness for signs of movement, when he saw none he dashed to the porch, climbed the few steps and pushed through the door, then shut it silently behind him.

He leaned back against the door catching his choppy breath and scanned the room. Nothing much had changed since his last visit, the tattered curtains had been replaced by an ugly green fabric and the couch had collapsed, now laying like a dead thing on the floor threatening to spill out of its crumbling wooden frame.

He crept through the lounge and kitchen, slid into the narrow corridor then edged along the wall. His pulse kicked up as he slunk over to her and edged her door open. The familiar smell of musk and sunshine hit his nose and his heart stumbled.

He found her on the bed, her lithe body wrapped in a white sheet, a sheen of sweat covered her forehead as her chest rose and fell in shallow breaths.

His heart swelled at the sight of her, too full, his feelings too big to contain. He wanted to rush to her side, shake her awake and kiss her lips. Touch her to make sure she was real. With quick steps he closed the distance to the bed and reached for her, his hand stilled, suspended in the air like a fly in a web. A raging war brewed inside him. He let his hand drop and allowed her to rest, to recover, to heal.

Ben inhaled, forcing air into his lungs, then climbed into her bed and lay next to her. Ariel mumbled and stirred but did not wake. He watched her sleep. The way her lips twitched and her hair stuck to her face, he listened to her steady breathing and held his breath each time she shuffled and twisted in her sheet. He had dreamed of being here with her, like this, for as long as could remember.

He gathered her in his arms and closed his eyes, never wanting to wake.

body moved against him and he grunted. The dream was too warm and too delicious to wake up. After a week of restlessness on Ishmin he didn't want to let go. She moved against him again, his eyes flew open as her body froze. Needing her warmth, he pulled her even closer.

Ariel squirmed in his arms and he reluctantly loosened his grip. She spun around and looked into his eyes.

"I'm dreaming," she said, her voice sleepy.

"No, you're not."

"I have to be, because you can't be real. You can't be here, in my bed."

"But I am." His heart leapt in his chest.

"Stop."

"Can a dream do this?" He brushed a lock of hair away from her cheek and placed a delicate peck on the exposed skin, still warm from her pillow.

Her eyes grew wider as they searched his face. Her hands reached for him, stabbing at his flesh.

"Ben? How?" She screeched.

He slapped a hand over her mouth to stop her rousing the silent house.

Bolting up, she pulled at the sheet and covered her body. She gawked at his naked torso for a moment too long, then shook her head. "What are you doing here? How did you get here? What's going on?"

His face split into a wide smile. "I told you so…"

"I told you so?" Her face crinkled and she hitched one brow. "You got my note?"

He nodded, grinning.

"So, does that mean that Mama is…"

"Slow down, Ariel. Is this the way you always say good morning?" He pulled her arm from beneath her, so that her body collapsed onto his. His lips grazed hers in a soft, tender kiss. His body tightened at her touch. He leaned back and looked into her eyes, his voice suddenly husky. "Hi."

"Hi." She stroked his face, the creases deepening. "How are you here?"

Ben loosened his grip on her and relayed the events of the previous week, his heart panged at the sight of Ariel's fear for her sister.

He stroked her face, hoping to brush away her pain, then drew her closer to him. "So, what should we do with our time? You know I can't leave this room at all. Maybe not even your bed."

She kissed him lightly, the touch unexpected, sending his body into a renewed frenzy. Ariel pulled away and studied him. When her eyes reached the sheet, her mouth fell open. "You filled my bed with sand."

"There was an entire beach between me and your bed."

"So, it's my bed you were after all along?" She raised an eyebrow, a smile ghosted her lips.

"Do you know how hard my bed is back on Dagon?"

"Can't say I'm surprised. You need a hard mattress to go with that thick head of yours."

"This thick head rolled around in the sand all night trying

184

to get to you." He flipped her over and pinned her down with his body.

Ariel squealed "You're an animal."

"And I made you a promise to share all my fleas." With that he put his hand in his hair and shook out a small pile of fine sand that coated Ariel's face, pillows and chest. She wriggled beneath him, shrieking. "What? Is this not part of the deal?" he jested as she tried to buck beneath him.

"No, you beast. Get off me!" She shrieked.

Foreheads touching, eyes locked, his smile alight.

When he grazed her lips with his, her body stilled. He delved deeper, the exquisite kiss delicate, deep and hungry. Without warning she pulled away from him and fell into a coughing fit, her small body contorting as her throat corded with effort.

"Sorry." His expression darkened.

"I'm fine, just a little tired and hungry and now my mouth is full of sand." She licked her teeth and grimaced. "I need to go wash it out."

"Is that an invitation? I would love to wash the sand from you." His stomach knotted and twisted at the prospect.

Crimson flooded her face as she sat up, then collapsed back onto the bed consumed by a coughing fit that saw her body curl up.

Ben clasped her hand, his eyebrows drawn together.

"I'm okay." She gave him a weak smile as a fine rain of sand sprinkled onto her floor. "Not sure you signed up to share any of my germs, though."

"I signed up for everything. Now sit down and wait here."

"Ben! Ben, you can't leave this room. You can't be seen." She called to him in a harsh whisper, her voice straining as he poked his head beyond the door.

"Coast is clear. I'll be right back. Don't move!"

"Ben! Ben." Her voice fell away as he stalked the empty corridor and made his way into the bathroom.

The taps came to life with a moan and water spilt into the bath, steam rising and veiling the small room in a foggy cloud. Back in Ariel's room he offered her his hand, despite her obvious reluctance she accepted it. He led her to the bathroom where small droplets had attached themselves to the walls in a thin layer of perspiration.

Ben pushed Ariel against the wall and reached for her blouse, he tugged on the material.

"No." She pushed his hand away.

Frustration rippled around him and he hissed through a clamped jaw, "Let me help you."

Ariel screwed her eyes shut and sighed. When she reopened them, she bit her lower lip then slowly lifted her hands above her head.

Ben peeled away the tight material which clung to her body like a second skin. His gaze swung to her breasts and his breath hitched in his throat. He ignored his own body which suddenly burned with heat and need.

Ben tugged at her underwear. With a silent look she permitted him to relieve her of the thin cloth. His lungs seized under a vice grip and he cursed his body for reacting to her as it had, savage, carnal, primal. He was indeed an animal. He wrenched his eyes away and sucked in a frayed breath.

Ariel's grip tightened in his as he guided her to the bath and steadied her as she climbed in, releasing her as soon as she submerged.

He sat on the edge of the bath, trying to memorise each one of her curves and exquisite femininity. He studied each scar, dimple, and imperfection beneath the film of translucent water. He watched her flesh tint pink with heat as his own burned with desire.

Ben squeezed a bead of shampoo onto his palm and raked the lotion through her wet hair, the strands falling, slippery and soapy through his fingers. His body shuddered as she relaxed against his touch, his restraint tested to its limit.

He inhaled the fruity fragrance as he scrubbed and massaged until a thick layer of foam had formed. Filling the hand bucket, he rinsed her hair, allowing the water to cascade around her until it ran clear.

Ben reached for Ariel's arm and ever so slowly, washed the length of her, tracing her shape, inking it into his memory. Her lips parted as he kneaded her body, savouring the silky feel of her skin under his calloused fingers. He fought his carnal urge to reach for her and kiss her, to satisfy his insatiable hunger for her.

He pushed away his strangled thoughts and yanked his hands away, instantly missing her. "You're done."

He stood up and tried to clear the rock that lodged in his throat. With shaking hands, he reached for her towel then pulled her out of the bath. Ben's gaze latched on to her body as water cascaded down in rivulets. He wrapped the towel around her and led her back to her room.

Ben watched Ariel dress, her nakedness disappearing behind loose fabric. He exhaled, his entire body relieved.

"Thank you," she whispered.

He nodded, clenching his jaw, afraid to speak.

"I feel better."

He turned to her. Her pale skin now flushed pink, the sparkle back in her eye. "You smell better." He crinkled his nose.

"At least one of us does."

He raised an arm, sniffed his armpit and grimaced. "You're not wrong."

They laughed as Ariel inched toward the door.

"Where are you going? I thought we were going to spend the day together."

"Getting away from you and your obnoxious body odour."

"Hey!" He pouted. "That's not fair."

She turned back to him and blew him a kiss. "I'll be right back. I just have to go get something."

"I don't want you to get anything. I just want you to rest."

"And I will. As soon as I get back."

"From where?"

"Just stay in my room. Don't be seen. I'll be back soon." She blew him another kiss and gave no other explanations.

Ben lay on her bed, listening to the quiet descend on the house. He felt at home in a way he hadn't in years. As though this place had known him as much as he had known it, like it had missed his presence.

He inhaled Ariel's scent that soaked her pillow. Sweet flowers and musty sweat. His groin ached from being denied once more. Images of her bare flesh in his palm reignited his yearning for her. Standing up uncomfortably, he paced the side of the room closest to the door.

Voices filtered through the open window, chattering and loud. Almost familiar. Ben dove under the bed, gluing his back to the floor, fear prickling his skin as he remained motionless.

The door creaked as it was pushed open. "Ben?" He heard Ariel's whisper, her sand covered feet approached the bed.

"Down here," he croaked and waited as she squatted down to find him.

"What are you doing?"

"I heard voices. I didn't think the sheet would provide enough cover." He winked and she rolled her eyes.

"Are you referring to your…"

He shrugged and smiled broadly. "I can't help what you do to me."

"I need you to get rid of it and wait here."

He pulled himself from under the bed and gave her a toothy grin. "No food references?"

"Just put it away!"

Ben closed his eyes and inhaled deeply, sucking in lungfuls of air and setting his thoughts on Dagon, on his cold stone house filled with loneliness. The bulge in his pants dissolved.

"Okay, now what?" he said, voice strained.

"Sit on the bed. I'll be back in a sec." With that, she bolted from the room, leaving him once more to wonder.

He didn't make it to the bed when he heard hushed voices and the weight of feet on the tired wooden floor.

He spun and his gaze fell on the threshold, where just beyond, he was met with a face he had dreamed about for years.

"Mum?" his breath hitched, and his heart pounded as he ran to her, stopping just short of her, suddenly unsure.

"Ben?" Her mouth fell open.

Mama Cath studied his face, brushing his chin with her hardened fingers, tugging slightly on his unruly hair, looking into his brown eyes.

"Ben," she cried, her tears slicing her otherwise beautiful features, then threw herself onto him.

He wrapped her in his arms, his eyes brimmed with unshed tears.

"How?" His mother pushed away and looked at him, bewildered, her hands still gripping, clawing at his arms.

"I'll let you two catch up." Ariel beamed at the pair and walked out of the room.

Mama Cath held on to Ben, as he led her to the bed. They sat in stunned silence, her mouth opening and shutting like a goldfish, her eyes bewildered in an unblinking stare. "Benjen," she wailed, "my beautiful son, you're here, and you've grown so much."

Her head fell onto his chest and he winged an arm around her shoulder, drawing her nearer. He breathed in her familiar scents.

"Mum." His chest heaved as he sucked in choppy breaths, fighting the torrent of tears that threatened to escape him.

"How?"

"Mama Beth." He settled for the short answer.

Mama Cath studied his face, a small smile tugging at her lips. "I should have known that wily old woman had something to do with this."

Ben shrugged, unsure what the right answer was.

"I have so many questions." She broke away from him but kept her eyes anchored to his face.

"Me too."

"But we have so little time." Her face contorted with sadness. "You have grown so much."

He gave her a faint smile.

"Your brothers?"

"Have been shuffled." The hope in her face diminished and her shoulders crumpled. His heart twitched at the half truth.

"Are you happy? Are you safe?"

"Happy enough." He shifted as her eyes fell on his hip, the scar rounding to his abdomen. Her eyes widened as she pushed past him and searched his back.

"Ben," she gasped her hands shooting to her mouth.

"That's in the past now." He took both her hands in his, soothing her. "What about you? Are you well?"

"Well enough." She sighed and as her breath left her, he noticed how old she had become in such a short period of time. Her lush thick hair had thinned, strands of white laced through her braid, her lips and eyes rounded by fine, deep-set lines and long shadows.

His chest tightened. "I'm sorry. I wish I could have stayed…"

She squeezed his hand. "I know my boy." Her eyes glistened and she cleared her throat. "Well... No point dwelling on wishes now." Her wan smile did not touch her eyes. "Tell me, do I have any grandbabies running around anywhere?"

Heat rushed to his face and stung the tips of his ears. "Mum," he whined at her.

"Don't! I need to know. I need something."

Despair etched itself into her face. She needed hope, she needed a piece of him, of any of them. He cleared his throat.

"I haven't..." He tore a hand through his hair and looked at his mother, taking her hands in his own. "Do you remember the last conversation we had? You told me to be gentle and true to myself. You told me to protect myself and what is mine."

She nodded, her eyes flinching to his back.

"I have been those things."

His mother studied his face searching for the answers he was reluctant to share. "Of course you have, you've always been good—"

"But—," he sucked in a long breath, "I am yet to mate with anyone."

They sat in the silence that exploded around them. Ben heard the rushing of his blood through his head as his heart struck in his chest.

"How is that possible?"

"I love Ariel. Only Ariel. I don't want to be with anyone but her." He clenched his jaw as he watched his mother digest his words. Her frown softened, the thin line of her mouth turning upwards, radiating.

"Of course you do." She clenched her hands together, holding them to her chest. "And she feels the same?"

His shy smile delivered his answer. She wrapped her arm around his and tugged him closer. "Just be careful and promise to make me some beautiful babies."

"Mum..."

"They would all have to look like her though." She nudged him and they both laughed at the notion, the sound infused with embarrassment, joy and sadness.

Mama Cath laced her fingers into Ben's. "I'm proud of you Benjen. You've grown into a good man."

Ariel's entrance into the room announced their time together had ended. They stood from the bed and he pulled her into a final embrace, taking in her warmth and love, allowing it to seep into him, saturate him. Her thin arms gripped his back as they held on to one another, reluctant to let go.

"I love you," he said in a choked whisper.

"Me too." She gave him a warm smile that radiated despite the sadness burning in her eyes. "Be careful, brave boy. Love her fiercely and when you are ready, send me some beautiful grandkids and know they will always be loved and cared for."

He managed a melancholy smile and he held her one last time. She placed a single delicate kiss on his cheek and pushed away from him.

As Mama Cath shuffled to the door, she took Ariel in her arms. "Thank you, Ariel, for this gift. I'll show myself out." She took one lingering look at her boy, who was now a man, and left behind her an empty silence broken by the gentle clap of the front door as it shut.

"Oh, Ariel," Ben choked closing the distance between them with a swift step. His lips found hers in desperation. He clung to her, tears saturating his face.

"Ariel, I... Thank you." He managed before he released her and slunk to the bed, his emotions in turmoil, as though an old wound had been scratched raw once again, a biting pain gnawed at his heart. He slammed his eyes shut and allowed Ariel to sooth his unravelling emotions.

Nightfall rolled over the horizon and brought with it a cool breeze that swept through the silent house. The hours had slipped through their hands like water even as they tried to hold on to each moment. Ben could not get his fill of her, his want became a need, like an infatuation, an emptiness he could not fill. Each touch requiring another, every kiss more hungry, more fierce, more tempting.

He held Ariel as he grazed his lips, a mere whisper of a touch. She pulled away from him and their eyes locked. "So, I know how you can repay me."

"Repay you?"

"Yes."

"For what?"

"For this morning."

"I thought that was a gift." He raised an eyebrow. "And anyway, I gave you a bath, didn't I?"

"Exactly."

"Ariel." He sighed. "I'm going to need some help understanding."

"You saw mine. Now…"

"Show you? My beast? Or was it a noodle? Or a sausage?" He laughed as she burned a light shade of pink.

"Yes." She bit her lip. "I want to see it."

"*It?*" Despite his humour his stomach churned and a shiver rippled inside him.

"Yes." She bit her lip again, her face flushed.

"If I recall correctly, you have already had the pleasure. Twice."

"Those times didn't count."

"How so?" His pulse hammered.

"The first time you were thirteen and the other time it was dark."

"But you did sneak a few peeks." He winked at her as pink gave way to a deep red.

"Oh, forget about it." She rolled off him. Ben grabbed her and rolled on top of her, blanketing her body with his.

"So fiery, Ariel. So impatient," he whispered his voice scratched as he brushed his lips along hers. "I've been waiting for years for you to ask."

He battled his way through the sheet then swaggered to the centre of her room where he stood to his full height, hands on his hips. Ben clenched his jaw and listened to his heart thrash in his chest.

Ensnared in her gaze, he met her challenge and offered one of his own. He felt thirteen again, the years falling away, the awkward fear and uncertainty skittering along his skin. He shook it off as Ariel crawled from the bed and approached him.

"So, this is how you want to play it?"

"I'm only playing by your rules." He tried to sound cocky but the tremble in his voice gave away far more than he had intended.

Every hair on his body stood in attention as Ariel approached then began to circle around him with slow deliberate steps, her gaze igniting the desire that simmered inside him. He stood frozen, his chest rising and falling like an angry tide.

Tendrils of heat spread through his body when her hand landed on his chest. His breath hitched in his throat when she wrapped a finger around a single black hair and tugged at it lightly. His gaze latched onto her mouth which curled with a dark smile.

She continued to circle, her hand dragging along the length of his abdomen, every muscle tightening beneath her touch. She caressed his upper arm, tracing it from his shoulder to his elbow and back again, goose bumps erupted along his feverish skin.

With a delicate touch she traced the dips and lines of his scared back. His fists clenched at his sides, his fingers twitched wanting to pull her away from his marred, broken skin.

Each passing touch, like cinders singeing his skin until at last she stopped and stood before him, pinning him with her fiery gaze. Her fingers lingered over his heart, the frenzied beat reaching out to her.

When her hand slipped to the elastic of his shorts, his breath lodged in his throat. Ariel lifted the fabric over the mounting bulge beneath and set him free, his shorts falling to his feet.

They stood motionless for a heartbeat until her eyes darted over him and her mouth fell open, breaking the spell.

Ben reached for her, making short work of her clothing.

He fell onto her and she moved readily to his touch. His hands stroked and clutched at her skin, his need for her demanding and urgent in a way he had never felt before. All thoughts drowned out by fierce desire.

"I want to be your mate," she whispered to him. "Now."

Ben stilled, his hand freezing mid motion. His brain stalled and heart faltered as whispers of consequence flooded his mind. He tore himself away from her despite his body screaming for hers.

"No. We can't." His voice raw, hoarse.

"Why? I'm saying yes, I'm ready."

"No." He shook his head and shied away from her, lifting his body from hers, fighting raw need and desperate hunger.

Regret nicked at his heart when her face collapsed, and she pulled the sheet over her naked body.

His eyebrows gathered and he dug an unsteady hand through his hair. "Don't be angry at me, Ariel. I am only doing what we agreed."

"But I am giving myself to you. Don't you want me?" Her voice clipped and broken.

"More than anything else in this world. But if we do this, I may never see you again. You know the risk we take." His thoughts clumped together like wet mud, jaw clenched in desperation.

He reached for her, but she flinched from his touch.

"Wouldn't you rather have a child? With me? What if we try on our fifth encounter and naught comes of it? What if we'll lose our only chance?"

Sweeping a hand across his chin, Ben turned to her, his heart heavy with his words. "Have you not been listening to anything I have said to you? I don't want to give you a child if *I* cannot be a part of its life."

"So you would rather me not have any part of you?"

"Ariel?"

"Is this how it's meant to be? You, on your island and I on mine? Alone? No pieces of you, while you go back to Ishmin, cycle after cycle, year after year, and try again with another? Others? How could I live knowing you have given yourself to someone else? That another might carry your seed, your child?"

"Ariel." He reached for her again, the distance between them suddenly too wide.

She shook his hand away. "If you'll not do this with me today, you'll not do this with me at all! I will seek another. I'd rather have a child to love, to cling onto than nothing at all. The consequences for me outweigh yours tenfold."

"Ariel, don't say that." Fear stabbed at him like a cold knife.

"I mean it!"

"Ariel." He spoke through clenched teeth.

"Come here and do what needs to be done. I know you want to. I've seen how you struggle each time you touch me. Touch me now. Please." Her voice quivered.

"Ariel." He softened.

"Please?" Tears welled in her eyes.

"I can't." He looked away from her small body which seemed to shrink before him.

"You won't!" She tugged at the sheet, her face reddening, embarrassment and anger sharpening her soft features.

"Not like this, Ariel. I—"

"You need to leave." Her eyes blazed.

"Ariel—"

"Go! Go now!" she screeched.

"Ariel, please, just listen—"

"Get out!" Ariel shrieked, wild eyed, nostrils flaring.

Ben searched Ariel's crestfallen face, his thoughts grasping at her words. His mouth fell open and he shook his head in disbelief, his brain desperately scrambling to make sense of it all.

Bursting from the bed, Ben grabbed his shorts, pivoted on his heel, and took off without a backwards glance.

His murky thoughts tainted with pain, his insides eviscerated. Fighting the aching collapse of his chest, Ben sucked in long sharp breaths and clenched his chest where his heart floated in an angry reckless sea, dislodged, bleeding, broken.

Ben trudged back to the beach, unable to hide himself or the emotions that bubbled over and threatened to spill into the too calm sea. He waited in the darkness, seeking out a shadow on the water, his escape. His goodbye.

He didn't admit it to himself, but a part of him waited for Ariel, he wanted her to come, to apologise, to accept, but her absence stabbed as harshly as the turmoil inside of him.

He heard the splash of an oar and the moon highlighted the silhouette of a man on his boat. Ben didn't wait for the man to come to shore, instead he slunk into the sea and swam to the boat, washing away his deeds, anger and bitter disappointment.

The oarsman pulled him onto the boat and his body landed on the hard floor with a thud. He lay there, the layer of water splashing his face as the boat lulled and crashed against the slight waves, staring at the moon, seeking an answer he wasn't going to get. His body churned and ached with chagrin and disbelief.

What had she done?

Upon his return to Dagon, Ben buried himself in more work than needed to be done. Brutal chores that smashed his body and occupied his mind as he laboured away the day light.

Nights were hardest, despite the ache of his muscles and his exhausted mind, sleep would not come. Rendering him a prisoner of his own mind.

In the darkness his mind drifted back to her face, her bewildered look and ashen complexion, the hung lip and clenched fists, knuckles white against the sheet. His stomach coiled with regret and anger, desire and pain.

He was only trying to do the right thing. He hoped that after three months she would see his intent and forgive him.

As Mating Season grew nearer his uncertainty gnawed at him, leaving a knitted, twisted ball of doubt inside him.

B en's clammy hands ran along his thighs as the boat
docked. Unable to wait, he pushed through the lines of
men to be assigned his tent. His body agitated, his skin prickled, on edge, he needed to see her, to resolve their issues, to
hold her. His body needed an end to the grief and tension, he
needed comfort, a single word that would mend the rip he
had created between them.

He raced to the dance floor and waited. Each minute like
a drop hanging from a leaking tap stretching longer and
growing fatter until it could no longer hold on to the rim. He
reached for a drink hoping the alcohol would soothe his
frayed nerves.

When the horn sounded his body jerked and jolted, he
peered at the entrance, his body rigid with anticipation.

His heart stuttered when he spotted her and their eyes
locked. Her beauty untamed and exquisite, like a blossoming
rare flower in spring. His face broke into a smile, but her
eyes remained cold, she looked away, her eyes darting over
the dance floor. She flinched for a second then licked her lips
and moved. He followed her gaze and ground his teeth, his
fists clenching at his sides.

He pushed away from the bar and thrust his way through the dance floor. Sweat clad bodies, obstructed him, slowed him down. Ariel reached the other man first. Ben growled as Liam closed in on her, hips ground against hers, hands closing around her waist.

"Ariel." Ben gripped her shoulder and spun her around attempting to unglue her from Liam's grip.

"Don't touch me," she hissed at him, her eyes fiery.

Liam smirked at Ben and licked his lips, his grip tightened around her. Ben's muscles stiffened and his mouth stretched into a thin line as he looked back at her. "Ariel."

"Go away, Ben."

Liam jeered at him as he glued his body to Ariel's, his groin grinding against her buttocks. "You heard the lady. Go away, pretty boy. You wouldn't want The Watchers to think you're forcing her to do something against her will now, would you?"

"Ariel?" Ben tried again as Liam drew her against him, his hand roaming the side of her body, resting just below her bosom.

Ariel remained silent as Liam kissed her neck, her face twisted into a slight grimace, her body tensing at his lips against her skin.

"Is this what you really want?" he hissed at her through clenched teeth.

"You know what I want. Now go away," she shot, her voice pinched.

Her words, like pellets, pierced his skin and he recoiled. Without further protest he turned around and left them, not turning back.

Ben didn't feel the bodies as he crashed against them. He trudged from the dance floor and towards the beach. He needed seclusion to lick his wounds. His pain sank like a heavy anchor down to the pit of his stomach, anger flared and burned beneath his skin while jealousy gnawed at his shredded heart.

His legs wobbled beneath him, threatening to give way when her voice reached him, carried by the wind. He spun around and saw Liam pulling her along.

Tendrils of rage spilled inside him, fuelling his body. His legs carried him, driven by heartache, by the need to see her. To see if she'd go through with her deed, if she would deal the final blow, the one that would crack and rupture and ruin him, that would taint the memory of her and all they'd ever shared.

He trudged through the sand, a sheen of cold sweat glazing his body as he finally understood why war had come all those years ago, why the world was broken.

Love.

He scowled as he thought of the word, his face creased in deep furrows. Love was just as cruel as it was beautiful, it burned cold and fierce, destroying and breaking everything in its path. It was a creator of pain and conflict, of anger and devastation.

He gritted his teeth at the thought and shook his head. To have believed anything else was foolish and naïve. Mama Beth warned him of its ruinous ways and her daughter was about to prove her right.

His throat filled with bile as he watched Liam drag her into a bungalow, whispering into her ear, his words made her beautiful face twist. Liam smirked and Ben's stomach clenched. He had seen that look on the faces of men before. Ariel was nothing more than a conquest and he was about to break her in ways she was not prepared for.

Ben swallowed his heartache and kept a short distance no more than a few paces from the entrance. This was her choice even if it was the wrong one, designed only to hurt him, created by the mind of an angry girl who lived in fear.

He watched Liam as he crudely threw his underwear off and pushed Ariel over a chair, her nude body on display like an object. He wouldn't revere her as she deserved but to hurt her, punish her, taint her. Ben squeezed his fists, his nails biting into the skin. Emptiness settled inside him pushing away every other feeling. He could almost hear the crack of his heart as it threatened to split and spill its entire contents, when she shot up from the chair and her voice drifted across to him, and suddenly his heart came alive, smashing against his chest.

"Liam, I don't want to do this." Her voice stitched with fear and regret.

"What are you talking about?" Liam threatened.

"I've changed my mind. I don't want *you*."

"I don't think you know what you want. Just let me show you how good I can make you feel." Liam's voice grated against his soul as he sprinted over to the bungalow door.

"Please, Liam." Her voice trembled, her wild eyes let loose a string of tears.

"I promise to make it quick." Liam closed the distance between them, his naked body on display, unabashed, his face burning, jaw clenched. "No need to cry."

"She said no." Ben stood at the door taking in Ariel's tear streaked face ashen complexion and shivering body covered by shaking hands.

Liam swung around, face rigid. "You? Again? Did she not tell you to go away?"

"Pretty sure that's what she is telling you to do now, *Liam*." Ben's balled hands tightened.

"I'm pretty sure that's none of your business, pretty boy."

"I will make it my business, and The Watchers' business if you do not leave right now," Ben hissed, glaring at Liam through narrowed eyes.

Liam's jaw clamped tight. His face a twisted mask of hatred as he pushed past Ariel, fishing for his shorts. He grabbed them and ploughed into Ben as he marched out.

Ben searched her face, his mouth a severe line, his eyes plagued with tortured emotion, hers swollen with tears. Without a word, he turned and walked away.

"Ben," she called to him, but he didn't turn back. He couldn't.

He trudged back to the ocean, his insides flooded with relief and bitterness. He found a rock coloured white in the moonlight jutting out into the ocean. He sat, feeling heavy and pulled his legs into his chest resting his chin on his knees. He stared into the black ocean and wished it would swallow him whole.

"Ben," her voice flared from the darkness.

"Go away, Ariel." He didn't turn to look at her.

"I'm sorry." Her voice quivered. "I was angry... I was stupid..."

"With him? Out of all people?" He threw her a look raked with disdain.

"Ben, I'm sorry."

"I thought you understood. I thought we had a deal. You can't go and change the rules whenever it suits you."

"I—"

"I don't want to hear about it, Ariel. Not now."

"Ben—"

"I need to think, and you need to leave." His body slumped as if deflated.

She put a hand on his arm and he jerked away. "Just go." He turned away from her, his face set with pain and anger and once more watched the crashing waves.

"I'm sorry," she whispered and she slid from the rock. He didn't move as she vanished into the night but as tension and anger gave way to relief and anguish, a single tear cleaved his burning cheeks.

He didn't want to see her and couldn't escape thoughts of her with Liam, which curdled his stomach, making it churn and ache. He could not escape, but he could hide. Just as he had done for the first few years in Dagon where, night after night he climbed into the uncharted forest of the island and pushed his body into helpless situations, wondering which would be the one to take him away from it all.

Ben packed enough supplies to last him four days and headed towards Ishmin's steep rock face. He had spotted a small nook from the ground. It would prove to be the perfect place to think and find solace from his restless thoughts.

He climbed the rough crag, the stone digging into his calloused hands, slicing the skin. He hissed at the pain and pulled himself upwards, his muscles screaming from exertion. Adrenalin coursed through his body washing away the feeling of emptiness.

He reached the nook and threw his bag onto the hard ground and pulled air into his lungs in harsh breaths. He lay down, dropping his head into his palms the draining adrenalin leaving room for more anguish and agitation that simmered around him like flies. He didn't want to love her anymore. He didn't want the thoughts of Liam to strangle him and shoot debilitating pain into his chest. Instead he wished they would be perfect strangers, that he could see her as anything other than the woman who sliced his heart open and left a bleeding wound. But he knew, in the deepest recesses of his shattered heart, that despite everything, he would forgive her.

The blue skies turned black then blue again. Hours slipped into days, days into nights, until without doing much but think, he had spent four days in his cave, wallowing in his anger and self-pity.

He descended the cliff face armed with two certainties.

She would have been searching for him, distressed and regretful and that he would go to her. He would not allow her to be Taken, that thought almost as brutal as Liam's hands on her body.

He reached the ground as long shadows painted the earth and the sun kissed the horizon goodnight.

He stood outside her tent, the blue fabric a curtain between them, listening intently, to her whimpering cries and sucking in of breath. His soul tore at the seams, glad for her remorse but sad for her pain. He wanted to balm the first and urge the other, to push on it until she bled.

He waited until the stars appeared and her whimpers fell silent then inched to the opening of the tent and pushed the flap aside. The darkness pierced only by a sliver of moonlight that drew a line on the sand. He stood waiting, listening, met only by silence. He slipped into the tent and crouched, pawing his way through the sand until he grabbed hold of her cot, the aluminum border cool against his clammy palm.

He lay on the sand beside her, listening to her shallow breathing. His fingers itched to touch her, to shake her awake, to demand her apology, to beg for her forgiveness. Instead, he let the night take him once more.

Ben opened his eyes to piercing light and her uncertain smile. "Hi."

"Hi." He kept his voice cool and face blank even as his heart surged and his stomach fluttered at the sight of her. As if he was seeing her again for the first time in years. As if this was their first meeting here on Ishmin.

Silence hung between them like the calm that ushers a violent tempest. Ben pushed himself off the sand, his back a white blanket of fine sediment.

"Why Liam? Out of all the men here?" He grimaced. His face drawn, light blue circles underlined his puffy eyes.

Her face fell into her hands and she shook her head. "Because he would have hurt you the most."

"He would have hurt you, too." Ben let the words settle around her in a tight noose, his jaw clenched at the unrelenting thought.

"Ben, I—"

"I know."

"It's just not fair, the thought of not having you. It cuts like a knife. It hurts to breathe. I'm not cut out to be without you."

"Ariel..." Her name ripped from his lips, pain lacing his voice.

"I'm sorry I've been so selfish," she wailed.

He waited while she unburdened herself.

"I know we made promises. And I know you were only keeping yours, but I got so scared I would be left with nothing. I don't know how to navigate this world without you in it. I don't know how to have your child without you by my side. I don't know if it's best to just be alone, never tasting your flesh, never *truly* being with you, than to have you for just one week and never again."

His heart stumbled at her words. Ariel pushed off the cot and sat up, her legs finding the sand. "The way you made me feel that night, the way you looked at me, I knew you wanted the same thing, and after you denied me, I was humiliated, ashamed." She sucked in a shaky breath. "Maybe you didn't want me as much as I wanted you, maybe I was wrong all along." Her voice cracked.

At that, Ben shuffled to her on his knees and buried his head in her lap, clutching her thighs. "No, Ariel. All I want is you. I have waited a lifetime for you, and I didn't want to lose you. Besides, if you would have fallen pregnant when you were not on the island, we both would have been doomed." Pain creased his face.

His fingers dug into her flesh and he rose so that her could pepper soft kisses along her neck.

"I'm sorry, Ben."

"I know." He kissed her tears. "I know. We've wasted so much precious time. Now we have to put on our show. They're watching."

"I thought you were angry with me."

"I am. But I still love you, and I can never let another have you," he whispered with frayed breath.

Ben pulled her to him, resting her on his lap before his mouth collided with hers, the kiss possessive, urgent, desperate. His hands twisted through her hair and trailed her back, the velvety feel of her skin wrenching a groan from a deep well of want inside him.

She broke the kiss and her gaze travelled from his mouth to his eyes and held him there as her hands unclasped her dress, the fabric falling around her shoulders. His breath stalled and heart stuttered. He reached for the dress and peeled it away from her body, possessed by the harsh need of her bare skin against his. Her underwear all that separated them, a final boundary that would have to remain between them.

He rested her on her back, taking in her beauty, and vulnerability. His heart swelled and he lowered himself onto her. Fighting the demented, urgent ache inside of him, he slowed, savouring her, tasting her, exploring every inch of bare flesh. His long, nimble fingers extracted from her low moans and gasps.

He found her mouth and stole her breath as she stole his, her hands wrenched through his hair as his heart thrummed and his heat pooled between them. He clutched at her skin, grunting and shattering around her.

When they had settled, he clipped the dress back on and

watched the light fabric as it fell along her delicate body, soaking their sins, hiding their secret.

"Ben, that was —"

"Beautiful. Ariel, you are beautiful." He kissed her, wanting so much more than he could take.

"Will it be like that when we… When you…?"

Ben's heart constricted, he kissed her shoulder then rose and offered his hand. "I hope so."

She took it and they stepped out and into the bright sun. He laced his hand into hers and they strolled along the beach, their steps lighter as the weight they had both carried lifted.

They sat and watched the waves play with the sand.

"What are we going to do?" her voice strained.

"I don't know."

She nodded, the gesture filing the silence with unshered words.

The hot powdery sand curled around Ben's toes as he glared into the dark horizon. Moonlight painted the water with silver strands that crashed against the rocks on the edge of Dagon's shoreline.

Movement caught his eye and he tensed for a moment as the lone figure approached. He recognised the broad shoulders and strong arms dangling like limp branches, the thick thighs and dark skin gleaming silver in the moonlight.

Antoine reached Ben and sat next to him in silence, his slender fingers sifted through the grains.

"You seem to have brought a heavy weight home with you my friend."

Ben squared his shoulders and attempted a wan smile, as if trying to disprove his friend.

"I see." Antoine remained casual.

He was shrouded by silence. It wrapped around him like a sea serpent, constricting, slowing down his breathing until he felt as if he would suffocate. He sucked in a long breath and turned to Antoine. "I feel like the sea. I'm wavering between anger and want, my feelings keep crashing against my rib cage and there's so much turmoil inside me…" He let his words fall away and ground his teeth as if afraid to spill his insides.

"You are sad."

"I'm angry." His nostrils flared. "I keep going back to all the what ifs and maybes, all the could have beens. How could she?"

"But in the end, she didn't."

"But she almost did, I can't even imagine." His stomach churned and twisted at the thought, his throat closed.

Antoine placed a hand on his shoulder and squeezed. He waited until Ben looked into his eyes then spoke. "But in the end, she didn't."

Ben's shoulders sagged as he exhaled and nodded. "She didn't, and then we... I..."

"I know."

"And next time..." At the thought his body flooded with heat and desire to finish what they had started. To know her body, to revere it. He cleared his throat, grateful for the darkness.

"You are worried."

Ben remained silent.

"You are ruined by anticipation."

His face snapped to the side and he eyed his friend's face, searching for answers. "What does that even mean."

"It means that you have wanted to indulge in a very particular pleasure for some time but have denied yourself. Now you have gotten a taste for anticipating this pleasure rather than acting upon it."

He frowned as Antoine continued his explanation. "You have become so accustomed to anticipating rejection and postponement that even the pleasure of anticipation has now been jaded and worn, and therein lies your tragedy."

"I still don't know what you're talking about." Ben turned his attention back to the crashing waves.

"I know you are worried, but there is a solution for your affliction."

He ground his teeth waiting for an answer.

"Time will solve all your problems."

"You are full of it, Antoine," Ben hissed. "We have no more time."

"Precisely." Antoine smiled.

"What you are saying?"

"What I am saying my friend, is that the time to lament is over and the time to anticipate has truly set in. There are no more obstacles or excuses, no more maybes and what ifs. You must at last act and delight in the pleasure you have denied yourself and end your suffering."

"And what if…" Ben cleared his throat. "My pleasure is not shared by…" He gestured with his hands, hoping the movements would make up for his awkwardness.

"On that you are on your own, friend, for my pleasure is garnered elsewhere." His smile widened and gleamed in the moonlight like pearls. "All will be just as it is meant to be."

Ben scoffed at his friend. "If you believe that you must be living in a different world to me."

"Or maybe I choose to believe that change is afoot and that a union of souls can break even the thickest of chains."

Ben's eyebrows pulled together and his lips stretched in a thin line. He nodded and wished he could hold on to the strain of positivity from Antoine.

"If you have nothing else to hold on to Ben, grasp onto hope, just as you said she must."

"And if I cannot?"

Antoine stood up, brushing sand from his legs. "Some people dream about the stars, others reach for them. You must decide what sort of person you are."

At that he turned and walked away.

He watched his friend leave then gazed at the sky,

wondering if the stars he sought to reach were always going to be just out of his grasp.

He batted the thought away and stood up, turned to make his way home when a low whistle sliced the silence.

"I can see why she likes you, must be that pretty face of yours." Liam's voice came from the darkness.

Ben ignored him and strode away only to have his way blocked by a group of men who seemed to have materialised from the darkness itself.

"I wish I was as pretty as you," Liam went on, a light swagger to his step, as the men formed a circle around Ben. "Maybe then she will finally open her legs for me."

"Watch yourself Liam." His muscles wound in his chest, his hands clenched in tight fists.

Liam scoffed at the threat. "Why? What are you going to do about it, *pretty boy*? No Watchers here to see. No friends to look after you." He stepped into the light, his face a mask of nonchalance.

"Liam." Ben's heart slammed against his chest.

"Did you really think *this* was over? That I would let you just take her away from me? Just let her walk away when I was ready to have my way with her? Do you have any idea how much pain I was in? How uncomfortable I was."

"Liam—" Ben's shoulders squared and his muscles tensed as the group closed in on him, inch by inch, sealing his escape.

"I really didn't like it at all." His eyes gleamed with menace as he looked around the circle.

For a singular moment there was stillness, crashing waves and heavy breath. The air heavy with animosity and distrust.

"Put him down." Liam's dangerous voice reverberated through Ben's bones .   ˌ

A sudden movement jerked Ben's body to life, a hand reached for him and he swung back, throwing his entire body weight behind the fist. It connected with a hard jaw.

Pain blazed up his arm as the man staggered backward and crumpled into the sand.

His victory was singular and short lived as blow after blow from shadowy fists landed across his face and body, his agile frame unable to deflect and protect himself as he threw weakening punches and faltering kicks. Starbursts split his vision and his legs collapsed as a brutal shot connected with the back of his head. A gush of pain jolted throughout his body and the taste of blood flooded his mouth. Bruised and winded Ben cradled his legs to his chest protecting his vital organs, hoping the brutal storm would abate.

"Enough, enough." Liam's voice pierced through his throbbing head and the rain of pain ceased. "Hold him."

Six pairs of rough hands seized him, pulling his body apart, pinning him to the ground.

Ben thrashed against them, but they scoffed at his feeble attempts.

Liam stalked forward and sat on his chest, the heavy weight crushing Ben, forcing the air from his lungs.

Liam's crazed face inched forward so that his hot breath skated over Ben's cheeks. "Now, pretty boy. I am going to make you a little less pretty." His brutal whisper grated against the rim of his ear.

Ben's eyes widened and his stomach rolled as he saw the jagged piece of glass that he produced.

"Liam, don't do this." Ben's eyes were glued to the glass as it inched ever closer to his face. "Liam. Don't." His heart smashed in his chest and he began thrashing, tugging and pulling against unrelenting grips.

"Shut him up," Liam growled, and a hand clasped his mouth.

Ben twisted his head back and forth, pushing his head back into the sand, seeking escape. The soft powder suddenly too hard, his muted screaming futile against the hand on his mouth. The jagged edge of the glass inched closer.

With a forceful shove, Liam's hand twisted and forced Ben's face to the sand exposing his right side. "If you fight, it will be worse." Liam's harsh voice abraded his skin.

Sand and salt coated Ben's nose as the glass met his flushed face. With slow precision Liam pieced his skin, the sharp edge entering just below his right eye. Ben's chest heaved as he tried to suck in breath, to push against the force, to scream against the pain.

Taking great pleasure in his work, Liam slashed a shallow cut stretching from the eye to the tip of Ben's lips.

He edged back as if admiring his work. "That's going to be a very pretty smile, let's make it even bigger."

Ben's stomach rolled and his breath came in shallow desperate gulps as Liam tore at the skin, pushing the glass deeper, slicing, lacerating, shredding his face, in slow torturous movements.

Pain rolled inside him like a flood, washing away all thoughts, leaving behind turmoil and devastation. His stomach reeled and fought the building nausea as his brain began to shut down, screaming out for the end.

Liam's weight shifted as he pushed back from his face his own twisted in a cruel satisfied smirk.

Ben searched for air, heaving in breath, but instead inhaled sand that clogged his throat and coated the inside of his mouth, mixing with congealed blood.

"What a pretty smile. Now, the other side." Liam's hand slid off Ben's face and into his hair, where he grabbed a fist full and rolled his head to the other side. Ben screamed into the hand still on his mouth as sand and salt rolled into the open wound. His heart thrashed in his chest and Liam's voice pierced the falling darkness.

"I'm going to make it so that no one will ever be able to look at you again."

Cold fear pierced Ben as he fought to stay awake, to fight, to beg, but the darkness beckoned, too strong, too alluring, too soft and pain free. Her tentacles wrapped around him, pulling him slowly to where pain didn't exist, to where thoughts didn't matter, to where he could be free.

A faint sound made Liam's body flinch and stiffen.

Another sound from a distance.

A yell? A cry?

"Looks like we might have to finish this another day, pretty boy." Liam's hand rammed Ben's head into the sand in disgust, then his weight disappeared as did the hands holding his body.

Ben rolled onto his side, air spilling into his lungs as bile built in his throat. He coughed and spluttered, red painting the white sand bellow him. Air flooded his body while the pain flared and expanded, raking his body in torment. Until at last he was shrouded in darkness.

He thought someone called his name.
　　Words.
The gentle feel of hands.
Air.
Pain.
Darkness.

Light burned through his retinas as he blinked and flinched in its harshness. Pain exploded through his face and behind his eyes and his hand shot up searching for the source.

A rough hand grabbed his wrist. "No, don't touch it, it's still healing and every time you move you crack the damn thing open." Luke released his wrist and Ben's hand dropped to his side.

He blinked, opened his eyes and found Luke's concerned face looking over him.

"Where am I?"

"In the hospital wing."

Ben's gaze swung across the room. He took in the white walls and glaring harsh light bulb that swung above him like a noose in the wind. He blinked again and his body throbbed in angry red agony. He winced as he moved and instantly regretted the action as raw pain tore through his face, and hot liquid sprung from his wound.

"Oh great, you've torn it again." Luke exhaled, unable to hide the concern in his voice. "Let me clean it up."

He dabbed a wet cloth over Ben's wound collecting the rivulet of blood that ran from the stitches.

"How bad is it?"

"Try not to talk, it makes it worse."

"Luke?"

"Stop moving—"

"Please…"

Luke's hand fell away and his face grew long and weary. "It won't heal well."

Ben's heart panged with the words as he tried to keep his facial muscles from reacting. "Liam used something blunt to create maximum damage. It's been stitched, but the cut is deep and ugly and uneven." He looked away, his hands knitting together. "I'm sorry."

Ben remained motionless allowing the feeling of anger to wash over him in a cold harsh wave.

"The Elders want answers."

"For what?"

"Ben."

"What good will it do? The damage is already done."

"He needs to be punished."

"It was too dark, I didn't see a face."

"Ben!"

"No! To what end Luke?"

"Look what he's done to you? He's an animal running loose, if you let him go, he'll become feral and there's no knowing what he would do."

Ben sucked in a long galvanising breath, his ribs aching as his chest expanded. "I choose forgiveness, compassion."

"Stupidity."

"Humanity."

"There's nothing human about Liam."

"Maybe, but he'll live in fear and uncertainty, he'll never know if someone's coming for him, he'll always sleep with one eye open."

"Can't you see that will make him even more dangerous? He'll be like a cornered animal, scared and frothing at the mouth, he'll attack and it'll be more brutal and more violent than anything you can imagine."

"No, he will cower for a while and then he'll forgive and forget."

"You don't know who you are dealing with, this is a mistake."

"It's a choice and I'm the one who gets to make it."

"One you'll live to regret."

"One that gives me hope, hope that humanity and decency can triumph over violence."

Luke stood at the edge of the bed and shook his head, his teeth grinding against one another like stone. "You're being stupid and naïve." He raked a hand through his unruly hair. "Even in the animal world there are consequences. You'll give him permission to continue with his transgressions, you'll give him leave to do this again, perhaps worse. Actions bare consequences."

"Well these are the consequences for my actions."

"And what did you do, that warranted this?" Luke

flinched as his gaze fell on Ben's face. Ben's heart sank to the floor even as Luke recovered.

"I can't say."

"Ben…"

"I can't—"

"Ben!"

"I fell in love!" He hissed the words in a harsh whisper and Luke fell silent, his face consumed with worry.

"And does Liam know?"

"I think so."

"And you're afraid he'll talk?"

"Petrified." Ben gulped down the words then cleared his throat. "Now we both bear each other's secret, one as deep and grave as the other. He knows his crime, he knows his punishment."

"As he knows yours…"

"Love isn't a crime."

"We both know that's not true." Luke's eyes fell to the floor and he rubbed a hand over his face. "Get some rest, I'll be back later."

"You're leaving?"

"Antoine and Jacob are outside. As are Oliver and Lucas." He sighed as he made his way to the door. "They've refused to leave ever since they heard you were here." He chuckled, a tired heavy sound. "I'll be back later."

Luke closed the door, behind which voices dripped into his room. The smile that split his face coursed a flash of agony behind his eyes. Ben clenched his teeth, the sensation pulling against his torn skin. Hot blood leaked from his face. He groaned and reached for the cloth Luke had discarded by his bed then pressed it to his cheek, the cold bit into his skin.

At the pain his mind drew a mental image of the wound. Curiosity gnawed at him, crawling beneath his skin and pulling at his resolve.

Ben pushed up from the bed and winced, his body heavy,

as if detached from his head, almost numb. He bit his lip and held the forming scream at bay as a layer of sweat erupted across his body.

When spots danced behind his eyes, he shut them, sucked in a long breath then stepped away from the bed.

A warm crimson rivulet oozed away from his wound and flowed down to his chest. His attempt at wiping the blood away resulted in a violent smear of red across his torso. The flow continued, relentless.

He pressed the cloth tighter, his effort doing nothing to stem the flow. He scoured the room, searching for a surface that would show him his face. The white space was just that, bland and white. The red bucket of water and trail of blood the only colour.

He growled, clenching his teeth the movement resulting in an eruption of fresh blood and pain.

He took a step closer to the door and it flew open.

"What are you doing out of bed? Get back! now!" Doctor Rob reached for him, wrapped a hand around his shoulder and pulled him back towards the bed then laid him down. Circling the bed, he examined Ben's face. "I have good news and bad news," the doctor started as he pressed the cloth against Ben's cheek.

"Good news first." Ben spoke through clenched teeth.

"The good news is that I brought fresh herbs to compact the wound. I can see that you have managed to wipe away what I applied last night." His tone was not amused.

"And the bad news?"

"You will be awake when I re-stitch your wound."

Ben grunted and nodded then lay back into the pillow glaring at the white ceiling, fingers grabbing the white sheet while the doctor prepared for his tasks, pulling out his tools from a drawer tucked beneath the bed.

"Now lie still and try not to move," the doctor grumbled as he threaded the needle and hovered over his face.

Ben sucked in a steeling breath as the needle pierce his skin. The thread rolled just beneath as the doctor tugged at it. Ben shut his eyes, willing his body to remain motionless, for his face to remain still as the doctor repeated the action again and again, sealing the wound.

"So how did you manage this anyway?"

"I fell on a sharp rock," Ben said through grated teeth.

"One hell of a rock. Must have been pretty magical seeing as I found a shard of glass in there last night."

Ben shrugged, offering nothing more.

The doctor pulled against his skin once more to snip the access thread. Ben's mouth flinched with the movement. "I'm going to put the herbs on now, do yourself a favour and try to keep them on this time. They'll help with the healing and suck out any infection."

The cold herbs soothed his heated skin, but only for a moment. As they lingered, they began to radiate a cold searing heat that burned against his wound as though someone had placed an ice cube on his face and set it alight.

The doctor caked the side of his face, the sharpness of Calendula, the tincture of pine from the Arnica and the over-powering sweetness of the Goldenrod, created a nauseating melody of smells that assaulted his senses and stung his eyes.

When he was done, the doctor pushed away from the bed, the mattress creaking with the shifted weight. "I have done the best I can for you, Benjen, son on Catherine. Please remain still, allow the herbs to do their job."

"Doctor?"

The older man tucked a long black braid behind an ear. "Yeah?"

"How bad is it?" Ben asked through clenched teeth, the raw pain spilling from between the gaps.

Rob stood for a long moment and considered his words, his blue eyes like a calm lake. "It's not good."

"Please." Ben felt the sting of tears as they pooled in his eyes.

Doctor Rob took his hand and squeezed it. "The scar you'll have will be long and ugly and will likely bring you pain for the rest of your natural life, but it is just a mark, it is not who you are. For some it'll take time to get used to but if you carry it like it belongs to you, no one will ever see it as anything other than a part of who you are."

Ben nodded, not in gratefulness or acceptance, just in understanding.

"I want to see."

"And you will, but first let the herbs work and get some rest, or next time I come here I'll tie you to the bed."

With that he released Ben's hand and walked to the door. "You have visitors, Benjen, but they risk infecting you, perhaps with their stupidity more than anything else, but at least until tomorrow they are to remain outside." His instructions were loud enough to cross both sides of the door. Ben bit down on his lip to stop from smiling.

"Doctor?"

The older man turned back to him.

"Can you help me rest?"

The doctor's face softened as he looked to Ben. "I'll be right back."

He returned moments later with a glass full of beige liquid. The doctor placed a straw in the poppy milk and put it to Ben's mouth. "Drink."

Ben sipped at the nutty drink, a tincture of soil wafted by his nose as he drained the glass.

Heat flushed his skin and his body felt a weariness that dragged him into darkness.

Frustration grew around him like a second skin. Bound to the bed and the room, the white walls closed in on him and pulled at his fragile mind. He relished the numbness of the poppy seed milk and sought to shut out the world as he waited like a pearl inside a shell, to heal, to grow and to be revealed to the world. Except that he knew that he wasn't a pearl but a beast, a marred, marked man, and no amount of shine would polish off the severed flesh of his face.

On the fifth day when Doctor Rob walked into the room, he peeled away the mask of herbs that covered Ben's damaged face. He nodded as he considered the area, fingering the cheek and tenderly prodding the skin. Ben winced at the movement.

The doctor churned his tongue between his teeth. The wound is looking good. The scab has remained moist and the swelling has gone down." His words were considered and slow as if he had spent much time thinking about them.

"So I can go?"

"In a minute."

"Why?"

Rob tucked his braid behind his ear and leaned back into his chair, folding his arms across his chest. "Ben." His eyes dropped to the floor and back to the boy's face. "Your scar will seem angry now, it might even seem like it'll never heal but you must remember that time changes things."

"So my face will heal."

"Not entirely, no." Rob's mouth stretched out into a thin line. "But given time, the redness will abate and the scar might thin out. It'll never entirely disappear, your 'rock' made sure of that, but it'll become more bearable, more flexible, more a part of you."

"More bearable..." his heavy chest tightened around him.

"That's not how I meant—"

Ben hopped off the bed, his body stiff and battered.

"I only meant to say that the itching will subside, the pain and discomfort of the damaged muscle and tissue around the area will move more freely."

Ben nodded only half listening. He reached for his clothes and dressed, pulling the shirt gently over his face. His stomach knotted and twisted, the anticipation to see his face driving his painful movements.

"I've sent your friends away. Your brother will accompany you home."

"I don't need anyone to hold my hand."

"I think that you'll find that you have no choice in the matter. I guess he wants to make sure you don't stumble on any more rocks on your way there."

Ben grumbled as he pulled on his shorts.

"Keep the wound clean and come back in a week to let me have a look at it. If you have redness or pain, come back."

"Anything else?" Ben stood with his hand on the door handle, impatience leaching from his body.

"Just remember to breathe."

"Thank you... For everything." He tipped his head, opened the door and found Luke leaning against the opposite wall to his room. He jerked up as Ben crossed the threshold. Ben didn't miss how his eyes lingered on his right cheek.

"Letting you out at last?" Luke flashed him his token mischievous smile.

"I know how to get home."

"I know." The smile faltered a little.

"So you can go."

"I will, but not yet."

"Fine," Ben grumbled and trudged away.

"Fine," Luke caught up to him easily and overextended his strides mimicking Ben like a child.

Ben rolled his eyes and continued home, his silence drowned by his hammering heart.

If Luke noticed his hesitation as he opened his front door,

he said nothing. Ben entered his house and closed the door behind him shutting Luke and the world outside. A moment later Luke opened the door and stepped inside.

"I want to be alone."

"Okay."

"I mean it."

"I know."

Ben threw his hands in the air and marched to his bedroom. From beneath his bed he pulled out a pounded sheet of corrugated iron. He had found it years ago, when it washed up onto the shore. His heart slammed against his chest as he took a long breath and held it up to his face.

His murky shape appeared distorted and uneven in the bent metal, a thick pink line sliced the otherwise tanned shape that looked back at him. He flung the makeshift mirror across the room and fell onto his bed as tears brimmed in his eyes, a scream brewing in his throat.

Luke coughed, leaning against his door frame.

Ben shot up and wiped his eyes. "What do you want?"

"I have something for you." He pulled a small silver shard from his pocket and held it out.

Ben's breath stalled. He sat staring at the piece of mirror unable to move or reach out or speak, his body too stiff, too still, too petrified.

Luke took a tentative step into the room and placed the mirror on the bed. "I'll be outside." He disappeared beyond the threshold, a moment later Ben heard his front door open and shut.

He sat eyeing the silver object on the bed as it taunted him, played with him, dared him. He reached for it, his fingers curling around the once sharp edges that had been ground smooth and coated with sand.

He clutched the mirror in his hand, slammed his eyes shut and when he opened them again, held the mirror to his face. His breath hitched as he studied it. His knuckles grew white around the small shard, staring at the stranger reflected back at him. His gaze travelled the long, jagged pink and white flesh that snaked from his right eye to the just above the lip, not yet a scar, but the beginnings of one. The skin around the wound still discoloured and swollen. His fingers shot to his face but hovered just above the marred flesh, unable to trace it, to feel it, to believe that it was part of him. He let his hand fall and his head dropped with it. He bit his lower lip, fighting the angry swirls that weaved in his stomach.

He fell to the bed and his hatred and disgust simmered on his skin like foam on choppy waters.

In the first week after his return home, Ben spent most of his time brooding and alone. Ignoring calls at his door.

On the sixth day of his self-imposed isolation, insistent knocking on the door pulled him away from his reverie.

"Go away!" he yelled and remained seated on the couch staring at the discoloured spot in the stone. He had noticed it two days before and for some reason could not stop staring at it.

The knocking continued.

He ignored it.

When the knocking died away his shoulders sagged and his body sank into the couch. When his front door swung open he leapt to his feet, his heart pounded in his chest.

Jacob, Antoine and Oliver walked into his house uninvited. They stared at his face eyes glued to his right cheek.

"Your admiring glances are beginning to embarrass me." He growled glaring at the intruders.

"As they should." Jacob laughed and took another step inside. "Come play with us, it's rest day."

Ben noticed the ball, it rested between Oliver's hand and

hip. He fell back into his couch, finding the spot on the floor. "I'm too tired, go away."

"You've rested enough, now come play."

"I said I am too tired."

"And I said we need a fifth body and you are it."

"Jacob—"

"Ben."

He leapt from his couch and marched around it coming face to face with Jacob, their breaths mingling as fury poured from Ben's flaring nostrils. "I said I need to rest."

"You seem fine to me."

The boys stood, crimson washing their cheeks as they stared each other down. Antoine placed a hand on Jacob's shoulder and the younger man relented and stepped back sighing and shaking his head.

"Ben." Antoine cut the silence. "No one here cares what you look like, none of us want to mate with you, we just need another player."

The boys eyed one another, the tension seeping from their bodies, the corners of their eyes began to crinkle and tilt up their faces spread in wide smiles until laughter shook their bodies and filled the room. Ben winced as agony tore through the merriment.

"It still hurts?"

He nodded at Jacob, whose smile faltered.

"It's fine. Let's go."

The boys hooted and clapped each other's backs as they ran from Ben's home and onto the path that lead to the beach.

22

Ben paced the length of his room, his heart crashing against his ribcage as he glared at the white shorts that mocked him. His clammy hands clenched the fabric gathering the shorts in a tight fist where they dangled, limp and lifeless.

The echo of footfalls on wood announced Luke's arrival. Ben snapped from his thoughts and looked up to see him standing in the doorway.

"Are you ready brother?"

Ben brushed a hand over his face, the mangled scar, now fully healed, bumped and grated against his fingers. He ignored the pang of dread that shot through him. "Just one more minute."

Luke nodded and stepped out of the room.

Ben stripped off his clothes. With his stomach in knots he slid into the white shorts, his trembling hands fastened the elastic across his hips.

His thoughts were consumed with Ariel, anticipation and dread crawled and crackled beneath his skin.

He stepped into the main room, his jaw locked, his fists clenched firmly by his sides.

"Let's go." He pushed by Luke, who stood waiting by the door, and led the way out and toward the beach.

The sand dipped and rolled disturbed by hundreds of feet. Men milled around, testosterone and eagerness filling the air as they awaited the boats.

"Hello pretty boy," a scornful voice smirked.

Ben jerked around to find Liam leering at him, a smirk plastered across his smug face.

Ben turned away.

"I see you have your game *face* on. Ready to *face* the ladies, are you? Will you be putting on a brave *face*?"

Ben dug his toes into the sand, concentrating on the hot particles filling the gaps between his toes.

"What's wrong friend? Too shy to *face* me?"

Ben clenched his jaw and ignored the remark.

"Well that's a slap in the *face* isn't it? And here I was, thinking we were friends."

Ben ground his teeth, hissing in breath.

"I guess I understand really, with a *face* like yours who needs—"

Ben spun around and shoved his chest. Liam stumbled backwards into a group of men who grumbled and pushed him back towards Ben.

"Mmm, you really are pretty now, aren't you?"

Ben's fist swung and connected with Liam's jaw. His hand exploded with fresh pain that he shook off. Liam stumbled backwards into another man, his face painted with surprise.

The man cursed and pushed Liam away for a second time.

Liam charged at Ben who sidestepped the blow. His assault landed on the edge of Antoine's shoulder. The large midnight man swivelled around, face taut, jaw set. He swung his tight fist, quick and potent, into Liam's stomach causing him to collapse to his knees, the air falling from him in a sharp hiss.

Liam's eyes narrowed, full of venom. He rose, dug he feet into to sand, then charged. Head and shoulders down, he tackled Ben to the sand, a stack of bodies falling along with them.

The crowd erupted like a volcano that had been dormant for too long. As if all one hundred days of anticipation and tension overflowed onto the beach in the form of punches and kicks, of shouts and yells. The crowd fought in a wild frenzy, shards of pain and splatters of blood filled the humid air.

The Elder Rohan climbed upon a raised rock and shouted over the group. "Settle. Settle now. What are you, animals? Savages? Yes, the fairer sex is fond of healing but none of you shall see them if you kill one another." The fight simmered like a wave reaching the shore, bruised and bloodied faces turned toward the Elder. "You are men, not animals, and you must act as such! I'm in a mind of forcing a full ban of this cycle." A disappointed grumble went up, Ben's chest tightened.

The freshly bathed men rendered unruly and wild. Hair flung in all directions, blood stained skin, bruised and broken, tarnished white shorts and sour sweat, yet never has Ben seen them more as men, more at ease, more the carnal savage animals guided by a primal urge to defend imbedded inside them all.

The Elder's mouth remained set a thin line as he scoured their faces. He nodded to himself then raised his voice. "It seems that you are all decorated in the punishment of this island, bestowed on you, by your own brothers, and so I will allow your departure. May you all entice them with your battle wounds and plant many seeds."

A roar rose from the crowd, palms slapped on shoulders as smiles cracked bloodied faces.

The men shuffled to the boats, sharing laughter and bottles while they smeared blood away and hailed each other. All the tension seeped away, left on the beach behind them.

⋘🐚

The sand beneath his feet felt courser. His heart thumped as he stepped away from the Keepsaker and towards the heart of Ishmin.

His gaze swept the horizon. Flickers of fire danced over the ocean bringing Ariel closer, ushering her towards him, to their final cycle. His body wracked with jitters as his hand brushed over his cheek.

"Are you worried, pretty boy?" Liam leered at him as he limped by, one eye swollen shut, a red blemish staining his jaw. "She won't find you so pretty now, will she?"

Antoine nudged his arm, drawing his attention from Liam. "You were never much to look at in the first place," he whispered.

Ben nodded, his face stoic. His gaze remained locked on the boats bringing his future to him.

The horn sounded across the island inviting the men to the dance floor and they ran like a frenzied horde. Ben's fingers feathered over his marred face while his mind languished with indecision. His feet burned with the desire to run, his heart tripped, hanging loosely in place by a solitary heartstring.

He swivelled and turned away, his legs carrying him away from the dance floor, from people and to the far edge of the beach, where he stared out into the ocean wondering how he would ever face Ariel. Petrified, his fists tightened, and his jaw ticked with anger and disappointment as he labelled himself a coward.

A second horn blew across the island. It sounded lonely and forlorn and within it he heard her name.

Ben steeled himself knowing Ariel had arrived on Ishmin. His skin prickled with the knowledge. He knew the stab of pain she would endure when she discovered his absence on the dance floor, and he knew her tenacity. She would seek him out. She would find him. Her approach inevitable, her touch, her discovery. His stomach braided and coiled at that thought.

He stood beneath the pale moonlight and waited for an end to longing and suffering, to desire and need, to fear and discovery, to lies and hiding in shadows.

"Ben?" At the sound of his name his body tensed and his breathing faltered.

He turned to her, the moon at his back, his face shrouded in darkness. His gaze landed on her flushed cheeks and rosy lips. Her hair spilled across her shoulders and down her back in waves.

He made no move towards her despite his entire being screaming with want.

Ariel took a few tentative steps and reached out to him, concern twisting her features. "Ben?"

"Ariel," he whispered to her, "don't come any closer." His heart stumbled as he talked.

Paying no heed to his request, Ariel slammed into him, the impact rendering him breathless. Her delicate hands wrapped around his larger frame and he winced at her touch. She tightened her grip around him and he softened against her. A gentle smile crept onto his face. He'd never known her to do what she was asked.

"Why didn't you come? I thought..." She looked to his face and her mouth fell open. "Ben?" She pushed away from him and examined his face, her eyes bulging. "What happened?"

He winced as her fingers feathered over his mangled face, his eyes falling to the sand.

"Just a scratch," he whispered, his voice strangled.

"Ben, what happened?" She choked as moonlight stripped away the darkness. "Who did this?"

"Everything we do has a consequence…"

"Liam?"

He tipped his head, his gaze drifting to the ocean.

"I did this?" she mewled as her face fell.

"No." Ben drew her to him and slipped, a hand around her waist the other coming to rest between her bare shoulder blades. His heart constricted when she didn't flinch or try to move away from him.

"Are you okay?" Her eyes glistened with unshed tears.

"I am now that you're here." His pulse hammered in his veins.

"Let's get you to your tent. You need to rest. You need to heal."

"No."

"Ben."

"No. All I need is you, tonight, now." He reached for her and swept a strand of hair over her shoulder. He sought out her lips, tentative at first, uncertain, afraid. But as her hands fell around his neck, and her body sank against his, the kiss became deeper and harder, tinged with a fervent pressing need. He drew her closer still, weaving his hand through her hair as her surrender evoked a desperate groan low in his throat and his body came alive.

He broke away, breathless, his gaze locked on hers. Ariel's hand slipped into his and all his uncertainties fell away. He spotted a bungalow tucked into the edge of the trees, and without hesitation led them over to the exposed building.

"Ben," she breathed his name. "Are you sure? You're hurt."

"Yes." His gaze darted over her face, the flush of her cheeks, the curve of her lips as she worried for him. "I am not waiting another day, another minute, another second. I want you, Ariel, now."

They breached the doorway, Ben drew a galvanising breath as he followed her inside. "No more show. It's time I make good on my promises." His voice sturdier than he felt.

She lowered herself onto the bed, her loose brown hair dragging along the sheets as she edged towards the centre. Ariel bit her lower lip, and when it popped out it was wet and glossy and all the invitation he needed. His resolve melted away and he fell onto the bed, prowling the length of her body.

He released the clasp, tugged at her dress and the fabric fell away, her flesh beneath flushed and needy.

When his fingers tugged at the elastic of the lacy under-garment, she did not stop him. Ever so slowly, he shed the last of her barriers and revealed her womanhood. His breath stalled as he raked his eyes along her body, glorious and beautiful. He glimpsed the beads of sweat along her chest, the triangle of dark hair between her legs, even as she tried to cover herself up.

"Don't." He kissed away her worry, drinking in her nudity, her splendour. "You are beautiful, Ariel."

With trembling hands, he removed his shorts.

Her hands explored his body, mapping it out with her fingers and inquisitive eyes. His heart galloped as he nestled himself above her. His skin feverish with desire, his movements suddenly clumsy, slow, uncertain.

"Are you ready?" The question rippled inside him as she nodded stiffly beneath him, her face brushed in crimson, her eyes alight.

His pulse quickened, his blood hummed in his ears as he buried his face in her neck, she smelt like the sea and sand and sunshine that lived beneath her skin.

They met together at last and his heart stopped suffocating, his doubts unravelled, his body drenched with wild hope. Enamoured with her, he wanted to have more of her, all of her, in every way that he could. To drink and eat and taste her. He sampled her offering, and his body trembled. All his pent-up desire smashed against her and he could not get enough. He languished in his weight on top of hers, the delicate expression of her face as it twisted and wondered and gaped and smiled. He wanted his sweat to mix with hers so that they became one, and when they did, they crumbled like sandcastles yielding to the tide.

They lay panting, glistening bodies entangled. He wrenched his body away from hers and rolled onto his back. She placed her head on his chest, her fingers curling around the few hairs that had sprouted there.

"Are you okay?" His gentle voice strained, uncertain.

Ariel lifted herself on an elbow, looked up and their eyes locked. "I am." She stretched and bushed his lips with hers, reassuring.

Still dismayed he asked, "Did I hurt you?"

Her hands curled around his midriff. "A little," she whispered, and his heart panged with regret.

"I'll try to be more gentle next time."

"Next time?" Her eyebrows came together in a pronounced V. "What makes you think that I will let you come near me again?" A hint of a smile crossed her face.

His body shivered with the heat of hers as her look set his body on fire once more. She giggled and the sound smashed into his chest, his body reacted to hers instantly, wanting, needing, aching.

"I don't think you're going to have any choice in the matter." He grinned boyishly as heat rose in his face. Ariel elbowed him playfully and he winced, his injured body remembering its pain.

"Sorry." She grimaced and kissed his bruised limb. "Is that better?"

He nodded and flinched, the bruising kiss scorching his skin.

Ariel kissed his damaged chest. "And that?"

He nodded, his heart chugging. "It hurts here too." He pointed to his chin, where a swollen red bruise decorated his jaw.

Ariel lay her lips on his damaged skin, her eyes welling with tears.

"I'm sorry…" she began, but he swallowed her words with his mouth, and she met him once more in his need.

"Enough! I've got nothing left to give."

"Quitter!" Ariel jibed at him as she sat atop him, bare.

"You've become quite the fiend." He kissed her sweaty forehead and sucked in a breath as she wriggled above him.

"We've wasted so much time. And soon we will be out of time." Her voice faltered. "You must give this gift to me, so that *if* we cannot be together, I will always have a piece of you." She clamped her thighs against his waist.

Her words sliced through him like a cold blade, his body twitched. His muscles suddenly rigid as the thought constricted his chest. "Don't say that. There must be another way for us. I cannot live without you."

"Nor I without you." She lay a soft kiss on his chest which tightened with her words. "But—"

"No. No buts." Ben lifted her and in a swift motion, rolled and lay her on her back, her naked body glistening with moisture. "Imagine if it's already happening. If deep inside of you a part of me is already growing." His pulse hammered at the thought.

He trailed a long finger to her navel and circled her belly button. He lowered his head to her abdomen. "Grow," he whispered, wished.

Ariel giggled and pushed him off, her cheeks flushed red. "Let's go swim."

"You go, I'm exhausted. Honestly, I don't know how you have the energy to still move around."

"This is why we are the superior sex." She stuck her tongue out at him and his gaze swept along her naked body. He took in the tanned complexion. Her curved shape edged by slightly protruding hip bones. Her long slim legs that converged over a small area, tucked away between her strong thighs, that already held so much power over him.

He tried to etch every inch of her into his memory as she slipped into her clothes. "Come with me?"

"I can't." He winked at her. "But don't take too long. I'm sure I'll recover quickly."

"You better." She giggled as she ran from the bungalow towards the rolling sea.

He watched as her shape disappeared and his eyes welled with tears. His breathing grew ragged and his stomach braided as a sob clawed its way from his throat. A sheen of sweat coated his body, a blend of fear and exertion. He cupped his hands over his face, his desolate tears smashing into his palms as he gave way to his grief.

For five days and nights they were inseparable, as if chasing time while it seeped away like fine sand in the wind. Days melted into one another as he'd drowned in her. Breathing only when she was in his arms. Imprinting her body onto his, her laughter, her voice, the tickle of her hair on his chest or her skin beneath his fingers.

His desire for her insatiable, his need for her like air. He never wanted to part with her and had never more wanted to give himself to another human, to leave pieces of himself inside her, to create life that would grow out of love, pure and beautiful. Perfect.

He watched her sleep for a while. The shallow rise and fall of her chest, her hair flared across the pillow, framing her delicate features. His body ached, a hollow pained thing as he felt time slipping away, He steeled himself, preparing for the loss of her.

He sat on the edge of the bed, his face resting in his palm, staring at the ocean as it rolled on without a master, perpetual and timeless.

"Are you okay?" Her voice shook him from his pained thoughts.

He turned to face her, his body twisting at the worry in her eyes. "I'm scared."

"Of what?"

"Of losing you." A debilitating ache quivered in his chest. Ben shot from the bed and walked to the arched entrance of the bungalow, leaning against the cold wall.

"That's never going to happen." Her voice carried across the room.

He didn't answer.

Her heat enveloped him before her fingers traced his chin and forced his face to turn to her, their eyes locked, her palm splayed across his cheek. "It will be okay."

He grabbed her arm and pulled her into him, wrapping himself around her, murmuring her name into her neck. His desperation leaked from the touch of his skin as he searched for comfort within her. Her taste, her touch, her scent, all a balm to his ache.

They watched the blue horizon turn a deep crimson, wishing time to slow down.

"Once we do this, there is no backing out." Her voice cracked as she spoke.

"I know."

"Are you sure you want to do this?"

"Ariel, I've been sure since the first day I met you." He drew her closer, needing her strength.

"I love you, Ben."

"I love you, too, Ariel."

They shared a kiss, flaming the fire that breathed between them and threatened to

burn their world to cinders.

23

He dragged in a galvanising breath and laced his fingers through Ariel's, his shaking hand wrapping around her clammy one.

"I love you Ariel, daughter of Elizabeth. I'll always love you, and no matter what happens on this day, the only regret I have is that we wasted so much time, that so much has been taken away from us and that I have been unable to give you more."

He slammed his lips into hers, a possessive, urgent kiss that stole her breath and her words, then led them along the beach.

His feet dug into the sand with each step he took by her side, the world vibrating around them, shaking to its core while remaining perfectly still.

The sun turned its back on them as it began its descent into the horizon, it beat down on them hot and angry as they stepped onto the deserted dance floor. Without the music and fire, the wooden floor revealed its ugly truth, scuffed and old, weary and bent, it cried beneath their footsteps.

They halted at the centre of the dance floor. Despite his racing heart and knotted stomach Ben stood tall, squaring his shoulders, straightening his back, his muscles tense and ridged. He tightened his grip around Ariel's hand and prepared himself for whatever may come.

"We would like to summon the high council," Ariel called out into the air.

The world stilled. Fear stabbed him like a cold sharp knife twisting in his guts and flooding his veins. His heart pounded with each passing second. Beads of sweat trickled down his brow.

An old man in a loincloth appeared like smoke from behind a tree. A fringe of grey hair framed his wrinkled face. He took an ungainly step forward, his deep velvety voice washed over them. "Who calls this council?"

"Ariel, daughter of Elizabeth and Benjen, son of Catherine."

"And what matter do you wish to bring before the council?"

"We seek permission to marry." Ariel's voice rang out in the deserted arena and the hair on the back of Ben's neck prickled. He stood stoic, waiting.

The Watcher nodded, his face grim. He brought two bony fingers to his mouth and whistled, the sound sharp and harsh.

From beyond the tree line, the whistle was taken up by another, fading in ferocity as it travelled from Watcher to Watcher, until it was heard no more.

A bell tolled across the island. The slow metallic ring reverberated over the water. It carried with it an invitation, a warning, an ending. Ben's heart jolted as the sound rang around him.

The crowd flooded into the arena. Murmurs of wonder carried, as men and women, some still in stages of undress, streamed into the meeting area where Ben and Ariel stood frozen in the centre, their hands laced, knuckles white, breaths held.

The Watchers, appeared from above, emerging from the treeline and behind rocks as if they were part of the island itself. Ben bit his lip, his insides churning as he watched them in silence. They encircled the arena and all its occupants from above and formed a human wall of dour faces. His gaze darted from one to the other. He took a deep breath trying to quell his hammering heart.

The human wall opened to allow a man and a woman to step through, the wall closing behind them.

Adorned in a red dress, The Watcher began, "I am The Watcher Tay, daughter of Audrey. Beside me stands The Watcher Eric, son of Clara." Her honeyed voice carried a note of venom as the crowd fell silent. "Step forward Ariel, daughter of Elizabeth and Benjen, Son of Catherine."

Ben's eyes turned to slits as Eric cocked his head at them.

The crowd that had closed around them tore apart, allowing them to pass, as if rubbing shoulders with either might infect them with a lethal virus. Hand in hand, they stepped to the fore and faced The Watchers.

"What is it that you seek?" Tay's voice flowed over them, her lips taut.

"We seek to be mates for life, promised only to one another." Ariel's words tugged at Ben's heart.

Tay burst into laughter while the crowd gasped at her words. With the dwindling of her laughter, Tay lifted her hands, awaiting silence. "If you choose to deprive yourself of the joy of mating with as many specimen as possible, and only mate with a single one for your entire lifetime, that is entirely your choice." She smirked at the girl. "*He* won't be allowed the same pleasure." Tay raised a single eyebrow at Ariel, tilting her head. "Ariel, daughter of Elizabeth, your sexual preferences are your business alone. Why did you call this court?"

"We seek to live together so that we can raise our children together." The crowd erupted once more. Ben's gaze shifted to Ariel whose cheeks burned red. He squeezed her hand, wishing he could carry her burden.

Tay's nostrils flared and she pinned Ariel with a cold, hard stare. "Do you have anyone who would stand for you?"

"My mother, if you wish to summon her."

"And mine," Ben called out, reliving for an instant his mother's embrace, her smell, her words.

Tay looked to Ben and scoffed. "Your mother? And how would you know the wishes of your mother?"

"When I was a boy, still by her side, she said she would do anything for me. If I'd had the chance to remain by her side, I have no doubt she would have continued to repeat the sentiment." Her lips pursed at the jab of his words.

"Summon them!" She waved and stabbed Eric with a cold look.

Eric wrenched a hand through his hair, his face grim. He seemed to deflate as he raised his hand and signalled to a figure at the back of the meeting area. The man was dressed in the olive-green garb of the silent army, long heavy pants that sat low against his narrow hips. His exposed back tattooed with his burdens.

Silence and duty.

The soldier raised his long spear and cawed. From beyond the dune came soldiers of the silent army. Men who were plucked from their homes at a tender age and raised only to serve under the Watchers, ensuring peace reigned throughout their Quarter.

They marched, muted by the golden sands, and took position behind the assembled crowd. A small party broke away and strode towards the ocean where boats and torches waited. Streams of vessels left the island in every direction as the silent guard set sail to summon the elders and the witnesses from every island of the Third Quarter. Ben's insides collided like waves against a rock face. Anxiety and pride broke against one another in tall harsh waves that clashed and frothed inside him.

When the flicker of torch light disappeared beyond the darkening horizon, Tay tutted at the two before her. "This time could have been used more wisely. All our guests could have been fulfilling their duties. Silly children with silly ideas, you know nothing of the world."

Ben's eyebrows gathered over his narrowed eyes, anger burning inside him as Tay admonished them.

She addressed Ariel and Ben, her overbearing smile parting her lips. "There is nowhere to go, and no way to leave. All the boats are gone. You two will remain here tonight." Looking to the crowd she added, "The rest of you may return to what it is you were doing, but be sure to be here at sunrise, for it's the seventh day, and judgment must be passed." Her lip curled as she finished, her words like shards of glass against Ben's heart.

With that, Eric turned to leave and the remaining Watchers vanished into the scenery.

The assembled guests dispersed, melting back into the forest and seas as Ariel and Ben remained rooted in place.

Tay growled and snapped her fingers. From beyond the tree line members of her personal silent army filed in. An army of her own making, renegades and law breakers. Their upper bodies exposed, most adorned a branded A, emblazoned across their chests, abominations as judged by the council. They wore black loin cloths and black masks that sat like helmets over their heads. Ben's grip on Ariel's hand tightened as they crept forward, surrounding the couple in a tight human barrier that reeked of stale sweat and digested fish. The men watched them silently through their black masks. Ben's jaw clenched and he resisted the urge to pull her to his body as the men leered at Ariel, flaying her with their greedy looks.

They sank to the wooden floor. He clutched Ariel to him,

his arms winging around her, pulling, protecting, needing her closeness.

"How can you be so calm?" she hissed at him, wringing her wrist. Her entire face drawn and clenched.

He looked at her, his body heaved and flooded with warmth, a wan smile on his face. "Because we've done it."

"Done what?"

"We told everyone what we want."

"But nothing's been decided, no resolutions have been made or passed." Her voice rose in pitch.

"I know."

"So why are you so calm?"

His insides quivered. "Because we have stood in front of the world and declared our love."

"And..."

"And is that not like marriage?"

Ariel's body stilled next to his. Her brown eyes searched his. "You think that our declaration was a marriage?"

"Wasn't it?" He raised an eyebrow.

She bit a trembling lip. "It doesn't mean anything if—"

"But that's just it, Ariel." He grazed her chin with his knuckles. "Is it not wonderful to know that should tomorrow bring the worst, for at least a brief time I could call you my wife?"

Her eyes welled up as she leaned into him, the kiss full of yearning and despair.

"I see you two like to put on a show." Tay's voice sliced through them. "By all means, I can wait."

Ariel grabbed Ben's arm, her fingers digging into his flesh.

"Get her up." Tay ordered. A cold shiver crawled along Ben's spine leaving behind prickles of fear.

Two soldiers broke away from the human barrier that surrounded them and walked into the circle. Ben scowled, his jaw ticked as they reached for Ariel.

"No!" she screamed, kicking them off.

"No!" Ben barked and shot to his feet, anger boiling inside him like lava, he clenched a fist and swung, connecting with one of the men. The sickening sounds of flesh meeting flesh bounced off his fist. The man fell to the ground wailing, Ben shook his aching hand which exploded with fresh pain.

His gaze fell on Ariel who clawed frantically at the soldiers, their hands wrapped around her, dragging her away. Ben leapt at the group, his fists clenched, his jaw tense. Pain erupted behind his ear, spreading its terrible tendrils around his head. He cried out and collapsed, head pounding. He fought to regain his feet, but the men closed in on him, a rain of kicks and punches landed on him from above.

Ariel's faint screams pierced the thunder of flesh and bones showered upon him, he strained to listen, but the downpour of fists overcame him. His body succumbed to the pain and the call of peace. His arms grew weak, his legs gave out and the blackness embraced him.

He woke to murmurs and the scuffle of feet, a group of soldiers surrounding him once more. With their backs to him they stood shoulder to shoulder, hip to hip, a solid human prison of flesh and bone, that dripped sweat and reeked of testosterone. They stood silent, these men, damned as much as he was.

He lay motionless, taking in slow breaths, his ribs ripping his insides with each movement of his chest. He gritted his teeth and caged the groan that threatened to escape his mouth.

A thud reverberated through the stage and his eyes searched the darkness. Men scuffed and shuffled across the wooden stage, then surrounded a shape on the opposite side.

"Ariel?" Ben called to her between living bars of human skin and bone, a toxic concoction of fear and worry saturated his insides, flooding him with rage and hatred. "Are you okay?"

"I'm fine," she called to him. "Are you hurt?"

"No," he hissed through ground teeth, struggling against the urge to fight his way to her, knowing all too well he would lose.

They fell silent as the soldiers surrounding them sniggered and chuckled.

"Good night," Ben whispered to her, earning a brutal kick in the ribs. He curled himself into a ball and waited for sleep.

24

B en swiped a hand over his swollen face, wincing at the pain which clawed at him like an angry animal, his eyes burned, begging for more sleep. Even the sky seemed restless as the sun blotted the horizon with hues of crimson and tangerine.

He stole glances between the muscular legs that surrounded him as he had done throughout the night. Ariel slept, motionless, safe, her chest rising and falling with the sea. Each time he caught a glimpse of her his own breathing eased.

A breeze swept across the island and carried with it the murmurings of newcomers. Ben peered through the gaps of his human cage and glimpsed the boats docking along the shore.

A gruff voice punctured the stillness of the arena. "Stand!"

Ben pushed himself up, his body protesting the movements, aching, heavy, tired, and yet, he stood tall, content, for he knew soon it would all be over.

"Move!" The butt of a spear jabbed his ribs and he grimaced, exhaling through clenched teeth.

The men escorted him to the left of the stage, where a

raised square podium had been set up overnight. He grabbed the edge and pulled himself up, his muscles screaming with the effort.

He looked around as he settled on his new perch and his eyes locked with Ariel's. She too stood upon a similar structure on the opposite side of the stage. Her hands folded across her chest, her face ashen.

He waved to her, his face cracking into a broken smile. His heart squeezed at her horrified face. Ben held her gaze and mouthed her name. She nodded, allowing him to hold her from a distance.

The sound of the horn cleaved through the emptiness of the arena. It shepherded the crowd in and with it the hope of a new beginning. Ben drew in a choppy breath and steeled himself for whatever may come.

The crowd meandered and clumped into the arena like a stream brought to a stop by a dam, then stood waiting. A trembling wave of anticipation.

The Watchers of Ishmin filed onto the stage, standing in two lines, flanking The Watcher Tay and The Watcher Eric on each side, as if they had sprouted wings. The women to her left and the men to his right.

Tay raised her hands and a hush fell. Curious eyes followed the purple-clad council members which filtered into the arena. Ben watched as they snaked around the crowd and settled into the rows of seats carved into the sand.

A silence descended on the makeshift court as the lovers were left to be examined by the crowd.

"State your names for the council," Tay began.

"I am Ariel, daughter of Elizabeth."

"And I Benjen, son of Catherine."

The council of elders bowed their head as one, greeting the young couple. They returned the gesture.

"Why have you called this gathering today?"

Ben spoke for them, his voice booming over the crowd

which gasped, faces contorted in surprise and horror. "We want to be known as husband and wife. We want freedom to co-exist and bring our children up together, learning virtues from both of us."

"Virtues?" Tay scoffed. "Men possess few of those." A murmur rolled over the crowd at her words.

"Few are better than none." Ben continued. "And these few have been instilled in us by our mothers." He let the words hang in the air as Tay glowered at him.

She began pacing like an agitated dog. "You know the rules of our lands, and you know why they exist."

"We do." Ben's voice rang steady and sure despite the turmoil thrashing inside him.

"And yet you challenge these rules?"

Ben scanned the crowd, within the sea of faces he found Antoine, his white teeth gleaming, his head held high as he rubbed shoulders with the Brown Robe beside him. Ben's heart throbbed. "Yes."

The Watcher pursed her lips and addressed the crowd. "You have all borne witness to these two abominations. They stand here today before The Council, before you, in an effort to derail our way of life."

"What?" Ariel's strangled cry cut her words. Ben's gaze landed on Ariel, imploring her to remain silent.

"Who stands for you today?" Tay called out, unperturbed by the interruption.

"I do." Mama Beth stood up. Clad in purple, she strode towards her daughter. "Elizabeth, daughter of Irma." Mama Beth stood tall as she met Tay's callous eyes.

"As do I." A second figure stood, she rose from the assembled mass and sliced her way towards Ben's platform.

"Mum!" Ben's heart pounded at seeing her face. Her long hair pulled back in a tight bun, her long green dress, worn with age, cascaded down her thinning body. He wanted to reach for her to hold her in his arms, to feel her warmth and share her strength. Ben clenched his fists at his side as a pair of guards escorted her towards his podium. Just out of reach.

Mama Cath gave him a reassuring look. A fraction of a smile touched her face as she took her place by her son's side. "Catherine, daughter of Thelma."

"Mama Beth," Tay's voice was laced with acid as she spoke the words, "why do you speak for this traitor?"

"She is my daughter."

Tay nodded. "Mama Cath, why do you speak for these traitors?"

"Benjen is my son." She had an air of pride as she spoke of him.

"Indeed. And what fine work you did raising these children." She didn't bother to hide her disdain. "Are there any others who wish to stand here today?"

A murmur rose from the crowd as a single figure pushed through. Liam emerged from the crowd shoving his way to the front. A long smirk sliced his healing face as he tipped his head to Ben then stood between the pair of women, looking up at Tay.

"I, Liam son of Ellen, am here to testify."

"In favour?"

"No. Against." Ben's nails bit his skin as his clenched fists tightened, his neck corded with tension.

"What say you, Liam?"

"This girl," He flicked Ariel a disgusted look, "has played with me since her arrival, yielding her power to torment me."

"That's a lie," Ariel screeched.

"Hush now." Tay raised an arm and silenced her with a cold look. Turning back to Liam, she continued, "How so?"

"She refused my mateship by attacking me, threatening to do it again, and to damage my manhood so completely I would never mate again."

A wave of sniggers rose from the crowd and a ghost of a

smile passed over Ben's lips, recalling Liam's body folded like that of an infant on the floor of Ariel's tent.

Liam scowled and continued. "I got her message, I stayed away. But then she returned to me. She invited my advances, played with me, showed me her body, asked for me to touch her, and then at the last, refused me again, for that pretty boy." He flicked his head towards Ben, his lip curling.

"That's not how it happened," Ariel called out, her face strained and red.

"If you interrupt once more, I will have the guards gag you." Tay's chilly voice sang out. She shifted her gaze back to Liam and continued. "So, you were denied?"

"I was interrupted. Given more time, she would have yielded to me."

"Are you certain?"

"Of course. I'm just as good a specimen as any other on this island."

Ben's jaw tightened with each word.

"Indeed. Do you see how this so-called love creates imbalance? It creates confusion and anger." Tay swivelled her gaze, latching onto Ben's marred face, her eyes tracing the ugly mark carving his cheek. "I see this anger led to Ben being punished for his offences."

Liam's face split into a dark smile. "Yes, he has. But what of her?"

"Do not concern yourself with her, for she is in The Council's hands. Do you have anything further?"

"I would like to make a request."

"Go on."

"Should it be found that they are abominations and no longer worthy of mating, I would like to take her."

"No!" Ben roared. Three spears turned and pointed at his direction and he froze, seething. Anger crackled beneath his skin, tangled with despair.

Liam sneered and returned his attention to Tay who pretended Ben's outburst was nothing at all.

"That is against the rules. Abominations are not to be touched."

"Those are the men. There's never been a woman marked."

"Indeed. It will be considered."

Ben's heart seized. He glowered at Tay, furious hatred pumped inside him. Tay remained focused on Liam awarding him with a pleasant smile that mimicked the smirk on his face. He bowed to her and his gaze landed on Ariel, who glared at him, her face a mask of horror and disgust. He blew her a kiss and dissolved back into the crowd.

As Tay thanked Liam for his testimony Ben's face twisted in a furious scowl, his body flooding with rage, a hot burning anger that wanted to burst out and hurt, torment and harm in the cruellest of ways. He gulped down his rage and focused on Ariel's face, seeking a way to calm his surging heart and rising fury.

Tay turned her attention to the two women standing before her. "What say you in their favour?"

"You must let them be together." The strength of Mama Beth's conviction surprised Ben. He studied the deep creases around her eyes and her deeply furrowed brow. "I have witnessed first-hand their dedication to one another since childhood. They belong together."

"But they threaten our entire way of life."

"They are only children, how can they possibly—"

"How can they?" Tay launched a scalding attack. "The old world gave way to urges, lust, desire, hatred. Men and women killed each other for this so-called love."

"But it is in our nature to love." Mama Cath gave Ben a gentle look. "We are creating an entire generation, which cannot possibly understand why they are walking around with a hole so big in their souls, they cannot feel fulfilled."

"Bah, nature." Tay waved her words away as if they were flies. "Nature is vicious and can be changed. We nurture our young and they receive enough love. Then we teach them independence. We send them into the world with the understanding that all of their needs, urges, and desires will be met throughout their life."

"Nurture?" Ben scoffed. "Your rules tore me from my mother's arms when I was still a child. There was no nurturing—"

"You were no longer a babe, but a man. You had all the tools needed for survival."

"But I was alone." His mind drifted to his first days on Dagon, when fear and loneliness had wrapped themselves around him while he'd slept, exposed, by his dying fire.

"You were surrounded by others," Tay spat at him.

"I was lonely, and only one person has been able to take that loneliness away." He looked to Ariel, seeking solace in her strained face.

"Do you have anything else to add before we bring this matter to a close?"

"What do you mean to a close?" Ariel shrieked "We've barely begun—" A brutal blow to the face silenced her words, the echo of skin against skin ebbed across the arena.

Ben exploded off his platform, surging towards her. Four guardsmen stood in his way, slowing his movements. He pushed the nearest one to the floor and punched a second in the face as he surged forward, hope creeping up in his chest as he got nearer. Pain exploded behind his eyes and his legs crumpled beneath him, his knees smashing into the wooden stage. He clutched the back of his skull, his fingers slicked over from the oozing warm liquid which trickled down the back of his neck. He gasped for breath as the world around him muted.

He heard his name on her lips, the sound tickled his skin and spread warmth around him. He squeezed his eyes shut and inhaled, the pounding of his head bearable, the world refocusing. Ariel screamed his name again.

He found her face drenched in tears which slid over the red welt of her cheek.

"I'm okay." He managed to utter, his ears ringing.

"See?" Tay began, apathetic. "We have not even finished the proceedings, and already your so-called love is bringing back the worst in us."

"This is not the worst." Mama Cath's voice nothing more than a harsh whisper, but it sliced through the crowd, clear and strong, in a way that Ben had never heard. "It is the best in us. For what is love if not life? It's passion, aggression, fear, desire, it's all that makes us human. We're born screaming into the world under pain and duress, we struggle for our first breath as we're wrenched from our mother's womb and into her arms. The first sensation we feel is love."

Mama Cath attempted to reach her son, but her path remained blocked. "They have done nothing if not demonstrate their bond. He'll fight for her like we fight for any we care about."

"We cannot take all that we want by force! It'll lead to our end again," Tay spat.

"He's not forcing her to stand by his side, nor did she force him to pretend to mate with her for the last year."

"Lies!"

"Love." Mama Cath smiled serenely at the frothing woman.

"Enough of this! It's time to conclude this mockery." The red-clad Watcher turned to the council. "You have witnessed their so-called love, born from lies and deception, fraught with hostility and violence. Should we allow them to violate our society with their poison? Has humanity not endured enough? Must we continue to diminish in our numbers? Must we fade out and let the sea take what's left of us?

"There's a reason we have these rules in place. They

protect our way of life. They protect our people. They protect us all from these acts of aggression. There's no need for this lust when we have mateship. There's no need to be greedy when there is plenty to go around. And there's no need for violence if there's nothing to fight for."

"But we must fight for those we love, we must fight—" Ben's dispute instantly silenced by another savage blow to the head.

"Ben!" Ariel's shriek rang out in the makeshift alcove.

Tay remained focused on the council, her seething face as red as her dress. "Rise. Rise now if you'd like to see these two punished for their crimes. Rise."

"Rise," Tay repeated as she glared at the men's wing which continued to sit defiantly behind Eric while most of the women stood united behind her.

Mama Beth's voice rose. "You cannot punish them for doing the only thing that's natural."

Tay swivelled and faced Mama Beth. "What do you know of nature? Even animals do not couple for a lifetime, and those who do have often been found to stray. After a male wolf impregnates the female, she seeks others to fulfill her other needs, food, protection, or just plain boredom. Our way of life ensures none of that is necessary. Why do you fight so hard to prove that this perfect system is flawed?"

"Because she's my child, and I too, love her."

"And should she survive today, you may take her home, and that's where she'll remain until her dying day, while this pathetic specimen—" she snarled at Ben's broken figure "— will join the silent army."

"Pathetic? You are the one that's pathetic. You're running scared of two teens after living an entire lifetime denying yourself the simplest of feelings."

"Feelings do not equate to survival."

"That's where you're wrong." Mama Beth pulled out her tobacco box.

"Oh?"

"I feel very strongly that if you don't let these two walk free, off this island, and into my care, one of us will not survive this day." The small metal box popped open as Mama Beth pulled out rolling paper. Expertly, she peppered tobacco into the white lining and rolled the cigarette before tucking it at the corner of her lips, then shut the box.

Tay took in the spectacle, watching Mama Beth's fingers create the thin cigarette. Her face curdled. She cleared her throat and began once more. "My dear council, I give you more proof, proof that love leads only to violence and death. This must end now. Our entire way of life hangs in the balance. It hangs in your judgment."

The men remained seated.

"Eric?" Tay looked to him, her voice rising. "Why don't you rise?"

Eric held her gaze momentarily then pushed himself from his seat.

When he spoke, it was not to her. "I am the Watcher Eric, commander of the silent army, watcher of peace, enforcer of law." His frame seemed to expand as he spoke, his smooth voice like a balm to the wounded. "You are right, Tay. We have been watching a spectacle, and you are the clown." The crowd gasped and Tay's face dropped. He turned to the council. "Please be seated, we are not done yet."

The members looked to one another as if seeking permission from the other, seeming like fish out of water, uncertainty colouring their features. "Please." Eric swept his arms across his chest and, one by one, they sat like falling rooks on a chessboard.

"Tay, daughter of Audrey, I'll not be made to execute your so-called laws. This army of faceless men you have built is your own twisted creation. It reeks of hatred and anger."

Tay's eyes flared as she levelled a glowering look at the man.

Ignoring her, he continued. "Those faithful to me, spears up!"

As one, green clad soldiers lifted their spears, aiming them at their masked brothers. Their cries and feet thundered as shrieks rose from the crowd.

"Stop! Drop your weapons at once!" Tay screamed at the soldiers. She turned back to Eric. "What are you doing?"

"What I should have done a long time ago. See, I too love my daughter very much and I'll not let you harm her, nor my wife of nineteen years." His eyes locked with Elizabeth, sharing a singular tender moment of goodbye.

A stunned murmur rippled across the crowd. Ben looked to Ariel whose eyes swivelled between Mama Beth and Eric.

"Your what?" Tay's eyes bulged indignantly from their sockets.

"These kids." He cocked a head towards Ben and Ariel, ignoring Tay's look of horror. "They're not the first to want more. They're not the only ones to find not just a mate, but a soulmate. We've lived like animals for too long and now we must reclaim our humanity."

"No! It'll destroy us."

"You can't punish everyone because Byron died."

At that, Tay shot him a menacing look. "Don't you dare mention his name."

"Why? Was he not just a mate? One among many?" Eric taunted her.

"Don't—"

"Did you open yourself up to all who came along? Freely and without malice? Without shame? Without choice?"

"I always had a choice. We wield all the power." Tay snarled at him.

"You wield nothing! Not when you force men upon women." His fist sliced through the air.

"Our species must endure. It must survive."

"To what end?"

"Eric?"

"There will be only one resolution and it'll be a peaceful one. You'll agree to our terms." He turned to the council. "You all will." It was not a threat nor a demand, but the calm demeanour of one who makes easy promises.

"What's your proposal?" Tay snarled at the man.

"A division." The word drew a murmur from the crowd.

"A divided earth? Are we not divided enough as it is? We already have our four quarters."

"Whose fault is that?"

She huffed at the accusation. "I only uphold the law. I'm not the one who made it."

"When it was made, it may have been necessary, but now it's no longer needed. The population has grown, the water is receding, and new ground has been found."

"What do you propose?" Tay hissed through a set jaw.

"Choice." He took a step closer to Tay, who recoiled. "A borderland, one which allows for the cohabitation of men and women, providing only that they be wed and remain faithful."

Tay scoffed at the idea. "And how do you propose that? How would you police the jealousy? The pride? The loyalty?"

"We don't."

"Savagery!"

"Humanity."

Her cold eyes burned as she gave him a scathing look. "And if this human world of yours spills into ours?"

"How could it?"

"You'll breed greed and filth within your ranks, you'll bring war, and with that our destruction."

"There will be peace. There will be contentment."

"Love is not peaceful. It's pain and agony, it's jealousy and uncertainty, it's heartbreak and hardship. Councilmen and women, you must hear me. We can't abide this. We must pluck out this cancer before it spreads. You must rise and stand with me. Rise to sustain our way of life. Rise to protect our children and our children's children."

Once more, the council members rose, and this time several of the men rose slowly from their seats.

Tay faced her audience, a rabid hunger dripped from her lips as she called to her soldiers. "Masked soldiers, defenders of The Watchers, Takers of Virgins and Makers of good men, take up your weapons."

The anxious crowd buzzed and hummed. Fear and anxiety leaked onto the beach as two silent armies pointed weapons at each other.

"Last chance, Tay, let them walk free," Beth called out to the crazed woman, her tone arctic under the hot morning sun.

"That'll never happen! Fools! Love is only for the weak!" Her shrill scream hovered over the swarming, restless mass before her. "Kill them – do it now!"

The frenzied horde, which had assembled to witness events, scattered like straws in a gust of wind, tossed and flung any which way. The wooden floor vibrated with the thunder of feet, and the skies filled with shrill cries and the clanging of metal.

Screaming and fear filled the air above Ben as soldiers draped in green and black exchanged blows, a rain of sweat and blood gushed onto him. He remained down, his scarlet fingers clawing at the wood, drawing him to Ariel, to safety, to hope.

A strike smashed his ankle, the pain scalding like boiling water, spilling into his stomach like acrid soup that needed expelling. A second blow landed along the side of his head pain spread into every part of his body. He fell onto his face. Figures blurred and colours leaked into one another until they painted an endless black canvass.

Ben had no sense of time, just the lulling of the ocean as pain seared through his leg and burned endlessly. It climbed through him in a slow crawl that hooked its jagged teeth into his flesh and bones and sinew. It filled every part of him until all he felt was agony and heat. Heat that coated his forehead with cold sweat and burned through his mind leaving no room for any thoughts or fear or worry. Just vast empty planes of agony.

He drifted with the boat, riding the waves of consciousness as they swelled and fell and broke and rose.

He glimpsed blue skies and a blanket of black, the rising of voices and the silence of infinite emptiness broken only by the swooshing of waves against the boat. The acrid smells of salt, fish and piss floated by him, and on occasion a rough touch crossed his forehead, mumbles of words that made no sense as he fell away from the world.

Ben had never known cold. He had known the feel of the fresh water as it hit his skin on a scorching afternoon. The water refreshing but not cold. Not truly. He shivered when he woke. The chill crept across his body like a slow glacier moving inside of him, biting the edge of his skin.

He shifted and moaned, his body wracked with pain.

"The fever's breaking, but the leg was te bad te save. I did wha I could." A gravelly voice explained. "You'll still feel the aftereffects of the infection. If I had to guess, could be another day or two, maybe then you'll be able te eat." The accented voice said, the man rolled his R's and swallowed his T's.

Ben tried to grasp onto the words, but they fell all around him like rain drops, hitting his skin then sliding off.

"I'll be back later with some water." The voice sighed. "With what they have planned for you boy, it would've been better te greet death."

A faint creak and a light thump followed, and Ben felt the presence disappear. He felt alone.

Ben pried his eyes open then blinked. His body shivered beneath a thick, soft blanket, a black thing with long black shaggy hair. It smelt both of the earth and the sea, a strange unfamiliar scent mixed with familiar nuances.

He pulled the blanket over himself, his fingers sinking into the soft luscious layers. The movement flared the pain in his body, and he stilled. His leg throbbed just above the ankle. He bit his lip to hold his pain inside.

It was then he noticed the change.

No waves crashed against a boat nor did his body lull or rock with movement, but rather he was on solid ground. Muted voices resounded around him. Humanity. A plethora of clunks and bangs tinged with the faint sounds of waves nipping at the shore.

His gaze swung around the space. For a moment he

thought himself in a cave but he was not encompassed by rock, but rather with earth, brown and thick and cool. The room was devoid of anything. A barren thing. He swivelled his head and found himself looking to the heavens; a black curtain drawn across the sky and speckled with stars. Wooden bars sliced across his vision, evenly spaced.

He looked around again, his mind trying to comprehend, to put together the pieces. He shivered and clung to the blanket seeking warmth. His eyes grew heavy and his mind numb, he sank into the darkness.

"You have te drink or you'll die. Though I have te say, I'm a bit surprised you've lasted this long." The gravelly voice returned and with it an insistent shaking.

He wrenched his eyes open. The man held a glass of water and he waved it in front of Ben's face. The water sloshed over thick, hairy fingers.

"You're awake then, aye." He smiled crookedly and held the wooden cup to Ben's mouth, tipping it. Ben gurgled and choked as a deluge of water flooded his throat and spilt across his face and slithered down his neck. "Like a babe then." The man shook his head and dipped the glass into a wooden bucket. "Are you ready this time?"

Ben nodded and wrapped his lips against the cup gulping the water, suddenly parched. He licked his dry lips. "Can I have some more please?"

The man refilled his cup for a third time and allowed him to sip the contents. "Thank you." Ben's voice rasped through chapped lips.

The man nodded and let the cup sink into the bucket then ran a hand over his thick red beard.

"You gonna stay awake this time?"

"Have you asked me before?"

"Aye. Not that it'll make a difference." The man scoffed.

"What's that supposed to mean?" A cold shiver crept across Ben's skin.

"Don't worry about that now. Can you sit up?" The man reached over and offered Ben his hand. "Here lemme help you."

His palm, as big as Ben's face, wrapped around his arm and yanked. Ben cringed and bit his tongue to keep from screaming. Nausea climbed up his throat and he sucked in a deep breath as he tried to hold himself at bay.

"Argh, sorry lad. I didn't mean to pull so hard. Don't know me own strength." He smiled and squeezed Ben's hand, shaking it. "I'm Connor, son of Aoife."

"Benjen, son of Catherine."

"Aye, they've told me yer name. Though I'm not sure if they'll let you keep it." He said it matter-of-factly, as if it meant nothing.

"What does that mean?" Ben's heart thundered.

"Don't worry yerself about it just now, hey? I need te look at yer leg."

Ben nodded and leaned against the wall. It crumbled beneath his touch, raining dark brown particles across his shoulders. The cool, moist earth flaked as Connor pulled the blanket away from him.

As he studied the ankle, he allowed Ben his first glimpse of the damage. The swollen limb stained with splashes of black, purple and green was wrapped between two pieces of polished wood that ran the length of his ankle to midway up his calf, held together with rough strips of fabric.

"Swelling looks like it's gone down again." Connor reassured him, as he examined the ankle which Ben didn't recognise as his own. "My splint will help, but I'm afraid they left it mistreated for te long and the bone began te heal before they got you te me." He shrugged.

"I don't understand." Ben ran a hand over his face, his

chest tingled, and he let out a frustrated blow. "Can you tell me what's going on? Where am I? Is Ariel ok?"

"Who's Ariel?" Connor's head cocked and a single bushy eyebrow rose like a fuzzy caterpillar.

"She's my…" Ben swallowed the words. "No one."

Connor's mouth pressed into a thin line that disappeared beneath his thick facial hair and he ran a hand over his beard as he nodded. "Aye, I see."

"Can you tell me what's going on?"

Connor reached for the tattered fabric which held together the splint and busied himself untying knots, until the splint fell away. Connor reached for the ankle and pushed against the blackened skin. Ben yelped at the touch, cold sweat erupted across his forehead and his hands shook uncontrollably.

"Aye, some time yet." He ran a hand through his curly red hair that hung low over his shoulders then rearranged the wooden splint. "Hold it."

Ben's vision swam as he grabbed the wooden pieces while Connor retied the fabric, fastening it against Ben's ankle. He hissed as it dug into his skin.

"Would ye like te try and eat now?" Connor studied Ben's face.

"Could you tell me where I am?"

"I'll bring you some dried meat and—"

"Please?" Ben reached for the giant redhead as he stood up. Connor examined him, green eyes flickering across his face while he ran his hand over his beard.

"Cernuava." Connor offered as he turned away.

"Where's that?"

"You're in the Second Quarter, Benjen, son of Catherine."

Ben's brain stuttered for a second as if it had short circuited. His mouth fell open trying to speak, yet the words wouldn't come, even when he tried to pry them from his mind by force. Instead, he sucked in lungfuls of air, trying to remember how to breathe.

Connor climbed on the stool and reached above him. He lifted the wooden bars that sealed Ben inside his earthly pit, then pulled himself out. Seated on the edge of the cage, Connor pulled on a rope attached to the foot of the small stool. It floated up and into Connor's hand. The red giant stood up and exchanged a silent look with Ben.

The wooden bars slammed back into place and Ben was alone once again. His racing heart, his only companion.

Ben's head rested in his palm as he lay back on his makeshift bed and watched the sun crawl along the horizon, casting long shadowy fingers across the moist brown walls of his cage. He lay still, like a dead thing, knowing movement brought agony.

His ankle throbbed' with constant reminders of its mangled state. A sheen of sweat covered his afflicted body and he pushed himself against the wall, seeking comfort. He sank into the cool moistness finding relief.

The bright sun did not provide warmth. A coldness hung in the air and clung on. Through the hole of his cage even the sky seemed a prisoner, a small circle cut away from the blue vastness he knew lay beyond.

Connor's arrival was pre-empted by a long shadow that dimmed out the weak rays. He lifted the bars, his red hair like sunrise, spilt across his wide hardened shoulders.

He lowered the chair then followed it into the cavity.

"Good morning, Benjen."

"Ben."

"Did you sleep?"

"I guess." He lied and swept a hand over his burning eyes. His restless body plagued by pain and nightmares.

Connor cocked his head. His hand disappeared into his vest and came out with a parcel wrapped in fabric. He shoved it at Ben. "Here."

"What is it?"

"Food. It'll help." He inched his hand closer still and held it until Ben accepted it. "Eat."

He unwrapped the fabric and found a piece of dried meat coated in herbs. His mouth watered at the gamey aroma. He bit into the meat, his teeth tearing through the hardened flesh.

"Good?"

Ben nodded as he ripped another chunk and chewed.

"You'll need yer strength with what's planned for ye." As before, his tone remained casual as if it didn't matter at all. "Silly if ye ask me. They should have marked ye while ye were still infected. It would have made the recovery easier and they could have put ye te work sooner." He shook his head. "Of course, no one actually asked me." He shrugged and his large shoulders dropped.

"What's going to happen to me? What's happening out there?"

"I'm just yer doctor."

"Please?" Ben's hand fell to his side, the meat half eaten.

"Is it true? Did you ask to live with a single mate? To raise her children?"

"Our."

"What's that?"

"Our children."

"So it is true?"

Ben answered with silence.

Connor burst into laughter, his entire body shaking with the sound that bounced off the walls. He slapped a giant hand against his knee. "Oh she must have been an amazing shag hey boy? Te give up all the women in the world for just one?" He wiped his eyes that swelled with tears. "Bet she was a wild one, aye? Did she su—"

The kick connected. Ben's heel dug into Connors chest with force. The giant man's eyes bulged as he grasped wildly at the air then toppled off his stool and smashed into the opposite wall.

Connor stared at Ben. His eyes wide, his expression bewildered, hair flying like a wild mane. A dark silence fell on the pit. Then a smile crept across the wild man's face. It grew and spread like ivy until once again he was consumed in a fit of laughter.

The giant shook, and his laughter tumbled in the small space. He rose to his full height and loomed over Ben.

"It's worse than all of that isn't it? Ye have an affliction even I can't fix."

Ben glared at him, his forehead furrowed with severe lines.

"You love her." The mirth fell away from Connor's face. "You've thrown your life away for love?"

Ben remained silent, staring, his face a strained mask of anger.

Connor shook his head as if confused.

"I didn't throw my life away." Ben's voice scratched through his parched throat.

"How do you explain this?" Connor gestured at the tight pit.

"Without Ariel I was never alive, and a life without her is not much of one."

"Ha. You lay with a girl and think you love her. That's hormones. Your body's chemicals sending your brain signals. All this because you stuck yourself someplace warm."

Ben's frown deepened and he scowled at the bigger man. "It's not hormones." Ben hissed through gritted teeth. "I've loved her all my life."

"I see." Connor ran a hand through his beard, the fingers skimming the red hair. "So not a foolish whim?"

"Why does it matter anyway?" Ben spat out. "Just tell me what they plan on doing to me."

"What ye'd expect I suppose." His shoulders swallowed his neck as they lifted around him. "Then again there's never been a case like yours before."

"A case like mine?"

"Love, and murder."

"Murder?"

"Aye," Connor's gaze swept over him, "though ye don't look the type."

"The type to what?"

"Kill anyone."

"I didn't."

"Save your pleas fer the jury."

Ben's frantic breaths threatened to suffocate him. "Who do they think I murdered?"

"The Mistress Watcher of yer Quarter."

The blood drained from Ben's face. "Tay? She's dead? How could that be?"

"Boy, ye're asking questions I can't answer."

"I need to know what's going on outside, please." Ben grabbed the man's arm but he yanked it away and climbed on the small stool. "Eat, Benjen. You'll need yer strength when they come for ye."

Ben wrenched a hand through his hair. "When will that be?"

"Soon I suppose, they're awaiting the arrival of a Mistress Watcher from Bonfrey."

"Where's that?"

"The place she calls home I suppose." With that he lifted his immense body from the pit, pulled up the stool and shut the wooden bars behind him.

"Get some rest laddy, I'll be back with yer lunch."

Connor's shadow disappeared, leaving Ben alone, seized with silent terror, which flooded his system with the excruciating need to flee. His immobilised body wanted to run. The adrenalin escaped in the form of warm reeking vomit that slid from his throat and conjured beads of sweat along his brow. Ben fell to the bed shaking and powerless, covered by a heavy blanket of dread.

S un up.
    Sun down.

He counted three days as he lay on his makeshift bed. He had decorated the walls of his pit with gouged holes and long nail tracks. His body too weak and the walls too high to scale.

He had screamed his throat raw on the first night of awareness only to enjoy a bucket of cold water that drenched his blanket and kept him shivering overnight. His hoarse voice carried less weight on the second day, and he was awarded by a shower of warm piss that soured his blanket and drenched his hair.

The sun woke him on the third morning. He stared at the blue sky and watched the clouds drift by. Ben envied them as they moved about leisurely above him.

The trap door opened and Connor's form cast its familiar shape across his bed. Ben watched as he lowered the stool and climbed inside, crinkling his nose as he descended. His usually cheerful face long and drawn.

"Good morning, Benjen."

"Good morning." His voice grated.

Connor's nose twitched and his face twisted. "You reek. Did you miss your bucket?" He pointed to the used bucket by the side of the bed.

Ben shrugged. "A gift from the guards."

Connor shook his head and handed him a parcel then retreated towards the opposite wall.

The parcel warmed his palm and smelt simultaneously sweet and sour. Fruit and malt married together to create a fog of memories and emotion. He unravelled the parcel and inhaled the bread, his heart pounded and his mind travelled back to Inan, to Mama Cath's kitchen where she would tear off pieces of bread for her three boys while they brawled around the kitchen.

Small crumbs rained on his finger as he tore at the crust. He threw the piece into his mouth and his eyes slammed shut at the delectable flavour, at the searing memories.

When he opened them, Connor's wore a distant look, his hand buried deep inside his beard.

"Are you okay?" A spittle of crumbs sprayed from Ben's mouth as he spoke.

Connor jerked up, jilted to life by the question and gave Ben a long sad look. "Today ye'll have to use yer leg Benjen. I'm concerned it'll damage the fragile bones and set back what progress ye've made. But I cannot hold them off any longer, they won't heed my words."

Ben nodded, his appetite muted. He wrapped the remainder of the bread and set it aside knowing it was unlikely to be eaten.

"Can ye stand up?"

"My doctor told me I should rest it."

"Yer doctor sounds like a wise man." A wane smile crossed Connor's face. "However, he isn't here now, I am, and today I'm a delivery man, and I must deliver ye for judgement. When ye return, I'll be yer doctor once more. I do believe ye'll require my services."

"How am I meant to get out of here?" Ben scanned the opening of the pit and grimaced.

"It'll be harder than getting ye in." Connor chuckled to himself as Ben's face whipped around searching the big man for answers. Connor held up his hands forestalling the question. "How about ye try to stand up."

Ben shuffled to the edge of the bed, his stiff legs moaning against the movement. He allowed them to dangle over the edge, then, with great care, lowered them both, keeping the weight on his good leg, the broken one hovering.

With rigid slow motions Ben pushed himself up. Unstable on one foot, he wavered like a flower in the wind before grabbing the wall and stabilising himself.

"Yer going te have te put it down eventually." Connor nodded to the mangled foot and Ben's jaw tightened. Pins of pain shot through his ankle as it swayed with slight movements.

Connor turned away from him, stood on the stool, then climbed out of the pit, his powerful back straining as he pulled his heavy body out.

He loomed over the pit and looked at Ben. "Yer turn."

Ben looked from Connor to the stool and back again. "I can't."

"Can't see ye having much choice now."

Ben sucked in a galvanising breath and hopped away from the wall. His ankle screamed with agony as it flayed around, his healthy leg threatening to buckle as his body erupted in sweat and shivers. He lurched himself at the opposite wall and hugged the dirt. The moist soil slithered between his fingers, crumbling beneath his palms as he fought for a hold. He drove himself into the wall until his flushed face buried in it and his body soaked up the coolness.

He gulped shallow earthy breaths and calmed his racing heart. When he thought himself ready, he craned his neck to meet Connor's uneasy stare. Ben reached for the loose rope bound to the stool, wrapped the length of it around his thick arm, then pulled the slack, ensuring it remained taut.

Ben scrutinized the stool and steeled himself for the task. His back left the wall at the same moment as he yanked the rope with force and leapt. He landed with a savage thud that jarred his broken leg. An anguished cry escaped his lips. He gripped the rope, knuckles blanched white, his bare toes clinging to the edge of the wooden stool. He teetered, unable to find his balance.

He clasped onto the rope even as his foot gave way and his back bent, threatening to topple over.

A hand clasped him and yanked, forcing his body onto the centre of the stool. He peered up to find large green eyes that looked at him with something akin to admiration. Connor nodded, a small movement that filled the bare space with his countenance.

"Thank you." Ben managed through ragged breaths and closed his grip on Connor's arm.

Connors thick brows gathered as he studied Ben's face. "Are ye ready lad?"

Ben looked to his dangling ankle and nodded.

"On three."

Ben locked eyes with the giant.

"One."

His fingers cinched around the thick arm of the redhead, digging into his flesh, his heart pounding in his ears.

"Two."

Connor yanked.

A momentary feeling of weightlessness was followed by excruciating pain. The cry fell from his lips as his body hit the ground, the air in his lungs expelled with a violent thud.

Ben screamed as pain drove through his leg. Every thought obliterated as the burning pain licked up the limb like scorching fire. He gurgled as he struggled to breathe, his body shaking. Darkness played at the fringes of his mind and he sucked in long helpless breaths. After a time the pain settled into a throbbing sharp ache.

Connor's large paw landed on his shoulder and patted him. "Ye did good lad, but ye must stand up now."

Ben's lips quivered as he grabbed Connor's offered hand and dragged himself up. With a gentle tug Connor helped him to stand up. "What happened to three?"

Connor shrugged.

Ben leaned against the big man and for the first time took in his surroundings. The foreign landscape alien and unfamiliar.

The ocean behind him, vast and blue, as beautiful as he remembered. His eyes glistened at the sight. Yet the beach boasted an earthy brown, almost unnatural.

"There are some better beaches along the coast, here is where the land tore apart, this is an unnatural abomination, created by man. Some think this beach is cursed." Connor explained.

"What do you think?" Ben's voice slurred with pain.

"Yer here aren't ye?" He shrugged. Ben found himself smiling.

His gaze followed the path as it sprawled lazily before them leading to a village which lay tucked before the rolling hills on the horizon. The sheer endless cliffs and craggy mountains of Dagon would dwarf these bumps in the earth.

The earth was painted green as it rose and fell like a sea on the land. But not the lush, vibrant tropical green of his home, cut by the mountains and sliced by the sun, but pale and garish, grown from moist soil and lashing rain. Protected from the sun by clouds and days of cold.

At the foot of the hills spread flat lands. Endless green fields

Connor took the first step towards the village shepherding Ben to whatever awaited.

"Let him walk," a cold flat voice called from behind them.

They turned to find a soldier clad in black, hidden behind his mask, his eyes cold and lifeless.

"He won't make it with his le—"

The soldier jabbed Connor with the back of his spear. "I said, let him walk."

Connor's eyes narrowed as he glared at the soldier then threw his chin forwards as he took a half step. The soldier scrambled backwards then recovered quickly, his spear pointed at the two men once more.

"I thought ye couldn't talk, silent army and all."

The soldier grimaced behind his mask his teeth flashed like those of a wild predator. "We can talk, we just can't judge. We keep our thoughts to ourselves and follow the orders we're given."

"Even when they're wrong?"

The soldier spat at Connor's feet. "Our orders are given by the wisest of the land put up by the very people who consider them so. My mind and my soul are silent, I have no regrets or fear. I do not judge actions, I act upon them. I'm silent because I choose to be, because I can be, and because my actions will speak louder than my words." He stepped forwards again, his spear inching closer to Connors midriff. "Now release the prisoner. He is to walk to his own judgment."

Connor exchanged a quick look with Ben and cocked his head, his mouth drawn in a thin line. "I have to let ye go now lad."

Ben's jaw ticked as Connor stepped away and released his hold. Ben's body wobbled, unsteady. He clenched his fists and put his ankle down. After a beat he attempted his first step. White hot pain shot through his leg and spread like flames to the rest of his body, his legs collapsed from beneath him and he heaved in a dry retch while his body accustomed itself to the new pain.

Connor looked from Ben to the soldier. "He can't do it."

"Then he'll crawl," the soldier hissed.

Connor clenched his teeth, his eyes trained on the soldier. "I need to deliver him for judgement, everyone has gathered.

There's no time for this." Connor bent down to Ben and laced his strong arms beneath his legs and back then picked him up as if his muscular body weighed nothing at all.

"I said put him down, let him crawl."

"I will not."

"I'll have you lashed for this."

"Ye go right ahead laddy, but if we don't get Benjen te judgement soon, we'll all be done for." Connor stepped away.

The soldier fell silent, his cold hard eyes glaring at the men. He growled then manoeuvred past them and marched ahead. Connor rolled his eyes and followed in his wake.

They meandered through a green pasture where strange animals roamed the fields. They bleated, the sound alien and unfamiliar.

"What are those?" Ben stretched his neck to have a better look.

"Those are sheep." Connor's voice, a mixture of amusement and nonchalance.

Ben stared at the animals clumped together in a flock, chewing grass. Their white coats dusty and stained. He stared at them full of wonder, until one raised its head and they locked eyes. Big, black innocent eyes that made him want to smile.

"What do you use them for?"

"Wool and food." Connor shifted Ben's weight in his arms. "In those fields beyond the village, we grow wheat, oats and barley. The land here broke in our favour, it is fruitful and lush, we have much available to trade with the other Quarters."

Ben nodded, his eyes wandered the unfamiliar landscape and his thoughts drifted to Ariel. How she might giggle with glee as she combed her fingers through the wool of the sheep and admire its sweet face. How she might run across the fields with bare feet which would sink into the grass and muddy earth. How her laugh might ring across the planes and her hair would ripple behind her in wild waves.

"Hurry up." The soldier's gruff voice snapped Ben away from his thoughts and he took in the village as they closed the distance.

Roads carved the brown earth and brick homes speckled the flat land. Piles of rock lay littered along the path waiting to be fashioned into more houses. Ben's heart panged as he thought about the quarry back on Dagon, of Luke and Jacob and Antoine. He hoped for their safety.

Connor meandered along the narrow paths of the village then stepped into a side lane which led to an open space. Surrounded by homes, the open area felt much like the arena of Ishmin. A shudder gripped Ben as he took in the raised stone stage, stained with old blood. A crowd gathered at its base.

Two men and two women—three clad in purple and one in deep red—sat on the stage. Grim faced and silent. A fire roared behind them.

A murmur went up as Connor shouldered his way to the stage. He squeezed Ben's arm as he deposited him onto the edge.

"Be brave, it'll be over quickly," he whispered as he released him then stepped aside. The soldier came to stand like a sentinel by Ben, saying nothing.

Ben felt all the inhabitants of the island turn their heads to look at him, his chest tingled with fingers of dread as one of the women stood up behind him silencing the crowd.

"I am Samantha, daughter of Jennifer, newly inducted Watcher of Ishmin, and I have been called to Cernuava, to see justice carried out on this day. Benjen, son of Catherine, your sins follow you wherever you go."

"Sins?" Ben questioned and was silenced by a scathing look.

"I will lead this court of the Second Quarter on behalf of

ı

Tay, daughter of Audrey who has been murdered viciously by the hands of Elizabeth, daughter of Irma." A cry went up in the crowd and Ben's stomach knitted.

The Watcher silenced the crowd and continued. "Ariel, daughter of the murderess Elizabeth has escaped. Scouts will find her and bring her to justice." Ben reeled with relief and anxiety, his body tingling with the pin pricks of too many emotions.

"Today we'll pass judgement on this lawbreaker. This small council of chosen elders has decided your fate. Our lands might be broken but the rules that govern them are universal and are in place to protect us all. The world is in turmoil, a small war wages in the Third Quarter due to your actions and those of your mate. Your refusal to follow the rules have set us back, and now there must be consequences to curb such rebellions, to end such behaviour and to calm the people so that peace can reign, and we can rebuild."

The crowd rippled with anger, their narrowed eyes fixed on him, set with predetermined judgement. He swallowed the fear that pushed its way up his dried throat.

"Stand up, Benjen, and say your piece." She glared at him blankly.

Ben swiped a hand across his chin and sucked in a deep breath then shuffled backwards onto the stage. "I can't stand." He shook his head.

The Watcher turned to the council. Their murmurs drifted by him as he steadied himself. She broke away and returned to the edge of the stage where she addressed the crowd. "We are agreed. Judgement has been decided."

"But," Ben struggled against his broken body, wanting to stand, fighting the agonising pain that gripped his leg, "I haven't been on trial yet, I haven't had my say."

The Watcher huffed, "Your trial took place days ago, you're here today to accept your judgement."

"But you need to give me a chance to defend myself." His

heart throbbed in his chest as hooks of fear pulled at him from all directions.

"I don't need to give you a chance to do anything. You know the law. You broke it and your actions brought unrest to an entire quarter. You have no defence, there are no words that'll change these facts."

Ben's fists clenched at his side, desperation welling in the pit of his stomach.

"Today you'll be branded an abomination and no longer carry your mother's name. You'll have your manhood severed and will be transported back to Ishmin to serve amongst the Brown Robes until your dying day. You are not worthy of being a man or spreading your seed."

Before he could protest, hands captured his shoulders and slammed his body into the rough, sharp rocks which dug into his back as he thrashed and screamed. Heavy hands landed on his legs and pinned them down, crushing is ankle. He roared in agony. His body battered against the hard stone as he fought with his remaining strength, stilling only when the scalding rod heated his skin when it neared his chest.

The metal bar glowed white, the letter 'A' enclosed in a circle, radiated heat that sparked a new wave of begging from Ben, the words spilling from his mouth like torrents of a waterfall, full of fear, incoherent and nonsensical. His soul screamed with petrified screeches, dreading the pain about to be inflicted on his body.

With a brutal shove the branding rod dug into his skin, it curled and stuck onto the metal as it sizzled and burned. Searing, brutal agony spread across his body, burning every-thing in its path. Starbursts exploded behind his eyes as they rolled to the back of his head. Ben screeched and screamed, thrashing, the pain threatening to break his mind, his thoughts drowning in agony, until he almost felt nothing at all.

With the same brutality of its introduction the rod was

yanked away from his chest tearing with it pieces of scorched blackened skin, leaving behind a deep reddened welt emblazoned deeply into flesh. The smell of charred skin clung to the air and the scent crawled up his nose and down his throat and coated everything, until all he tasted was his own ruined flesh. He gagged and choked, the hands around him disappeared and he lay dazed and delirious, his body fighting the urge to shut down, to escape the pain, grunting and gasping.

"And now we must complete his punishment." Samantha's voice sliced through the hushed silence and signalled for the soldiers to grab Ben once more.

"Wait!" Connor stood up and took several steps towards the stage. "I wish to speak before you proceed."

"Say what you must, son of Aoife."

"He has not been prepared—"

Samantha waved a hand at Ben, "He doesn't deserve to be, he can be cleansed after."

Connor nodded. "Aye, but that is not tradition."

"In this case I think it can be wavered."

Connor scratched through his beard and examined Ben's broken body. "I think ye would be making a mistake. I wish for ye te consider postponing his alteration."

"For what purpose?"

"Let me assure ye, if ye take this action now, ye might as well throw him te the fishes and allow him te rot. He won't survive much more. He'll serve no purpose if he's dead and death will be far te good for this abomination. Brown Robes are an asset to us all. Let me heal him so that he can be cleansed, and his punishment can be carried through in the proper manner as per the law."

The crowd waited in charged silence and Samantha nodded, seemingly considering Connor's advice, then turned back to the other council members who clustered together.

Ben rolled on the hard stone, falling in and out of

consciousness, his body jerked and lolled, stiffened then loosened into limp limbs and grunting misery.

Samantha stepped to the edge of the stage. "Connor, son of Aoife, you are a healer of men are you not?"

"I am." Connor dragged a hand through his beard.

"And you think this man could be healed?"

"I do."

"Then the burden is upon you to heal this abomination and ensure his well-being, so that when I return I can carry out his sentence in full and take him with me back to Ishmin where he shall live out the rest of his life as a Brown Robe. Where he'll be silenced and burdened with the needs of others, never to plant his seed or grow his bloodline. To be forgotten."

Connor tipped his head once, his eyes flickering momentarily to the figure lolling around on the stage.

"It is done. I'll return to Ishmin and leave in my stead members of the silent army who will be my eyes and ears. Upon their word I shall return when it is time. We are concluded for today, thank you for holding witness and holding your brother accountable."

The crowd dispersed in low murmurs until all that were left were Connor, Ben and three figures lurking in the shadows. Connor swept his eyes over them. They turned away and disappeared.

"Ben? Ben are ye alright?" Someone whispered to him, or maybe they were shouting. Ben's tongue seemed glued to the top of his mouth and his eyes did not want to focus. He tried to speak, he wanted to scream but all that he managed were pathetic moans muted by snot and tears and coated with pain.

A movement brought more pain until his mind splintered and sheer white turned to black.

Morning brought Connor, and with him, the milk of the poppy and that brought long painless sleep and wild vivid dreams. Days fused into nights as sleep allowed his body to heal and his mind to crawl inside itself. On occasion he tried to hang on to moments like glimpses of the moon, or the sun hanging high in blue skies, or black speckled nights or the howling of wind.

Time slipped away like water into the earth, his body bearing witness to its passage. His hair grew beyond his shoulders and his muscles withered, his body grew stiff as he lay and sank deeper into his dreams. He sipped on his milk and his mind took him to her, and in his dreams, he tasted her. She lingered on his skin and her voice permeated his being with laughter so delightful he wanted to burst and cry and scream, but each time, she would fade away and all that remained was the memory etched on his flesh, on his tongue, searing his very soul. So vivid and colourful that he was left reeling when he woke back into reality.

The pain had eased into a hum that lived permanently under his skin like an incessant fly that buzzed around until it gradually faded into white noise. His burn scabbed over, but his heart remained ripped raw and empty. His pit filled with weariness and anguish.

Ben groaned and rolled over, the blue skies hung above, tormenting him as his gaze swept the pit that has become his world. A wretched place of solitude where he could be alone with her.

Connor's large shadow fell over the pit and Ben bit his lower lip, his stomach coiling in anticipation, licking his lips as he awaited the drops that would take him to her.

Connor climbed inside and sat on his stool, his face drawn, he pushed his fingers through his beard and sat in silence.

"Where's my milk?" Ben growled at him.

"Ye cannot have any more, yer wound is healed."

Ben ran a hand over the raised scar of his chest and grumbled from deep in his throat. "I want more. I don't want to be here. I don't want to think!"

Connor ran a hand through his beard and shook his head. "I'm sorry Benjen, I don't have any for ye."

Ben shot from the bed and pushed himself against Connor's larger body. His jaw clamped, he hissed through his teeth, "I. Need. More. I'm. In. Pain." He locked eyes with the giant, then pushed away falling back onto the bed.

Connor's face twisted with sadness and he pulled his hand away from Ben's. "It is my job te heal ye, and yer body is coursing with the poppy and yer mind is confused. Ye need te be clear so ye can think. Ye need te be clear so ye can understand what's going to happen te ye, and ye need to be clear so ye can move and walk and be free of here."

Ben rolled onto his back. "As long as I'm here, as long as I'm away from Ariel and forced to serve as a Brown Robe, I'll never be free."

"That's the poppy talking."

"We both know it isn't." He ground his teeth, his body cramping with need. "I've already told you, without her I might as well be dead."

"But *they* do not want ye te die, they want ye te repent."

"I have nothing to repent." He sniffed and slammed his eyes shut. "Loving Ariel is not a sin, loving her keeps my heart beating, and if there's no hope, if I am to meet her at Ishmin and watch her with others, I'd rather spend the rest of what's left of my life in dreams. And when the time comes and they come to take me, I shall let the ocean take me first."

Connor stood up and climbed the stool, looking down at Ben. "There will be no more milk and no more pity. Ye'll rest and sweat the poison from yer body, and I'll come for ye and ye'll walk."

"No."

"Aye, I cannot heal ye if I cannot assess the damage caused te yer leg. I don't know if I'll ever be able te heal it and if it doesn't heal, then my duty will never be fulfilled and ye will remain my burden, unable to perform as a Brown Robe." Conner shrugged then winked as he pulled himself out of the pit.

"Wait," Ben called after him, "my milk, I need it."

Connor's shadow disappeared even as he kept wailing his name.

When he returned he brought with him another man. They climbed into the pit in silence. Connor leaned against the wall and the newcomer sat on the stool by the bed. The space felt cramped with the large bodies inhabiting it.

The newcomer glared at Ben.

"Who are you?" Ben's eyes narrowed as he scrutinised the man.

The newcomer ignored the question. "I hear you have been making demands."

Ben's gaze flickered to Connor who shrugged, then back to the man still glaring at him. "Not demands. I need poppy for the pain."

"I think the pain you're in is beyond the mending of the poppy, or even the great Doctor Connor over here."

Ben rubbed his hands over his face hiding his twitching jaw. "Just give it to me."

"I'm afraid I can't do that."

"You mean won't."

The newcomer tipped his head.

Ben clutched his blanket, his knuckles white against it. "Just a little bit, to tide me over. Everything hurts so bad." His lips quivered as he spoke.

The newcomer sighed and folded his arms across his chest then straightened his lanky body as he shook his head. "Still weak."

Ben frowned, his teeth grinding. "What did you say?"

"I'm pretty sure you heard me, *Benjen*." He smeared out the name, taunting him. "You're still weak and pathetic. Mama Cath would be so disappointed with her perfect baby boy."

Ben stilled and studied the man sitting before him, attempting to push through the fog that had lulled his senses for so long.

"Do you know me?"

"Better than you know me obviously." The man exhaled, his nose flaring with the action. "That's okay, when I left, you were still so young."

Ben shifted on the bed, his eyes roamed over the man's face. Cool emerald eyes rimmed by dark circles stared back at him. His mouth fell open and he swept sweat from his brow. "Mason?"

The man turned to Connor, a smile spread across his face. "Told you he would recognise me, now cough up."

Connor grumbled and he rummaged around in his vest then pulled out a ripe red apple. He threw it at Mason who caught it with a quick move.

"Mmm." He smelt the fruit. "It's been months since we've had any fresh ones." His teeth severed the apple, juice dribbled down his chin as he bit into it.

Ben pushed himself up to a sitting position, his mouth still ajar and studied the man in front of him who slurped and bit into the apple.

His brother was not as he remembered him, his lanky frame fuller and broader, no longer a scared boy but a man whose deep-set eyes remained as they had always been. "Mason?"

"Yes, Ben."

"What are you doing here?"

"I could ask you the same question."

Ben inhaled and clutched the bridge of his nose. "Look, can you help me or not?"

"Oh, I plan to." Mason sat back, leaning against the wall as he ate the apple, crunching and sucking with each bite.

"Okay, okay. So you'll get me some more poppy milk?" Relief leaked out of Ben.

"You like it?"

"It helps me."

"And now I'm here to help you."

"How?"

"You'll see." Mason stood up and gestured to Connor to follow him. The two men climbed out of the hole leaving Ben's hollow screams to echo against the walls.

In his delirium he visited his home. Voices mocked him from the dark abyss of his broken mind. Mama Cath cried his name while Luke shook his head in disappointment. Jacob's long pointed finger scorned him as he laughed at his fate and Ariel's desperate cries tore at his soul as she lamented his death. They clawed and screamed at him until his body cried with sweat and shivered with pain and he cackled and laughed at the walls closing in around him.

Sleep returned and hunger gnawed at his stomach.

The moon drifted in the shimmering night sky when the roof of his pit flew open and Mason scaled down the rope and onto the stool.

"What's wrong?" Ben jerked up from the bed and studied his older brother.

"Here." Mason handed Ben a shiny red apple and a portion of bread.

Ben snatched the food and pushed the stale bread into his mouth. He chewed the doughy slice and forced it down his throat even as it threatened to clog it.

Mason sat on the stool, his elbows leaning on his knees while he watched Ben. "How do you feel?"

Ben rubbed his hands on his grubby blanket. "Better."

Mason nodded. "Tell me about our mother."

"What do you want to know?"

Mason sighed. "Everything. I remember so little of her, like somehow she's dead though I know that she isn't."

Ben nodded, understanding his meaning. "She is brave and stronger than I ever imagined, and she misses you and Logan. Your absence has carved the lines on her face and drained the colour from her hair." His shoulders slumped as he thought about the last time he saw his mother.

Mason's face twisted into a tortured grimace. "When you see her again, tell her I am well. That I miss her and I will hold her in my arms again."

Ben scoffed and looked at his feet. "Sure."

Silence fell between the brothers.

"Ariel, daughter of Elizabeth? She is the cause of all this? I still remember her as a child, much the same way that I remembered you until recently."

"She is not a child anymore. And neither am I."

"You love her?"

"She makes me feel alive and brave and petrified and completely out of control all at the same time. When I am around her it's like everything falls apart and pulls together all at once. She makes me feel whole." Ben's words drifted. "Or at least she did, before..."

"You don't think she would feel the same now?"

"It's just that..." Ben ran a hand along his body, the scarred face and torso, the mangled leg. His body told a story of defeat and brutal torment.

"If she somehow managed to love you, it was never for your looks brother, for we all know I am the most handsome of Mama Cath's sons." Mason's face split into an uncharacteristic grin and for a second Ben had the urge to wrap his arms around him.

"I think Logan might have something to say about that." He scoffed and Mason fell silent. "Do you know where he is?"

His brother remained silent.

"Is he alive?" Ben's body flooded with hope and his heart thumped like a wild drum. Mason's gaze locked with Ben's for a second before he dipped his head downwards. The silence returned thick and heavy around them.

"When did you get here? What do you do?"

Mason swept a hand across his chin. "The Shuffling, you know, just after I turned twenty."

"But you were on Dagon. There is an order, you should have stayed. Logan too."

"What should have happened... Could have happened..." He shrugged. "Yet here we are."

"What aren't you telling me?"

Mason sighed, a shadow of a smile crossed his face. "We all followed our hearts, you just took it a step further."

"Logan?"

"Benjen." His voice held an unveiled warning.

Ben scrubbed a hand over his face. "Your Job?"

"I tend to the herds and sheer the flock when it's time."

"That explains the smell." Ben crinkled his nose.

"Pretty sure you're smelling yourself. I wash every day." Both men looked at Ben's near-empty bucket and the momentary jesting vanished.

Mason stood and climbed on the stool. "Stay strong brother. Keep your head down but your chin up. You'll find that nothing is set in stone and even when we think our path is set there is always room to carve a new one."

Ben nodded at his brother. "What was her name?"

Mason scoffed then pulled himself out of the pit, dragging the chair up behind him. "Good night Ben. See you soon."

In the morning Connor and Mason slid into the pit and stood leaning against the walls.

"Are you ready brother?"

Ben's eyes narrowed as he looked at his brother. "For what?"

"For a taste of the outside."

Ben's gaze darted from the two men and up towards the circle of blue. "There's nothing for me out there."

Mason sighed, "I thought you might say that." He turned to Connor. "Grab him."

As one, both men reached the bed. Mason's hands closed around Ben's legs while Connor wrapped his arms beneath Ben's, hooking them as he yanked him up and out.

Ben struggled against his assailants, thrashing in their arms. He felt like a twig about to snap, thin and dried out. Connor pulled himself out of the pit, his fingers digging into Ben's flesh as he dragged him up while Mason heaved from beneath.

The light dazed him.

He lay on the dark sand and flailed like a fish out of water, feeling like a stranger in the world. The outside seemed suddenly too big and wide and despite himself he wanted to crawl back into his hole in the ground where the dark walls felt safe.

The two men stood over him as he rolled onto his stomach and clawed his way towards the pit, dark sand sifting between his fingers. Their heavy sighs rolled above him. Hands closed around his ankles and dragged him away. He dug his fingers into the sand groaning, begging, leaving long furrowed trails as his prison drew further away.

"This is for your own good Benjen."

With their grip still firm around his ankles, the two men grabbed his wrists and carried him into the ocean. Gentle waves lapped below him as the two men drove further into the sea until it grasped at Mason's hips.

"Let him go." Mason said.

Ben hit the water like jagged rock.

The freezing water permeated his skin, stealing the heat from his body. Salt stung his dry lips and settled inside his mouth, coating his tongue and sliding down his throat. He gasped, fighting for air, until his knees found the ground and he pushed himself above the waves that danced around him, calm and unperturbed by his interruption.

He hauled in breath, sucking in nuances of briny water and muddy earth, of sour sweat and unfamiliar aromas carried by the sweet breeze that chilled his wet body. He crawled to the shore where Connor and Mason stood stoic, watching, staring, saying nothing.

Ben collapsed. Waves rolled over him as his head rested on the sand. The sun beat above him with no warmth and the breeze smothered him with icy wet kisses that burned his skin.

He lay there until his teeth rattled and his eyes burned, and his muscles wound themselves tightly, seeking warmth from his bones.

"Whenever you're ready." Mason called to him his hands folded tightly around his waist.

Ben groaned and dug his fingers into the moist sand. They clawed and pulled until he had dragged himself away and to dry sand then rolled onto his back. Within moments two large shadows loomed over him.

"Why did you do that?" he asked through a shivering breath.

"You stank," Mason stated before throwing a towel at his drenched brother.

Ben sat up and peeled his pants off then dried himself as best he could. Connor lay a long shirt and a clean pair of pants at his feet.

"You're not going to help?"

"Ye're not a cripple and I'm not yer mum." Connor shrugged.

"My leg—"

"Has healed, ye'll have te try it out eventually."

Ben grumbled as he twisted and turned on the sand fighting the fabric which clung to his wet body. When dressed again he turned to his brother. "What now? You're going to throw me in the water again?"

"Now ye go te work."

"Work?" He quirked an eyebrow.

"Yes, work. Ye have been in the earth te long, ye have buried yourself alive. It's time te re-join the living."

"Why? So, they can take me away?"

"Boy, ye are thicker than ye are broken," Connor said exasperated as he ran a hand over his beard.

Mason ignored Connor's outburst. "Here." He threw two sticks fashioned into crutches at Ben. They were sanded smooth with a protruding bulge designed as a hold.

Ben studied them and rolled onto his knees, his neck muscles corded and his arms ached as he pulled himself up. He stood on one foot, wobbling against the crutches.

"Good." Mason smiled at him. "Now come on." The two men walked away.

He sucked in a long breath and stabbed the earth with the crutches, flinging himself forward as he did, suspecting that should he refuse, more pain would follow.

Mason and Connor strolled up the path, snippets of laugher swept by him as he followed in their wake, his arms burned and his skin gleamed with a sheen of perspiration. His mind, clear for the first time in many weeks, drifted to his first day at the quarry, the ache plaguing his body, his heaving breaths as he lifted and pulled and broke through the stone. How his muscles screamed at him to stop and yet he had found the strength to go on, to complete his task. But most of all he recalled how the work exhausted him, making his mind too weary to think or miss or need all that he had left behind.

He fell in a pathetic heap of bones and flesh at the edge of the field where Mason and Connor stood waiting. They offered no help. He calmed his laboured breath and waited.

Mason squatted and looked at his brother, his face carved into a grim expression as he spoke. "You are *not* a prisoner."

Ben's gaze fell on the two soldiers that had followed them

at a distance then cocked a single eyebrow at his brother, his mouth pulling to the side.

"You're being held hostage by your mind, you can find freedom here."

"The pit and filth I live in are not imaginary, nor are those soldiers waiting to tell their mistress about my health. I know what you're trying to do, but my fate is sealed. Releasing me from the pit and setting me to work does not grant me freedom. Once they come for me, the only freedom I will ever know is death."

"You're free as long as you fight."

"And what is it I am fighting for?"

"Perhaps that is what you need to rediscover, because while you have been dreaming your life away people have been losing theirs to protect the life you asked to create."

"What are you talking about?"

"Your actions back on Ishmin have rippled across our world. A war wages, one that demands change or death. Your war will come to our shores. Whether you want to accept it or not, you and Ariel have broken something that many are going to try and reseal with words and brutality. If you don't get yourself together and fight, you'll be their greatest weapon. A broken half man that tried to love a woman once. If you or Ariel fall, we all fall."

"Ariel, is she alright?" Ben's skin prickled at the sound of her name.

"I don't know."

"How long?"

"How long what?"

"How long have I sat in that pit?"

"About three months now since your arrival."

A brutal angry pang stabbed at Ben's heart and he blew out a severed breath. "Three?"

"At least, maybe four."

Ben's body seized as his heart thundered in his chest. "That means—"

"It means nothing."

"It means Ariel has—"

"No."

"But—"

"There's much you do not understand and much that's happened while you buried yourself in self-pity. You have friends here, you have allies, keep your eyes open and mouth shut. Blend in, work hard, become forgettable." Mason's gaze snapped over the soldiers.

"Who—"

"Hush!"

The group fell into a hushed silence while two figures approached them. Ben squinted through narrowed eyes then let out a snort and shook his head.

Connor shot him a look. "What's so funny?"

"I'm dreaming and none of this real." Relief saturated his body.

"And why do ye think that?"

"Because I am seeing things again." Ben's mouth curled in a grin and his body sank into the earth.

Mason turned to Ben and punched him on the arm.

Ben rubbed the reddening patch and cursed. "What was that for?"

"Illustrating that you're not sleeping, but if you feel like you might be, it's time to wake up."

Ben grumbled under his breath and watched the two figures until they stopped by his feet.

"Ben," they said in unison and bent over him, "at last."

Ben brushed a hand over his face and licked his dry lips. "Are you really here?" He looked at their faces, scrutinising.

Antoine squatted, face to face with his friend, he placed a hand on his shoulder, "yes. We are."

"But..." He gestured to Danny whose Brown Robe had

been discarded and replaced with the everyday garb worn by all the men of Cernuava. His pale face sullied with dried earth. "How?"

Antoine face fell as he spoke. "In the chaos you fell, I rushed to your aid but there were too many guards around you, too many sharp objects. When they lifted you into the boat we followed. It was easy to undress the dead. A mask over our faces and our silence secured our safety. We came to ensure no harm befell you." His eyes tracked the fresh scar emblazoned across Ben's chest then his gaze cast downwards. "I'm sorry we failed you."

"Ariel? Did you see her?"

"Your mother pulled her away towards the beach. In the chaos she was lost, but I feel that she made it to a boat and taken to safety."

"You *feel*? You didn't see?"

Antoine shook his head, his lips pressed into a thin line.

"What of Mama Beth?"

Antoine's eyes flickered over the field, his silence heavy between them.

Ben wrenched a hand through his hair then brushed it over his face.

"I know how things might seem but, for now let us celebrate that you are here among the living, surrounded by friends and out of that dreadful pit." Antoine squeezed his shoulder and stood up, his fingers brushing against Danny's as he did so.

Perhaps it was Antoine's words or the wind that blew across the field, carrying with it the sweet perfume of flowers from far away meadows beyond the oceans, but he felt her. She called for him to return to her and he knew that somehow, he would.

Days dissolved into months, spent with Mason, Antoine and Danny tending to the herds. Evenings spent alone in his pit with his gnawing thoughts and shredding fears that skewered his insides and filled him with doubt.

With time, his guards had vanished, preferring to pass their days with the men of the village. Their disappearance brought him solace. He hoped perhaps he had managed what Mason had suggested and became forgettable. He walked freely among the fields and the men of the village returning to his pit to sleep, eat and to hide during their Mating Season festivities, when the village became a ghost town occupied by the elderly, those deemed too young to mate and two men, who like mice, hid in the rafters of the doctor's office.

The coldest months passed, and the sun returned bringing blue skies and the ripening of produce. Men cut the fields and Mason had taken the sheep to be sheared. They came back into the fields naked, shivering and fat with unborn lambs.

Ben chewed on his meat and looked up at the blue sky wishing the time away. The silence, once familiar, now gnawed at him, alone in his pit he had too much time to think. He missed Connor's full laugh and Mason's sour looks while they were away fulfilling their mating duties. The bars of his prison flew open and a young boy of no more than fourteen loomed above him with wide, terror-stricken eyes.

"They told me you know about the herd. I need your help."

He threw a stool to Ben who blinked at the boy.

"Come on." His red face streaked with tears.

Ben climbed the stool and pulled himself from the pit then followed the boy who ran ahead up the path. "This way."

He hobbled in a half run, his crutches helping his descent into the field.

"Please hurry."

"What's wrong?"

"I need your help, she's about to die."

"Who?"

"Hurry."

Ben barged into the field, the high grass tickling his thighs, the blades parting as he pushed through behind the boy.

The ewe's tail twitched, and she bleated a desperate unhappy sound. Her big brown eyes hooded with signs of tiredness.

"What's wrong with her?" Ben looked at the ashen boy.

"I don't know. She just fell over. She's been uneasy all day and just now she has fallen. They'd have my head if she dies."

Ben's chest ached for the boy for he knew his despair well. He sat by the fallen beast and ran his hand along her neck, which strained and twisted. Another desperate sound fell from her. He stroked the swollen belly and found the liquid which had erupted from her. Her guttural bleat tore at his core as he looked to the boy.

"She is giving birth. Something must be wrong with her baby."

Ben ran a hand over his face, "Get it out then."

The boy took a half a step back, the last of his colour drained away as he shook his head and looked pleadingly at Ben.

Ben's jaw ticked. He examined the ewe palpating along her belly which moved and twitched beneath his fingers, he found her opening and searched for the lamb. "What do I do?"

"You need to get the baby. From inside." The boy's panicked voice rose to a near shriek.

A calm logic set over Ben. The ewe bleated in pain and he pushed a hand inside, seeking her baby. Within the warmth of her womb, he felt the lamb, but not a nose and face, but the warm wet backside and tail, with both legs tucked beneath her.

He expelled his hand and the ewe kicked back, her lips curling with a scream.

"It's stuck," Ben said.

"Get it out, before they both die." The boy's ashen expression landed on the suffering sheep.

"How?"

"I don't know!"

Ben drew in a long breath and reached blindly for the lamb, he discovered one trapped leg and pulled gently to release it then repeated the process with the other. As he withdrew his hand, liquid erupted from the sheep who gave another strained bleat.

Two tiny hooves emerged and Ben tugged gently, helping the lamb out into the world. The small body fell to the ground and lay in a blood-spattered, goo-covered pile and remained motionless.

"Is it dead?" the boy's voice trembled.

Adrenalin smothered Ben's momentary delight, no longer certain whether he was witnessing life or death.

"I don't know." Nerves ran up from his stomach and tickled his throat choking him with uncertainty.

"What do we do?"

The ewe bleated, panicked, her big brown eyes teary and pleading.

Ben reached for the fallen lamb's face, pushing away the fluid from its mouth and nose. They waited for what seemed like an age when the lamb opened its eyes and took a breath.

The boy cheered and the ewe bleated a relieved, delighted sound that resonated around the field.

His thoughts drifted to Ariel, how he had whispered against her naked skin, begged for his seed to grow inside her. Hot tears surged uncontrollably down his cheeks as if lamenting a death, and yet it was the opposite, he could not breathe for the sheer excitement of it all.

The lamb stood on wobbly legs, its mother licking and circling her baby.

"You did it." The boy laughed and clapped his shoulder. "Stay here, I'll go get help."

"Help?"

"We need to move them to a pen, we must make sure they bond. I can't carry both." His eyes flicked over Ben's ankle.

Ben nodded and the sun kissed his face as he watched the lamb suckle from its mother. He was filled with a great sense of hope, for he knew he had witnessed the creation of life, an existence that braided two souls with love, real immediate and primal.

The mirth usually etched on Connor's face was replaced by a stony expression as he approached, flanked by four soldiers. "Benjen, ye must come with me."

"What's going on?"

"You only speak when spoken to, abomination." A soldier slurred at him from behind his mask.

Ben grabbed his crutches and stood up then followed Connor down the path and towards the village, the four soldiers surrounding them as they walked. Ben's stomach churned as they meandered through the cold stone buildings. He had not set foot in the village since his branding. Smoke rose from chimneys and nausea danced in his throat threatening to erupt. He sucked in deep slow breaths as Connor led him deeper into the village.

He followed him through a green door worn by sunlight and time, they walked through a small waiting room housing three green plastic chairs. Connor turned to the soldiers. "Ye three can wait here."

"You don't get to give the orders doctor, we go where he goes." The one in command sneered and pushed Connor, ending the conversation.

The group followed Connor into a thin corridor, he opened a door and ushered Ben inside. Ben's gaze swept over the narrow bathroom noting the shower tucked into one corner and a bucket and blade resting by the sink. Then landed on Connor's ashen face.

"Strip."

Ben shut his eyes and inhaled. He pulled himself to his full height and straightened his back. "No."

The word smashed against the stone and a flicker of a smile tugged at Connor's mouth before it vanished again.

"Don't make this hard Benjen." Connor warned. "Strip."

Ben didn't move, he dug his crutches into the floor and tilted his chin up. "No."

The commanding soldier pushed into the room and shoved Connor aside, then pointed his spear at Ben's face, the blade inches from his left eye. "The doctor has long forgotten that you're a prisoner, but I haven't. Strip, or I shall cut out your eyes, pluck them with my blade and shove them down your—"

"Ye cannot harm him. Ye know the instructions." Connor straightened up and looked directly at Ben as he spoke to the captain.

The soldier grunted a frustrated guttural sound and looked at Ben through narrow slits. "He doesn't need both eyes."

"He does, and all his fingers and toes. There's only one body part he'll not need as a Brown Robe, but it isn't ye who gets the pleasure of removing it."

The soldier grunted and made to turn away, then in a swift movement swivelled, spun his spear so that the hilt faced Ben, then buried it with a forceful shove into his stomach.

The air fell from his lungs as the soldier swung a second time, the wooden stake smashing against Ben's ribs, a third smash across his neck splashed pain into his face and shoulders. "Hold him." The soldier commanded.

Two soldiers pushed into the cramped room and smashed Ben against the wall, pinning him against the cool tiles.

"His new robe will cover the welts." The commander's gravelly voice skated over his skin leaving goose bumps in his wake.

The icy tip of the spear pressed into the back of his neck, and a sharp hot breath escaped him and clung to the tiles. The cold blade nudged at his skin then trailed down shredding his shirt. It fell open, sliced away like flayed flesh.

"Try not to move." The commander jested as he drove the blade in deeper, then continued, until he cut through Ben's shorts and pulled the destroyed fabric away, leaving him naked.

"Turn him around and get him on his knees," the captain ordered.

The two soldiers yanked Ben's hair, spun his body around and forced him to his knees. Ben flailed and thrashed his knees shredding against the hard stone colouring it a dark red.

"Doctor." The soldier gestured to Connor who moved forward and grabbed the blade from the bucket.

"Benjen," Connor called to him, placing a hand on his shoulder and looking directly into his eyes. "Ben."

Ben froze and looked at his friend.

"*This* isn't the right time to fight."

"What do—"

"Save yer strength. Ye're going to need it." Connor ran a hand through his beard. "Please."

Ben hissed through an iron clad jaw, his head fell in surrender. His body slackened against the soldiers.

"Release him." Connor looked to the soldiers who ignored him. "He won't fight."

The soldiers' grips tightened around Ben's arms, their knuckles whitening.

Connor shook his head then raked a hand through Ben's long locks. He grabbed clumps of hair and hacked through the long strands, letting them fall to the floor like autumn leaves. When he had sheared it as best as he could, he lathered soap into a foam and coated Ben's head. With slow precise strokes Connor ran the razor against Ben's scalp. The silence in the room hung like a heavy dark cloud, severed only by the splashing of the blade rinsed in the bucket after the last of Ben's hair disappeared beneath the blade.

Connor lathered his throat and jaw and just as meticulously removed the growth which has spurted there over the months.

Connor wiped away the remains of the foam with a rough towel and took Ben's hand, clipping each fingernail, cleaning the mud and dirt gathered beneath. He did not protest, did not fight or pull or try to run, but he was not defeated. His back remained straight, his head held high as inch by inch they tried to strip away what remained of him.

Connor looked to the soldiers who still held Ben in their grasp. "Are ye going te hold him while he showers?"

The soldiers looked to their leader who tipped his chin and they dropped their hold. Ben remained on his knees and waited for instructions.

"Ye must wash." Connor handed him a bar of soap and signalled to the shower.

Ben stood up and hobbled to the shower, his crutched abandoned. He twisted the lever, water spilt from the shower head, so cold at first, he almost flinched. Once the stream warmed Ben stepped beneath it, letting the rivulets beat off his head and trail down his body. The water, stained red, pooled at his feet. He ran a hand over his naked head and his fist clenched around the bar of soap.

He began to lather his body, his hands navigating on

their own along his thin arms and protruding hip bones. Connor's kindness had always been tempered by the guards' cruelty, and despite his afforded freedoms he had always remained a prisoner, deprived of meals ensuring he remained weakened.

Heat soaked into his blistered, scarred skin and his mind faded into dullness conjuring images of Ariel, her delicate smile and piercing eyes, her long graceful fingers laced through his as she led him to whatever future awaited.

He rinsed and towelled himself off with the moist towel, then followed Connor to a third room. The entourage of soldiers trailing behind.

The room was bare save a single cot that lay directly in its centre. A pair of brown shorts thrown across the blanket that covered it.

"Get dressed."

Ben slipped into the shorts and waited.

"Ye've been cleansed and prepared for yer ceremony tomorrow. Tonight ye must lay here as Benjen, for tomorrow ye leave yer name and identity in this room and join the Brown Robes." Connor tilted his head towards the bed and Ben slipped inside silently, covering his body with the blanket, his gaze boring into the ceiling. He would heed Connor's plea and save his strength for the morning, for that's when his fight would begin and end.

"Get up." Connor's harsh whisper jolted Ben awake and obliterated his dreams. He opened his eyes, the night an infinite dark tunnel. "Stay quiet, move quickly, there's little time."

Connor was already pulling him from the cot and toward the door. With an arm wrapped around the bigger man they glued their backs to the wall, Ben's eyes wide as he searched the darkness, all signs of sleep left behind in his cot. His mind raced trying to catch up.

"The guards?" Ben's heart ricocheted inside him.

"Taken care of, for now." Connor squeezed his shoulder and whispered above him. "When I give the signal ye run, as fast as ye can Benjen."

Ben nodded unsure if Connor saw the movement in the all-consuming darkness. His skin prickled and his heart thudded too loudly.

Connor tapped his shoulder, and they burst away from the wall and surged forward, his lame foot dragging behind him, Connor guided them through the narrow corridor and into the waiting room.

The door burst open, and they stepped into the deluge of water pelting from the angry sky. Lightning cleaved the darkness with white branches that illuminated the four soldiers slumped against the wall, seemingly asleep.

"Go," Connor shouted over the roar of the storm.

Ben didn't dare look back as Connor's powerful strides dragged him along, propelling him away from the village and towards the sea. Coarse muddy sand turned grainy beneath his feet. A bitter gust nipped at his flesh, biting his body and stinging his narrowed eyes.

"Hurry!" The word crashed into the roar of the choppy ocean before them. Adrenaline flooded through him, driving him forwards.

His feet hit the water. Icy, inky black waves pounded at his body as he pushed ahead.

"Not much further." Connor released his grip as they thrust further into the water. "Swim. Stay with me."

They moved deeper and deeper into the rough waves, the wind screamed in his ears, his body burned with the cold, his breath heavy and desperate. He pushed against the current, the frigid water threatening to drain away the last of his energy.

He searched the dark blanket, Connor long vanished in the rising seas and endless blackness. He drifted, the raging waves carrying him aloft. Icy shards of fear pierced his heart and he screamed above the roaring sea. "Connor!" He was answered by a wave which flooded his mouth with salty water.

He thought of death. After months spent in his filthy pit, slowly eroded into half a man, drowning would bring freedom, it would bring release. For a time, he had wished for nothing but death but now that it called to him, he didn't want to go, he wanted to see tomorrow, to fight, to have a future dictated by his own choices.

He found air and sucked it into his lungs then surged forward through the violent water. The sky rumbled above him and he rumbled in return, unleashing a roar which tore through his entire body and challenged death itself. Arms grabbed him and yanked. He was plucked out of the water and released onto the wooden floor of a rocking boat. He gasped, filling his depleted lungs through chattering teeth.

Hands pulled at his clothes and undressed him, then draped him in a warm blanket which he clasped and pulled tightly around his body, drawing whatever warmth if offered before the rain soaked through it, rendering it heavy with droplets.

"Now my friend I have finally repaid your kindness." Antoine's face twisted in a strange mask of worry and glee.

"Antoine, you're here?"

"Yes, Danny too." He heard the smile in his friend's voice, and his heart squeezed in joy and fear.

"I will see you home yet."

Mason's voice suddenly soared over the thundering storm. "You must go! Once they discover you're gone, they'll give chase." He squatted before Ben and clasped his hand.

The boat jolted, tossing its passengers around. Ben tightened his grip on his brother. "Come with us."

He shook his head. "Tell Mama I'm alive and well, tell her I'll see her soon. There's much work that needs to be done here."

Mason wrapped a hand around his brother and drew him into a strong embrace. The brothers held each other briefly in the darkness, leaving the silence to say all that was between them.

Mason turned to Connor who sat hunched on a bench fighting to fill his air lungs with air, "look after him."

"Aye, I will."

Mason's grip loosened and his hand fell away, he stood up and turned towards the oarsman. "Get them home safely."

"Mason." Ben called his brother, "Should I tell her the name of the woman that keeps you here?" Ben tried for a last time.

"Arabella, daughter of Olivia." The boat rocked as Mason leaped into the violent, dark waters and disappeared behind the cresting waves.

The group sat motionless as the oarsman navigated them away, knowing dawn was a few precious hours away and the sky would turn blue and the yellow orb above them would shine like a beam, exposing them.

Ben's body remained rigid, his muscles tense, his heart thundering and yet, despite the slew of emotions flooding his body, a small smile tugged at the corner of his lips.

Ben's feet touched the sand, the hot grains weaved between his toes and the sun caressed his skin. The familiar scent of Inan carried by the breeze swept over him and his eyes brimmed with tears. His legs gave way and he fell on his knees, his stiff pants soaking up the warm water as waves tickled his legs and welcomed him home.

A man he had never seen before extended his arm, grinning, "Welcome."

Even as he took it, he heard his name, it radiated through the air and smashed into him, familiar, loving, gentle.

Mama Cath sprinted towards him. Sand flew in every direction as her feet smashed through the sand. As she neared him, she slowed then came to a complete standstill.

Her eyes widened while they took him in, scouring his body from head to toe. He gave her a wan smile and she collapsed onto the sand, her hands winging around him, her body quivering against him as she shed hot tears.

He closed his arms around her and pulled her closer. Two skeletal forms in a pitiful, desperate, joyous, embrace. When he released her, tears ran down his cheeks. "Mum," he whispered through chapped lips.

"Ben, you're home." It was a relieved sigh and a pained cry all in one. "Look what they've done to you." She ran a hand over his shaved head, the bristles catching against her skin.

"Mama Cath, let me get him to the hospital." The unfamiliar man placed a gentle hand on her shoulder, she placed her palm over his hand and nodded, allowing him to help her up from the sand.

"I'll take him." The growl came from behind them, and Ben's face cracked open in a large smile while Mama Cath and the newcomer stepped back, startled, as if they had only just noticed the giant.

Connor came to stand by Ben like a protective bear over his cub, Antoine and Danny flanked his other side.

"Mama, meet Connor."

Mama Cath smiled and tipped her head in hello.

"And this is Antoine and Danny." He gestured to his other friends.

Her smile stretched and tears pooled in her eyes as she greeted them.

Ben got to his feet, Mama Cath brushed his jaw with her fingers then laced her arm in his, and led them away from the beach.

"Where's Ariel?" he asked as they followed the path. An echo of something familiar.

"We'll find her as soon as we get you settled."

"Find her now." He stilled and shot his mother a desperate look.

She squeezed his thin bicep. "We will."

Knots tightened in his abdomen as they walked deeper into the new Inan. He found traces of his childhood in the village, where buildings still stood, and orchards still grew. But he also noticed the scorched, blacked skeletons that were once homes, new settlements and new paths that diverged into places where thick shrubbery once grew.

But most of all he was enthralled by men and women

walking freely, hand in hand, sharing laughter both delicate and raucous, harsh and soft. Surrounded by happiness he selfishly wanted it for himself.

He noticed the snatched looks and ignored the whispers as they ascended the path. They were a mismatched group, a kaleidoscope of lives that had landed on their shore.

"This is yer home?" Connor asked, his tone appreciative as his gaze followed a group of giggling women.

"Mm hmm." Ben grinned at the giant whose eyes looked to be falling out of their sockets.

"I see why ye fought so hard te get back here."

Ben chuckled as Connor ogled Inan and all that it had to offer.

Mama Cath pushed ahead and stopped at the hospital door. She whispered to the man who nodded and smiled, standing in wait. "Alan here will show your friends to their cots and have them fed."

"I'm not going anywhere." Connor stepped closer to Ben who turned to look at his friends.

"I'm fine, go get some food and rest."

"They can go." Connor gestured towards Antoine and Danny. "I'm not going anywhere."

"Are you sure?" Antoine shuffled his feet.

"Go. I'm fine, as you can see." Ben made a show of rolling his eyes and the small party chuckled.

Antoine and Danny followed Alan through the door, Mama Cath caught it and held it open for her son. From inside leaked the smell of smoke and sweat and testosterone.

Ben studied the hospital wing, his mouth falling slightly ajar. Cots littered the floor, sleeping men occupied some, piles of clothes laid on others. He scanned the space, his brows pulling together. He noticed the charred doors and damaged walls. He looked to his mother.

"Just temporary, till everyone finds a new home. It takes a while to rebuild." Ben nodded his thoughts drifting to Dagon, to Luke and his quarry, to his own home probably occupied by someone else.

"Where's Ariel?" he asked as Mama Cath led them through the suddenly charged room. The men all stood silently staring at Ben. His mangled foot dragged slightly behind him as he straightened his back and held his head high.

"We've sent word, she'll be here soon."

Ben clenched his jaw, anticipation growing within him, coiling around him like ivy.

"In here."

The white room had somehow remained perfectly intact, untouched, unused. Sterile and cold. A shiver ran up Ben's spine.

"On the bed."

"Mum—" Before he could protest further Connor lifted him up and set him on the bed as if he was a young child.

"Connor!"

"Yer welcome." The big man ignored Ben's agitation and flashed him a smile.

"I'll go get you some soup, and then you must rest." Mama Cath tried and failed to hide her smile.

"I want to see Ariel."

"I've told you, she's coming." She sighed. "Now, you'll eat, and you'll rest, and she will come."

"Fine," he grumbled and watched his mother leave.

"I can see where ye get it from." Connor's eyes lit up.

"I've no idea what you mean." He smirked at the big man.

"How're ye holding up, Benjen?"

"I'm fine."

Connor tipped his head, cocking a single eyebrow.

Ben exhaled and pursed his lips as he glared at Connor wondering if the big man could hear his pounding heart. When the stare became unrelenting, he threw his hands up in the air and sighed. "Fine! I'm overwhelmed and I can't wai—"

The door burst open and his mother stepped inside with a bowl of soup. She shoved it into his hands.

"Eat."

She watched as Ben sucked down a spoonful then turned to Connor. "Come, there's soup for you too and a cot for you to rest after your long journey."

His gaze shot to Ben.

"Go you big softie, I'm fine. I'm home." His smile was genuine and rich and Connor visibly relaxed.

Mama Cath turned to Connor, his massive shape looming above her. "Thank you for bringing my boy back to me." She clasped his hands in hers, her eyes brimming with fresh tears.

"Aye, he kind of made it impossible not te."

The two stepped outside and left Ben with the silence of his thoughts and the thundering of his heart.

He put the bowl down, unable to eat while consumed by thoughts of Ariel.

He wondered how much she might have changed given how much his time on Cernuava altered him. He lay back resting his head on his palm, the white sheet soft and comforting, his body tingling with apprehension and fear. His heart chugged and stumbled at the thoughts that plagued him since his escape.

A loud bang woke him.

Her whisper carried to him as if still in a dream, his world threatened to tilt as his name on her lips wrapped around his heart and squeezed.

"Ben? Ben, can you hear me?"

Her voice flooded his senses with hope so fierce his heart threatened to seize. He sucked in a steeling breath. "I'm hungry, not deaf..." He caught the look in her eye through half-opened slits.

Ariel landed her punched on his upper arm.

"Ouch." He winced, not a trace of humour in his voice.

"I'm sorry, I'm so sorry."

"It's alright, Ariel. I'm alright." He wanted her to come closer so that he could wrap himself around her, but she was too far, distant. His heart panged with emptiness.

"I'm so sorry I left you. I'm so sorry they took you. I thought..." Ariel's face broke into tears. Anguished relief spilled from her.

Ben pushed his body from the bed, the sheet spilling from his torso. Ariel gasped at the sight. The air around them stilling.

He sucked in a frayed breath, steading his quivering hand as he reached for her and coaxed her chin so that she looked into his eyes, her delicate soft skin setting his on fire. "I'm here now, and we're going to be alright."

"Ben—." Her eyes kept falling to his chest, her mouth agape. "Ben—," she repeated, her fingers reaching for the angry scar emblazoned across his chest. He didn't flinch as she traced the thick scar tissue blemishing his chest. The raised 'A', an angry stain.

He gave her a weak smile. "All they did was put your name on my body. It reminded me every day why I shouldn't stop fighting. Not until I'd see you again."

She let her hands drop then leaned in, her scent enveloping him as her soft lips grazed his. His heart soared, skin burned, and his body ached for her familiarity.

When she pulled away, she traced his stark jawline with a finger and locked eyes with him. "There's something I need to tell you."

His heart sank and his stomach knitted. He slammed his eyes shut and when he opened them again, he tried to find sincerity in his words. "It's okay." He cleared his throat and swallowed the large lump that had lodged itself there. "You thought I was dead. I don't— Ouch! Will you stop doing that?" He rubbed his arm where Ariel had landed a second punch.

"Why would you even think that?"

"I'm delirious," he covered up for the faltering of his heart with jest, his body flooded with relief, his mind spiralling between hope and despair. "What is it?"

"I have something to tell you. Well, more like show you." She bit her lower lip and got up from her chair. "Wait right here."

"Not like I can go anywhere, anyway." He didn't want her to leave, not when she had finally come, not when he had finally seen her and touched her and felt like she still might be his. Not when she had barely even been by his side.

He fell back onto the bed, his gaze followed her to the door, anticipation crawling beneath his skin. He already missed her, needed her, mourned for her. His heart pounded in his chest as he waited for her return, as time stretched out like a vast endless ocean.

The door edged open and Ariel stepped back inside. In her arms a baby girl. She approached the bed, whispering in the baby's ear.

"Ben, meet your daughter, Elizabeth."

His world stood still as the words sank slowly like an anchor to his very core. "My daugh—*Our* daughter?" He looked at the baby who stared back at him and a savage broken sob forced its way from him as his heart slammed against his chest, growing with each fierce pound. He gaped at the baby and his gaze swung back from mother to daughter. The baby girl had her mother's wild hair and slender face but, in her eyes, he saw himself.

Ariel nodded and her smile faltered. "Would you like to hold her?"

Ben bowed his head, unable to speak, his body shivering.

"Go give daddy a big cuddle." Ariel smiled at the baby and gave her a quick peck on the forehead as she placed her on Ben's chest and into his arms.

The unfamiliar weight like a piece of a puzzle that fit perfectly in his arms, one he had no idea he was missing until that instant. The baby's warmth radiated into every part of him and she smelt of the sea and of wildflowers.

"Hi baby girl," he cooed. "Hi, Elizabeth." Ben wrapped his hands around the baby, who pawed playfully with his face, her tiny fingers pulling his lips and nose. He watched her with fascination while she blew raspberries and cooed easily, snuggling against him. "Elizabeth." He exhaled her name, looking to Ariel with wonderment.

"I didn't think you would mind."

"No. It's perfect. She's perfect." He stared into Elizabeth's face in awe, taking in her features, her hair which had thickened and curled just beyond her shoulders, the large eyes —*his* eyes—looking back at him through Ariel's face.

The baby lay her head down and let herself settle into the rise and fall of Ben's chest. Soon her breathing slowed and she lay motionless.

Ben looked at Ariel, his eyes big with questions and fear. "She'll be fine. You both will. Now sleep while you can. She took her first steps today so you'll need your strength to chase after her."

Ben's mouth fell open and Ariel leaned over and sealed it with a kiss.

Ariel climbed into the bed and lay alongside him. His heart expanded and grew. His body inundated with tumultuous emotions, warming him like rays of the sun, spreading inside him, taking hold. After being lost in the dark for so long he knew that at last he was truly home.

EPILOGUE

Ariel's screech tore through his soul as he watched her helplessly, her face contorting in savage beautiful pain, beads of sweat leaking down her flushed tired face.

"One more big push," Mama Cath reassured her in a calm voice.

Ariel's foot braced against Ben's strong chest as she pushed, her shrill cry saturating his senses.

His breath stalled as he glimpsed the mop of hair on the baby's head, followed by a tiny scrunched-up face. It looked so small and fragile as it slid into the world. His gaze flew to Ariel who fell back onto the bed drained and elated and he wept, his heart expanding, growing, unravelling.

"It's a girl." Mama Cath said as she handed him the baby still coated in blood and afterbirth, and something broke inside him allowing joy so utterly unlike he had ever experienced before to filter inside him.

He locked eyes with Ariel as he placed their daughter on her chest, his heart full of awe and relief, for her torment was over. He kissed her forehead tasting the saltiness of her sweat.

"Are you okay?"

She looked at the baby on her breast and her face broke into a tired serene smile. "perfect."

"Just like her mother." He beamed at her awed at her strength, resilience and ineffable beauty, "You are amazing and fierce. Thank you for giving me my daughters, Ariel. I love you."

"I love you too Ben."

He rushed from the room and found Elizabeth who played with Rosalie and her boys, Connor looming over them all, his face strained and protective.

"It's a girl!" he called to the group who looked up elated. "Elizabeth, come, meet your sister."

The two-year-old lumbered over to her father, a wide grin spread across her face. "Told you it was a girl, daddy."

"Yes, you did."

"What's her name?"

"Let's go ask your mum."

They edged to the bed where the new-born latched onto Ariel seeking warmth, wrapped in a light cloth that had long ago greyed with time and use.

"Hi." Ariel wiped her brow and her face cracked into a tired smile full of delight and weariness. Elizabeth's eyes grew with wonder as she studied the baby.

"What's her name, mummy?"

Ariel locked eyes with Ben and a peace unlike any he had ever known fell upon him. "Her name is Hope."

THE END

ACKNOWLEDGMENTS

Thank you to my husband, Clarke that despite everything still stands by me, encourages me, believes in me and drives me to continue and tell stories in the only way I know how.

To my incredible friend Megan Marshall, I love your support and encouragement and how you love this book as much as I do. To Cassy Warren, this story would not be what it is without you and your incredible input. I love that you love my characters as much as me and give them your heart. You are a wonderful friend and partner in crime. Chris Reynolds, thank you for all the feedback and time invested in this book, you've given me so much to be able to create this world and your input and friendship are invaluable to me.

I would love to thank my amazing friend and beta Dawn, her enthusiasm knows no boundaries, her genuine love for books, reading, and helping authors is contagious and humbling. You inspire me to be better with each and every book!

To the amazing Jennifer Demeter, thank you for creating such an incredible cover. Thank you for your patience and enthusiasm in bringing to life Ariel and her world. You've exceeded all my expectations.

My sincere thanks to every one of you who played a part in bringing this dream of mine to life.

ABOUT THE AUTHOR

Want to know more about the author and keep in touch?

You can find her here

ALSO BY YAEL MAREE

Standalone

When We Vanish

Series

Mating Season Book One, Ariel

Mating Season, Book Two, Ben